Hill Country Property

Jim Sanderson

Livingston Press
The Univerity of West Alabama

ISBN 13: 978-1-60489-152-2, trade paper
ISBN 13: 978-1-60489-153-9, hardcover
ISBN: 1-60489-152-1, trade paper
ISBN: 1-60489-153-X, hardcover
Library of Congress Control Number 2015934860
Printed on acid-free paper.
Printed in the United States of America,
Ebsco Media
Hardcover binding by: Heckman Bindery
Typesetting and page layout: Amanda Nolin, Joe Taylor,
Proofreading: Teresa Boykin, Joe Taylor, Amanda Nolin, Tricia Taylor
Back cover layout: Amanda Nolin
Cover photo: unknown photographer
Cover design: Amanda Nolin

This is a work of fiction:
any resemblance
to persons living or dead is coincidental.

Livingston Press is part of The University of West Alabama,
and thereby has non-profit status.
Donations are tax-deductible:
brothers and sisters, we need 'em.

first edition
6 5 4 3 3 2 1

Acknowledgments
Chapters in this novel have appeared in the following altered forms:
"Becky." Main Street Rag (Charlotte, NC), summer 2010.
"Bolens." *American Studies Association of Texas Journal.* (Baylor University,
      WacoTexas) 2008
"Divorce Laws." *The Concho River Review* (San Angelo,Texas). Spring 1992,
      and "Divorce Laws." special commemorative issue of *Concho River
      Review*, Best of *Concho River Review* (San Angelo, TX). Spring 2002.
"Emma & Shorty." *Getting By: Stories of Working Lives.* Eds. David Shevin &
      Larry Smith. Huron, Ohio: Bottom Dog Press,.1996
"A Life in Venice." *New Texas '91.* Ed. Jim Lee. Denton, TX: Center for Texas
      Studies. (University of North Texas), 1991.
"Like in the Movies." *North Atlantic Review* (Stony Brook, NY), no. 9, 1997,
      and *Faded Love.* Ink Brush Press, 2010.
"Property Rights." *Phoebe: The George Mason Review* (George Mason
      University, Fairfax, Virginia). 18.1 & 2. Fall/Winter 1988.
"Taos." *Riversedge* (Edinburg, Texas). Spring 1991.

Hill Country Property

*Once again, for my parents,
Marjorie and "Sandy" Sanderson.*

Chapter 1:
Becky

It is 1985. I am in my new pickup truck watching Kay Menger's marriage unravel. With nothing to do but watch, I remember that I had tried to strengthen my marriage by having an affair with a smelly woman who trimmed her toenails by moonlight. The sad part was that my wife didn't care that I was having an affair with this particular woman or anyone else. Sexually or otherwise, in the equation that my now-ex-wife uses to account for her life, I just don't count . . .

It is 1985. I have been able to drink legally, get drafted, and smoke small amounts of marijuana without fear of being prosecuted for a felony for over fifteen years. By the state's definition of legal, I am an adult. But as a baby boomer, I don't feel like I am adult. The reason I can't feel adulthood is the generation before me. My mother and father are not the cause of my maturity retardation. My wife's parents are.

Forty-one years before 1985, my father-in-law had his trigger finger shot off by a German sharpshooter and had decided to make something of himself. Thirty-seven years before, my mother-in-law had come out of the movie *Red River*, seen what she thought was a real cowboy, married him, and thus had redesigned her romantic and erotic life.

The nightly Gulf breeze catches the smell of Kay Menger's freshly cut grass and blows it through the window of my six-month old 1985 Toyota pickup, which I have parked down the street. I sit in my pickup, watching, resting my camera in my lap, and ducking my head when a car comes by. From the full summer moon and the street lamp on the corner, I can see that Kay Menger's front yard looks like the yards of the other recent divorcees. With no one to help and less time for the house, the ex-wives I watch let the yards grow shaggy and fill with kids' toys. It takes two yuppies to tend Austin's over-priced suburban lawns.

On my first pass by Kay's house, just before dusk, I saw muddy Ninja warriors and G.I. Joes lying in the lawn's bare spots. The toy soldiers still lie there, in the dark, wounded in action or hiding and waiting for an enemy. The youngest's tricycle with its bent frame and misaligned handlebars is still parked under the pecan tree where he left it. The pecan tree's branches droop from the weight of its sour-smelling, ripening pecans. The hedges need trimming, and the awning needs painting. Some anxiety about what the place looks like and what the married neighbors think no doubt creeps into to Kay's crowded mind, but she's probably too preoccupied with making a living and caring for the boys, now that the hubby is gone, to let neighbors' thoughts weigh in the balance of her decisions. In the driveway is a BMW. Most of the new computer engineers, doctors, lawyers, and real estate developers who live in this neighborhood—and raise the price of property in Austin—have a Mercedes, BMW, Cadillac, or Chevy Suburban parked in their driveways. But this is not Kay's BMW. Her husband got theirs.

The porch light comes on, and the front door opens. I take off Henry's old hat, put it beside me, and scoot down in my seat until I can just barely see over the dash of my Toyota pickup. Henry died while he was still my father-in-law, so he never knew me as his ex-son-in-law. He would have had fun playing detective with me (sort of like hunting, he'd say), but he wouldn't like the reason for it.

A man, clearly not Mr. Menger, steps out of the door and into the porch light. He has no shoes on; he carries those in his hand; and his shirt is unbuttoned. Kay Menger stays in the doorway, and the porch light makes her negligee translucent and shows off the trim figure of a mid-thirtyish woman, a woman my age. With a body like hers, I can see why her soon to be ex would just naturally expect boyfriends. The man leans toward her, and she steps up to him. What starts out as a good night peck turns into a full tongue-in-the-throat kiss. They wrap their arms around each other, and he leans her back against the door frame. His hand lowers to her butt. I raise my camera and take the shot. Ah, infrared. It will capture them and give me the money to buy a little peace. Then Kay pulls away from him and smiles.

He doesn't want to leave, but he has to. She can't risk his staying. Came over for Sunday dinner, right after going to church with his family. Stayed the afternoon. Stayed through *Sixty Minutes*, then through Sunday night prime time. Stayed until the kids were in bed.

The man steps down a few steps, turns, and smiles at Kay. She raises one flat palm to her lips and blows him a kiss. He turns away and starts to walk down the sidewalk, but he suddenly raises one foot, grabs it, and starts hopping on the other foot. A wounded, neglected Ninja warrior, hiding and waiting, had gouged Kay's boyfriend with his sword. The boyfriend turns to face Kay again. She giggles. Then he gets into his BMW. I take another picture and write down the license plate number.

I wait until Kay's boyfriend is well down the block before I put on Henry's old Stetson, start my Toyota pickup, and leave Kay to her dreams. It was an amicable divorce until Kay's lawyer told her to ask for the kids, a sizeable chunk of child support, and half of her husband's retirement and savings. So, her husband got Buck Cronin and thus me to help him out. Now Kay will be lucky to get the kids. She won't be able to make the house payments on her own. Kay will have to drop out of this neighborhood and will discover the price of Austin property. While the rest of the state suffers from an oil bust, Austin is booming with people who have discovered its clean water, pleasant views, and liberal attitudes.

These new Texans don't suffer through a marriage, so divorce is also booming in Austin. And chain smoking, hyper-tense, happily married Buck Cronin is the meanest, toughest divorce lawyer in Austin, Texas. Since my own divorce and resulting poverty and underemployment, Buck Cronin has regularly hired me to find nasty facts for highly contested divorces. What God joined together, Buck Cronin and I can put asunder. Buck uses my *research* only if he needs it; he likes to have it ready if the proceedings get ugly. He is expensive, but his clients usually beat the shit out of their ex-spouses. In my hippie days, I believed in free love, but now I know it's never free.

For me, though, help is on the way. Buck's good wife, Shelly, has found a friend of a friend who would be *right* for me. She will be my first real date since leaving Victoria.

And Becky is coming back for a visit. For some reason my ex mother-in-law's return soothes me. She finally wants to see the kids that she left nearly thirty years ago. She figures that she has paid for their love.

Only I know that Becky is coming. Only I have seen her since she left. Though I didn't know it at the time, tracking her down for Henry was the start of my training as a private investigator in the divorce business.

Because she insists, I'll let her be a surprise to my ex and my brother-in-law. Becky and I are conspirators, and for once, with her, I may be able to put people back together rather than take them apart. Of course, she may further unravel her family, but she may re-knit the loose strands that her husband Henry left when he died. Maybe I am one of those loose strands.

I start my truck and put it in gear. On this Sunday night, seemingly protected by their money and their gentle natures, the Austin suburbanites settle in for another hard week, sneak a peek at their cute kids sleeping, or silently hump in their bedrooms. But they don't know that I snake through their neighborhood like a premonition of their futures. I smell their freshly cut carpet grass in the gentle Gulf breeze. It smells like unraveling dreams.

* * *

After listening to Henry, reading his letters, checking postmarks and return addresses, I discovered that Becky Bolen had studied film at U.C.L.A., had been promoted to full professor at Oklahoma State University, and published a book about Samuel Fuller. Yet, when I at last met her and asked her how she could leave her family, she giggled and said she had simply decided to become a villain. Until I read her book that was once her dissertation, I had never heard of Samuel Fuller. Since then, I've rented videos of nearly all his movies.

Becky told me about her father, old Carl Baumann. I can't help but think of him as old. He was what Americans, with all their racial and ethnic cruelty, used to call a real "square head." He was from one of those old German families that came to central Texas after one of the big European upheavals and, as a young man he moved to the city, San Antonio, to engage in a prosperous livelihood and a family. He found a nice German girl already in San Antonio and had two girls with Doris. When he was promoted to the manager of Piggly Wiggly's grocery store number 8 in 1932, Carl Baumann moved his family to Highland Park, a housing development on the southside of San Antonio. The neighborhood had well-kept, shaded green lawns and ornate houses with porches in both the back and front yards and steep English-style or squared, tiled, Spanish-style roofs.

Becky remembered the house she grew up in at 811 Hicks on the south side of San Antonio as made of large, flat native limestone, which she used to rub with her small hands, making them rough and chalky. Her house had a cement wishing well and a brick goldfish pond in the backyard and large pecan trees to climb in both the back and front yards. "Mamma" had rows of flowerbeds full of lilies and roses along the backyard fence. Becky could remember liking the house and remembered a certain German pride and stubbornness in her Mamma when she said, "my house." But most important to Papa, old Carl Baumann, fashionable but modest, middle class Highland Park had good, friendly white neighbors, no "Mexcans" or "Negroes" to bother you or bring the property values down.

In 1946, right after Detroit switched from making tanks for World War II back to cars, Carl Baumann, the Piggly Wiggly store number 8 manager, decided to buy his first new car. He asked his two daughters, Mary, whom he called Schatzi, and Rebecca, whom he never called Becky, whether they wanted a radio or a heater in this new car. Schatzi, a working girl at eighteen, and Rebecca, a high school junior at sixteen, both squealed for a radio. But, when he went down to order the car, in his practical old German way, he decided that his daughters were wrong. He ordered his new Dodge with a heater but no radio.

Doris sympathized with them but took old Carl's side because she always did, because, as she said, he was almost always right. Schatzi said it was just like Papa. Rebecca went to the movies. Rebecca always went to the movies.

Though Carl was scared of her riding the bus all the way to downtown San Antonio—Mexicans, black men, and the veterans hung around downtown—he let her have this luxury. Rebecca had defied her father enough for him to know that it was useless to keep her from the movies. To Rebecca, the movies and the theaters had always been worth the risk of angering her Papa. She especially liked the Majestic, built in 1925 and even more ornate and gaudy than the Aztec or Texas. She would go into the theater as soon before the feature started as the aisle attendants would let her. Encased in air-conditioning, still a luxury in San Antonio in the 40s, Rebecca would look around in the dim light at the castle ledges, balconies, and sky-blue dome. And, when the lights dimmed even more for the start of the feature, she shot a quick glance at the blackening dome to see the imitation stars that looked like pin pricks in the roof letting a little sun in.

At first, she didn't really care what she watched, but after a while she picked her shows with discretion. She didn't admit what she liked to her friends. While they went to see Ingrid Bergman or Robert Taylor or Robert Montgomery or Robert Walker and raved for two years about *Mildred Pierce*, she liked the tough men in westerns, war, or gangster movies. Inside her heroes' toughness, she found something endearingly pathetic. She was never romantic about her heroes, saw them with all their flaws, but admired their stories nevertheless. (Later, in her dissertation, Becky would argue that if John Wayne or James Cagney or, later, Robert Mitchum and Kirk Douglas wouldn't have been so pathetic, they would have been classical villains, not heroes.) Because her interests were peculiar, because she wanted no giggling girlfriends annoying her while deep in her concentration and meditation within a movie theater, Rebecca always went to the movies alone.

Skipping a grade to graduate at seventeen, Rebecca, at old Carl's urging, put off ideas about college and, like Schatzi, got a job with the telephone company, a good safe job for a woman. She could keep it until she got married or, if she didn't—God forbid, but then you had to be realistic and practical in those days—it would be a good job for an aging old maid. After a year with the company, at the end of an afternoon at the movies, she met a rough-looking cowboy named Henry Bolen.

* * *

Rebecca had just seen *Red River*. She came out of the Majestic air conditioning and immediately felt the San Antonio humidity melt the makeup on her face. She glanced up one last time at the banner stretched across Houston Street. Dark hero John Wayne, the kind of hero Rebecca liked, stared down from one end of the banner toward Montgomery Cliff at the other end of the banner. "The grandest movie of the year in the grandest theater in Texas," the banner said over the two stars. She walked down the block toward the bus stop, ignoring the glances and occasional whistles from the veterans and the airmen from the newly created Air Force training base way out on the west side of San Antonio.

Across the street and three blocks down from her bus stop was Neisner's five & dime. Rebecca checked in her purse and saw she had enough change for a cherry Coke. She crossed the street to Neisner's and re-entered air-conditioned air. Since old Carl Baumann had been letting her come to the movies, Rebecca liked to slip into Neisner's. As usual, she first looked into the glass cage of the Duke of Chimp, Neisner's latest in a series of chimpanzees. This latest Duke was getting older and feisty, his diapers—which he had to wear because of his failing bowels and bladder—were soiled and the cage stunk, and he picked at the hat he wore and at the scabs on his elbows. He would be gone soon. The owners of Neisner's kept Dukes in glass cages until they got old and ugly and scared the kids or until they got strong enough to bang against the glass and put small cracks in it. But, they always had a Duke because kids would drag their parents in to see the monkey like the ones in the Tarzan movies, then want a cold drink from the fountain.

As Rebecca watched the Duke, she felt someone standing behind her and turned to see a tall cowboy. He had on a silver belly cowboy hat, a white shirt, red tie, and tan colored suit. She looked down to see his shiny boots. The hat and the boots were obviously new. The suit, with sweat stains under his arms and across the chest, was older; the shirt, with its damp collar sticking to the cowboy's neck, had a tattered collar point. "Chimp," he said and smiled.

She nodded, ducked under his chin, went to the soda fountain, and sat in a booth. He followed behind her and sat at the counter. Too coy to look over her shoulder, she reached into her purse, got out her powder box, flipped up the lid, and looked in its mirror at him. He swiveled away from her to face the mirror behind the counter. The soda jerk came up to her and caught her looking in the mirror. She gasped as the cowboy turned toward her, then she ordered a cherry Coke.

The cowboy stepped across to her and said that he would buy the Coke. He stood above her, she looking up at him, noting the baked-in, hardened smile lines around his eyes and mouth. "Sit down," she finally said.

He sat in the seat across from her and pulled his wallet from out of his back pocket with a thumb and the stub of an index finger. She caught herself staring, but he smiled, slapped his wallet down in front of him and raised his hand. "A Kraut shot that off," he said. "You heard of the Normandy Invasion?"

"I read about the war," Rebecca said.

"You don't look old enough to have been reading that long ago." He smiled.

"I'm older than I look, and I read pretty well too." He kept smiling. "Did it hurt?" she asked.

"Hardly knew it was gone until three days later."

"You were in the army?"

"Yeah."

The soda jerk brought her cherry Coke and the cowboy's banana split. He smiled at it. Rebecca sipped through the straw in her Coke and looked across at the mountain of ice cream with its streams of chocolate running into the cowboy's glass dish. He picked up his spoon in his fist, looked at her, then curled it into the proper position, and took a big bite of ice cream. "Thank you," she said.

"Listen, would you mind if I take off my jacket? I'm still warm."

"Go ahead," Rebecca said.

He pulled both arms out of his suit jacket at once and wadded it up and pushed it behind him. Next, he unbuttoned his collar button and, with his forefinger, loosened his tie. His white shirt clung to his sweaty chest. "Damn," he said, looked down at his banana split, then lifted his eyes to the top of his sockets to see her. Then, he unbuttoned his sleeves and pulled and rolled them until the sleeves were up around his large biceps.

When he finished undressing, Rebecca was sucking down the last bit of cherry Coke and his ice cream was melting. "You want a spoon," he said as he looked down at the mountain of ice cream sinking into the mud-looking lake that was threatening to overflow the glass dish.

Rebecca shook her head, then said, "Yes."

Later, as Rebecca ladled out the last bit of mud-colored, melted ice cream, the cowboy leaned back into his side of the booth and spread his arms across the top of it. "I just bought my first stallion."

Rebecca knew about the ploys of high school football players and hard-up veterans but was unprepared for a cowboy with a stallion. She knew that, when she smiled, her face must have given off the signal to the cowboy that he was doing just fine with her. "What do you do?"

"I raise horses. Got my own land," he said.

Professor Becky Bolen could look back and know what old Carl Baumann thought. An older man would be settled, more serious, and responsible, nothing better for a young woman, who has silly thoughts crowding out the practical ones, than a mature man. And, Henry did seem rich. He had a new hat, new boots, and a new horse, and he did seem mature and responsible.

* * *

Toward the end of that summer, Henry finally invited Rebecca to his property. They drove due north on Texas Highway 281, then turned off on Ranch Road 12 toward Fischer. The dust from the gravel of Ranch Road 12, which had to wait another five years before it was paved, swirled in through the open windows of Henry's pick-up truck, and Rebecca swallowed the dust and suppressed her choking. She remembered how excited she was at finally seeing Henry's grand estate, how she was tempted to keep her eyes shut until they drove through the front gate. And before he turned into his gate, Henry stopped his truck, said to her to look both directions to see the view. She looked at the prettiest part of Texas for the first time. And, as he drove through his gate, he pointed out the brush that he had cleared back from the edge of the road.

Henry dropped his '36 Ford pickup into second gear and climbed toward his house. Henry explained, when Rebecca walked inside, that the poles would be up, the electricity would be in soon, and there was plumbing and two butane stoves. The daughter of the Piggly Wiggly manager was not rich, but had lived comfortably—this house was the closest thing she had ever seen to poverty.

After the house, Henry showed her the horse barn with the one stallion that he just bought. "Where are the others?" Rebecca asked.

"I sold the mares to get the stallion, but I'll have more."

They drove around on the roads that Henry blazed himself with a borrowed bulldozer. They walked to Fischer Creek for a picnic in the shade. After a short nap in the crook of Henry's arm, she felt the dampness of his sweat underneath her head. Rebecca looked at the creek, walked down the gentle rocky slope to it, squatted on the root of a cypress, and sprinkled the cool, spring fed water on her face. She turned to Henry, her face growing red but coolly saying, "Wouldn't it be nice to take a swim?"

Henry accepted the sinful hint with neither a slanderous nor a prudish smile. Rebecca got embarrassed and ducked her head to hide her blush. Henry stood and turned his back and said, "I won't look. You take off what you need to."

Rebecca was too young to know much about men, but while Henry's action seemed gentlemanly, it also felt disappointing. She took off all her clothes, waded into the water chest deep, shivered from the coolness, crossed her arms in front of her chest, and said, "Okay, now you come in."

Rebecca did not turn her head as Henry undressed. She studied the man's white nakedness under his shirt and trousers. He dove in in his undershorts and swam to her. She shivered as he stood up in front of her; then he ducked her head under the water. She shot up out of the water and grabbed him around the back of the neck and kissed him long and hard and felt the green water flowing against her back as much as his kiss. So, this was sin, she thought to herself.

They kissed, and Henry let himself feel her breasts. Then he swam away, up the current. She swam after him, and both of them laughed as they turned around to let the current carry them back. They hugged again in the cool water, then Henry carried her out of the water, sat her down on his clothes, and kissed her gently. She decided that, although he looked poor, had only the one horse and the house without electricity, he would make money, and what's more, he was so damn romantic.

After they made love in the shade of a cypress tree with the breeze making the shadows of the leaves dance on their naked white bodies, Henry stood and turned his back while she dressed.

Becky would guess years later that Henry, like old Carl, wanted propriety, not ecstasy. With his back to her while she pulled up her high-rise briefs, she saw the nervous twitch of the muscles in his shoulders and neck. An older Rebecca could imagine him wondering if he had guessed right, if he had reacted right, if, in the age of earned sex, he had initiated a marriage contract with this eighteen-year-old baby.

* * *

After five mares, three springs of colts, nights without electricity, and months of Rebecca's budget balancing, Henry took her to see Jack Hillier, the only doctor in Fischer and a part-time real estate investor. Good Doc Hillier, no doubt aware of Henry's trouble with starting a family, because of Sam Penschorn's and Pete Proctor's gossiping down at Marie's Tavern, declared Rebecca sterile. "It just doesn't take on some women," he told Henry. He was polite enough, sympathetic enough, though Rebecca needed no sympathy for something she wasn't sure she wanted. She noticed hanging heads and the restrained innuendos from Henry, Doris, Old Carl, and even Schatzi. She almost heard the sympathetic looks that crept onto their faces when her back was turned.

So Henry decided to adopt. He took, he said, "what no one else wanted: a three year old Mexican boy still shitting his pants." Henry changed the boy's name from Raul to Kyle, after Kyle Rote, the football player who shared a year of high school with Rebecca. Rebecca knew that Henry, for all his cussing of Mexicans, had no idea about the basis of prejudice. In fact, he had a hard time distinguishing any differences among people. He was just an expert at adapting to the environment. And if the prejudice of his German neighbors and father-in-law demanded he cuss Mexicans, so be it. When Old Carl Baumann objected to this little wetback boy, Henry realized that he had the old man's daughter and no longer needed his approval.

Rebecca, unprepared as she was for motherhood, read up on Dr. Spock and expected trouble from a three-year-old taken from the only home he had known and put in another one without nuns. She was prepared to be gentle with the boy, to withstand temper tantrums, but none came. Kyle, from the moment he stepped into Henry's house, got down to business. He never seemed to be a child. Even at three years old, he realized he was lucky not to be even poorer or dead. On Kyle's fifth birthday, Rebecca found out from Doc Hillier she was pregnant. When the baby girl was born, Henry insisted on a "classy" name like Victoria.

* * *

The summer of 1955 was in the middle of a seven-year-long drought in Texas. The ground dried up and split open. Farmers and ranchers were ruined. Horses had nothing to eat but the hay their owners bought them. And the winter of 1955 had a record-setting norther blow into central Texas. One night that winter was the moment Rebecca decided to redirect her life, to listen to the voice she knew was speaking the truth, what in her was to become Becky. Rebecca sat in her living room huddled next to a butane stove. The house had electricity, as Henry had promised, but it still could not keep out the winter drafts. She hugged her eighteen-month-old baby girl, who had a touch of fever, to her chest and told her son about the sick mare Henry was tending to. First the horse pulled up lame and then, as with most horses, once her feet went, her stomach went, and now she was dying. Henry was in the stable with her trying to force-feed her medicine and get her on her feet. Henry couldn't afford to lose another horse.

Rebecca shivered and pulled the baby tighter to her.

"Will Venus die too?" Kyle asked.

"We hope not," Rebecca said. You had to be honest with Kyle. He had his hunting cap on with one fur-lined ear flap pulled down over an ear and the other side sticking straight up.

"What happens if she does?"

"We don't know, Kyle. Are you sleepy yet?" Victoria let out a muffled cry, and Rebecca patted her back. Kyle pulled his blanket tighter around himself and went back to scribbling in his Lone Ranger coloring book.

As she then saw it, in the age when you had to earn the right to have sex, abstinence and marriage were the only options open to a nice girl. At eighteen, with active but untested hormones, abstinence seemed far worse than marriage, but at twenty-five with the rest of her life determined because of the search for proper sex, Rebecca was reconsidering abstinence. She felt guilty about her mental debate because unsuspecting Henry, out in the barn agonizing over his sick horse, had no idea how far his wife had drifted away from him. Henry wouldn't believe the thoughts of the nice girl he took from Carl Baumann.

Young Rebecca figured that Henry was just as she saw and knew him at that moment in 1955. He wouldn't change, would never have more than what he now had and, though he did love her, he could not love any more passionately or thoroughly than he then did. And he could never understand or know what she did. A library card, monthly trips to San Antonio for a movie, and an occasional dance on Marie's back porch were not enough to satisfy the curiosity of Rebecca Bolen, who had graduated early from high school, had been urged to go to college by her teachers, but had been told by Carl Baumann that college for a girl was a waste of time. Abstinence was possible. But she had two arguments for staying: one in her arms and one making blue and red streaks in his Lone Ranger coloring book.

On a Sunday the next summer, during a visit to her parents, while Henry gave Kyle a ride around San Antonio in his brand new second-hand pickup truck and Victoria was asleep in her Mamma's old bedroom, Rebecca told old Carl Baumann what she was secretly thinking about. They sat around the yellow, plastic-topped kitchen table, sipping on iced tea, old Carl tinkling his ice against the edges of his glass and sucking in on his cigar. Schatzi, dressed in knee-length shorts rolled up to her thighs and a sleeveless blouse, slumped in a kitchen table chair and hung her head over the back of the chair to let her hair dry in the breeze of the whirring water cooler, which Old Carl had just bought. Because the kitchen got the hottest from Doris' cooking, because he loved his wife, Old Carl put the water cooler in the kitchen. The rest of the house could use electric fans. Doris washed dishes. Rebecca would have preferred that her aging, still unmarried sister not be present, but she saw no polite way to get rid of her.

"Papa," Rebecca said, "I'm not happy."

Doris turned around from her dishes, wiping her wet hands in her apron, as though she sensed what would come next. Old Carl pulled his cigar out of his mouth and looked at the wet end. "So who is?" he asked.

"I would be, if I could borrow the money for the cruise

to Cuba," Schatzi said.

Old Carl banged his pipe on the table. "No trips to Cuba."

"It's a one-time deal. I can go with my girlfriends at the phone company," Schatzi said.

"No," old Carl said. "You live here, the answer is no."

"Papa, listen," Rebecca said, "I'm not happy living with Henry." Doris took a step closer to the table.

Schatzi straightened up in the chair, looked around at her parents and sister, then stood and said, "I think I'll curl my hair." As she walked out of the room, Rebecca looked at Schatzi's thighs, grown flabby after nearly ten years at the telephone company, and wondered what she did about sex, how she avoided it, if she did.

"I'm getting old," Rebecca said.

"Phooey," Old Carl said. "Twenty-five," he said and looked at Doris, then laughed. "She's getting old, ha."

"I'm not old yet, but I'm getting old without seeing or doing any more than what I did before I was married."

Doris walked to the table and sat down. She looked, to Rebecca, as if she were about to cry. Rebecca thought this look strange because she could only remember her mother with a passive, restrained look on her face—no laughter, but no tears. Rebecca looked closer at her mother, saw the empty eyes and the open mouth, and thought, My God, Mamma knows all about this.

Old Carl smiled in the wise-ass way that old German fathers smile, and looked across at his daughter with a loving but firm stare. "This is a phase. It will pass. It happens in all marriages."

Rebecca turned to her mother to see if it were true, to see if this was just a phase. Tears were just about to spill out of her mother's eyes, and Rebecca, too, felt like crying because she saw, in the empty face with gray splotches on the tired and drooping cheeks, that it was not just a phase. You never grew out of your regrets. Rebecca never wanted to look like her mother. "Oh,

Mamma," Rebecca said, then turned to Old Carl, "I want to get a divorce."

"Ha," Old Carl said and banged the flimsy kitchen table with his palm.

"I want to stay here with my kids until I can find a job."

Old Carl hit harder this time, shocking poor Doris. "*Kein* divorces." Those hard German eyes fixed Rebecca in place. "You have two babies. What about your *jungen*?"

"What about me?" Rebecca asked her father, then turned to look at her now crying mother.

"Who marries a woman with two babies and a divorce?"

"I don't want a new husband. I just don't want the one I have," Rebecca said to Carl.

"So what is so wrong with him?"

"Nothing. I'm just not happy."

"*Nein*, you go back to him."

"No."

"Mamma, you tell her."

Rebecca turned to look at her mother and said, "Please, Mamma, don't answer him if you don't want to."

But Doris was now crying and could say nothing. "See, see, you made your mother cry," Old Carl said to Rebecca, stood, walked behind his wife, and rubbed her shoulders.

"Mamma, Mamma," Rebecca said and reached under the table to pat her mother's knee.

Doris looked up at her daughter and asked, "You know what you give up and what you go against?"

"You hear what your mother says?" Old Carl said to Rebecca, hearing a warning rather than an honest question.

"Yes Mamma, I know."

"You know nothing," Old Carl said.

"I know I will move out with my babies and stay where I can," Rebecca said.

"Then you will not talk to me. You take away food, and a good house, and a good responsible father from those babies, and you will ruin them. I have seen this," Carl said.

"I will do it," Rebecca said to her mother and herself as an affirmation, then repeated to Carl, "I will do it," as a warning.

"You be careful," Doris said, and Rebecca saw Old Carl squeeze his wife's shoulder.

"How will you feed them?" Carl asked.

"I will." Rebecca reached across the table for her mother's hand, but Doris nodded her head once, pulled her hands away, then turned her head away from Rebecca.

Old Carl left his wife and walked to his daughter. His voice grew calm. "You see too many movies. Things are now hard. Love goes away. But, nobody makes you any promises. Now, you just have to go on." He patted her shoulders and looked at her. "Ask your mother."

"Please don't answer him, Mamma," Rebecca said.

"Sometimes it hurts to hear the truth," Old Carl said.

Doris gained control of herself. She straightened in her chair and grabbed the table with both hands. She swallowed hard and closed her eyes. "Your father is right," she said.

"Is he right that I should stay with Henry or is he right that it is a hard world?"

Rebecca hesitated to give Doris a chance to answer for herself and her daughter and not her husband. Doris looked at her daughter, and then, as though Old Carl's stare could pull up her head, she looked at her husband and said, "Both."

"Oh, Mamma," Rebecca sighed.

Doris stiffened and let her face go back to its passive, restrained look. "Give it more time," Doris said, and Rebecca cried for her bondage to Henry and for her mother's strange bondage to Old Carl. Then Doris cried, and Old Carl patted his wife, then his daughter on their backs to comfort them through the harsh truths he thought he had just explained to them. And he said just loud enough for them to hear him, "Women!"

* * *

Rebecca went to the movies. Years later, after thinking and looking at all the newspaper movie ads from that month and year, Becky still could not find what film she saw. Becky wanted a movie to mark this moment of life but just could not remember it or find it. Young Rebecca was hardly paying attention. The images flickering in front of her were illusions, lies; she knew that, but they didn't have to be so different from reality. They weren't completely different from truth, Rebecca thought in the dark theater as she cried, unable to absorb this mystery movie. She thought about what John Wayne, Alan Ladd, Burt Lancaster, Robert Mitchum would do. Right and wrong were right and wrong, she concluded. But the strength or will to do something, and then to suffer the consequences, was perhaps more important than right or wrong things. At twenty-five, Rebecca decided to free herself from sex, from men, from the age of earned sex, from the urge to do what was right. She would become a villain. Sydney Greenstreet, Jack Palance, Richard Widmark, even Barbara Stanwyck were just as pure in their own way as any hero.

That afternoon, after the movie, Rebecca waved to her parents and Schatzi from the cab of Henry's new second-hand pickup, her baby in her arms, her husband in the driver's seat, and her son standing in the seat between them as they drove back to Henry's Hill Country property with its dying horses, dark house, and pretty scenery. She waited four months.

In the fall, on a day when the wind shifted and the air stood still in humid anticipation of the coming dry norther, while Henry had gone to town to sit at Marie's and drink beer with Sam Penschorn, Pete Proctor, and Doc Jack Hillier, Rebecca left. Two-year-old Victoria, who slept through all the dramas of her early life, was asleep in the kids' bedroom, but Rebecca pulled Kyle into the kitchen to explain to the seven-year-old about what was going to happen to his mother.

"Kyle," she said to the boy, who was dunking an Oreo cookie in a glass of milk. "You have always been your father's boy, and so you're like him. You can take things as they come. You're hard to hurt. So, I'm going to explain this to you."

"This why I don't get a Davy Crockett hat?"

"No, this is serious."

The boy gulped down an Oreo, pushed the milk away from him, crossed his arms, and prepared to be serious. Rebecca almost laughed at him.

"I'm going to leave, Kyle."

"To San Antonio?"

"No."

"Can I go?"

"No, you've got to stay with your father."

"Okay."

"I've written a letter to explain to your father." She pulled it out of the pocket in her blouse and handed it to Kyle. "I want you to give it to him."

"Okay."

"I want something else, too."

"What?"

"Watch your father, and your grandparents, and yourself and make sure you all take care of your sister."

"Sure." Kyle held the letter out in front of him and looked at it. He turned the envelope over in his hand, probably wishing he could read well enough to understand it. Rebecca watched him, shocked that she had gotten through this farewell so well without much regret, then started to cry.

"I have so much confidence in you. And, I know

what a good boy you are, so I'm going to leave you alone now with your sister. And, you watch her until your father gets home. And then you always watch her." Kyle started to cry because, as stoic as he was, he sensed the climactic nature of this scene.

Rebecca, telling herself for weeks not to grow too sentimental and thus torment herself with guilt, could not keep from hugging Kyle then kissing him on the cheek. Then she gave completely in to sentimentality and quietly opened the door to the Victoria's bedroom, Kyle standing behind her, to take a last look at sleeping Victoria.

She picked up her packed suitcase that was waiting at the front door and walked down the gravel road from Henry's house to newly paved Ranch Road 12. When she got to the end of the road and stepped on Ranch Road 12, she turned around to look at the house and saw Kyle standing on the front porch watching her. She gave a full, roundhouse wave, and he returned the wave. She stuck her thumb in the air and got all the way to Big Spring, Texas before dawn, but before she went to sleep in Big Spring, she walked into a truck stop and got her first job as a waitress. She gave her name as "Becky."

Becky saw the pill, feminism, and drugs turn the age of earned sex into the age of unearned sex. Villainous Becky enjoyed herself in the new age: sex, movies, and college. She also sent letters, with no return addresses, to Schatzi and then Henry. Schatzi's letters stopped and ol' Carl himself had to call Becky and tell her that her sister had committed suicide. Doris let her know when Carl died. Then Doris died. Then I showed up at her office, said I was Roger Jackson, her son-in-law, and pleaded with her to come see Henry Bolen and her kids before Henry died.

I told her something she didn't know. In 1959, with the horse farm failing because of the famous fifties' drought and Henry's mismanagement, Henry went to Carl Baumann for help. Rebecca's father gave him $5,000 and co-signed a note for another $3,000, and told Henry that all debts for Victoria's desertion were then paid in full.

Becky laughed. "Those poor old men," she said.

And then I told her that I had this strange idea that, if I he could reunite Victoria with her mother, then Victoria might not leave me. Becky refused my request. After all, she had decided to become a villain.

Chapter 2:
Daryl and Clara

I pull into the driveway of my rented townhouse surrounded by other townhouses rented by people like me, an economic niche below the people who live around Kay Menger. A few headlights shine in driveways down the street and then shut off: other night workers like me. I don't sleep too well.

As I stick my keys in the door, I hear, "Hey buddy," from behind me. My stomach tightens. I stick a key through the first and middle finger of my right hand and get ready to take a swing at the guy. This could be a husband, somebody I've caught with my camera. It could be Kay Menger's new boyfriend. I refuse, so far, to carry a gun.

I turn and see that it is my new neighbor, George. "Hey, man," George says as he hulks toward me. "You think I could camp out on your couch?" George is six-three, thin, and well-built.

"What the hell?" is all I can think to say.

George stops and stuffs his hands in his pockets. "You've seen that woman I been running with, right? Twenty-two, second best piece of ass I've ever had. But she's got no responsibility whatsoever."

When he first moved in, George invited me and the lady next to him over for dinner. Dinner was quail gumbo. He had shot the quail during the last hunting season–though I wouldn't doubt that they were poached–and later he admitted to me that the roux was store-bought. The lady next door wasn't too impressed with his dinner or either of us.

"Where is she?" I ask George.

"I was playing pool. She comes in with a friend and wants to borrow my truck." George slouches and shrugs his shoulders. "So I give her my keys. It comes closing time, and I can't find her. A buddy gives me a ride home. Goddamn, when she gets back . . ."

I cradle my keys in my hand and open my door. George follows me in.

George played tackle and linebacker next to Tommy Nobis for the '63 and '64 Longhorns. He is still an old-school jock, from a time when football was not the way to fame or fortune, but still something resembling a game. He has the easy grace and humor of a jock, and also a jock's simplicity. I find him comfortable.

As I go into my bedroom and dig though my linen for a sheet and blanket for George, I hear him from the living room. "I thought it would be easy," he says. "You come home after work. You buy the little boys toy soldiers and toy guns; you buy the little girls dolls. Now, none of it works." He makes good money as a salesman. He has to to support his former wives and houses. Thank God I've never taken photos of either of his ex-wives. "Roger, when you wake in the morning, if you hearing bitching and screaming, think nothing of it. If she wasn't the second best piece of ass I ever had . . ."

I bring George his linen and help him spread it over my couch. "Female problems," he mutters.

"That's my business." George laughs because I told him my business. I leave him and go to my own bed.

With George on my couch, I lie on my back and put a pillow over my face. I hear George snoring and try to sleep. George and I aren't doing too well in the age of unearned sex. Tonight, at least, I have something to look forward to. Hope makes me relax. I stopped thinking of Becky as a villain. She now seems more like a casualty, just like ol' Carl, Doris, Schatzi, and Henry.

The night I proposed to Victoria I couldn't sleep either. So I left her asleep in her room and snuck back into Henry's dark living room and felt my way around it. I got to the front door and walked out to Henry's veranda. I pulled a joint that I had been saving and savoring all day out of my pocket and lit it up. "I didn't know you smoked," I heard and nearly swallowed my joint.

Henry was sitting in a rocker and staring out over his land. All I could really see was his Stetson making a smooth arch as he rocked back and forth. I slowly got up and pressed the tip of my joint with my thumb and forefinger. "I guess I shouldn't start," I said and stepped toward Henry.

I could see his Stetson turn toward me. "That wasn't a cigarette was it?"

I shuffled my feet, "No sir."

"I'd prefer you not smoke it on my property," Henry said. His hat shifted as he bent to one side of his rocker. He straightened and held a beer can toward me, "Here, have a beer. It's legal."

I stepped closer to Henry and grabbed a beer. It wasn't really cold but drinking it and talking to Henry gave me something to do while I waited out that night. "Thank you, Henry," I said and heard a swoosh as Henry popped another top.

"Problems inside?" Henry asked, and I saw his Stetson jerk toward the house. Then he started to push himself up, "Is Victoria okay?"

"Victoria's fine, no physical problems." Henry sank into his chair. "I couldn't sleep. I've got things on my mind."

"Women problems, I bet." Henry giggled. "It's a bitch." Henry giggled again. "But you really ain't got it so bad. With women, I mean," Henry said.

"I guess I love your daughter," I told Henry. I heard no answer, just the steady rocking. Then I dared to bring up the forbidden subject. "I suppose you loved your wife."

All I heard was more rocking. "The first woman I really loved was a Mexican," Henry said as though he didn't hear me or had disregarded my question.

"Did you marry her?"

Henry chuckled. His rocker gained momentum. "No, of course not. Would have been a godawful, terrible mistake. I was just a piss ant kid at the time."

"But what about Becky?" I asked. But she was not the story that Henry wanted to tell or was willing to tell that night.

"Consuela," Henry said. "She was a whore."

Presently, when I'm in my dark townhouse, I sometimes I think he's with me. So we, Henry's spirit and I, sit around at night thinking, remembering, getting pissed off, and hoping for a time when we can finally be glad for what we did have.

* * *

You can see Balcones fault off the west side of IH 35. To the east of IH 35 is the best Texas farmland. The clear creeks in the Hill Country spill down the fault and become deep, wide, cypress lined, mostly dammed rivers: the Guadalupe, the Frio, the Nueces, the Blanco, the Colorado.

When I met him, Henry lived near this eastern edge, just west of IH 35. West on IH 10 or Texas 290, you can't see the Hill Country end like you see it begin off IH 35. The cedars and scrub oak get shorter and thinner, then disappear. The hills become mesas and arroyos then stretch out into miles and miles of West Texas.

West Texans took their Christianity seriously. They had a mean god. For only something intent on punishing men could have or would have created a landscape that had no green, no trees, no natural marks, just an occasional swell in the ground; that had no water, not even in the sky.

The heat could curl the atmosphere around into a tornado. A thunderstorm, with lightning out to strike anything without cover in the flat land, could drown you any time of year. Hail was the size of biscuits. All spring long dust could choke you. Rain could mix with dust, and the mud would fall from the sky. To live in West Texas at the start of this century, you had to take joy where you could find it. The people figured there had to be a God as stark, as simple, and as mean as the weather, so they found what joy they could in Him and prayed to Him.

Henry's mother was such a person, a good Baptist. Her farmer parents, thinking that they and God could make things grow, brought two-year-old Clara to a farm in between Odessa and Pecos at the turn of the century. With the help of her parents, Clara soon saw God in the flatness.

Henry's father, Daryl Bolen, however, was a cowboy. His kind didn't have a god like the Christian farmers. They just figured that life was naturally tough. So they became as tough, and as crude, and as unreasoning as the land they saw. But like most cowboys, Daryl could see his future, himself at fifty: bow-legged, probably drunk, penniless, toothless, useless. So he quit laughing at the farmers and started looking at their daughters. When he married Clara, he at first tried to believe in her Baptist God but then gave up and resigned himself to letting her have her way. And with the same weird genes for wrong decisions as those he passed on the to his son, Daryl, always a cowboy but now married, bought a new suit and a saddle at a shop in Odessa. Then the grass died, and ranching became useless around Odessa. Soon after, Odessa became the center of the oil patch. Henry was born in 1917, shortly before the oil boom.

When he was seventeen, during a night without anything to do, long before a car was a necessity for a teenager, Henry snuck back to the alley behind Slick

Tom's billiard hall with Melinda Sue Wengler. In that long, dark age of earned sex, Henry Bolen pushed his flat palm under the hem of Melinda Sue's summer dress and along the side of her long, never shaven leg. As he hooked his then intact trigger finger over the top of Melinda's panties and began to pull them down, he wondered just what he should feel, just what he would see. It was the greatest excitement he had ever had.

Melinda Sue Wengler, a Baptist girl, stuck in and confused by the age of earned sex, must have also wondered just how she should feel. She could have had no idea as to how she should think about something that felt as different as this. No doubt her mother, not yet sensing the need to inform her, had never told her about the hideousness and danger of letting teenage boys feel up her dress. Perhaps, poor Melinda Sue was a bright girl and able to reason that things that felt mysterious or different like things that looked or smelled different, like the sky before a storm, probably meant danger. Or maybe, the rough God of West Texas whispered in her ear to keep her legs crossed. So as Henry lowered her panties to her knees, she screamed as loudly as she could.

Henry jerked up, barely getting his curled forefinger out of Melinda's panties, almost losing it then rather than to a German soldier ten years later. More confused now, Henry tried to think this out, tried to figure what first made her spread her bean pole thighs then let out with a scream. While his mind whirled in a confused rather than moral tornado, a strong claw squeezed into the soft spot between his neck and shoulder. He twisted to break the grip and saw Tom Jordan, the owner of Slick Tom's Billiard parlor, gripping his shoulder with one hand and reaching for him with the other.

He got his shoulder out of Tom's fist, but Tom caught him around the neck with his other arm. "I ain't done a thing," Henry yelled, then saw Melinda—her skirt just below her waist, her torn panties just below her thighs—fold her arms over her face and convulse with sobbing. "But I ain't done but what I was led to," Henry got out before Tom circled another arm around him and started dragging him down the alley. And, with his head sticking out from between Tom's hold on him, Henry was able to see Melinda curl into a tight ball, like a doodle bug, and cry and shake all over. "Melinda?" he sobbed back at her.

* * *

Later that night, Henry sat in a cell in the town jail and peered out at the wooden door that separated him from a conference room where his parents were deciding his fate with the police chief, a minister, and the school principal. While Clara cried, the men decided that he might be dangerous in school. The principal would expel him but keep quiet about the circumstances. The minister would come by for weekly conferences until Henry was cured. And Daryl Bolen and the police chief thought he should get a job.

Far past midnight, when good Baptists were in bed asleep and the oil field trash roamed the downtown streets looking for some way to spend their money, Daryl and Clara drove Henry home. From the backseat of the car, Henry watched the heads of his mother and father. "It's the influence of all these oil men," his mother said. Daryl, as always, nodded his head and didn't comment.

They lived in a two bedroom shotgun house next to Monahans draw, a natural drainage ditch that the city used as a sewage dump during the winter months. At Clara's urging, they walked quietly, so as not to wake the other people who had chosen to move alongside an open sewer. They walked into the living room, and Henry pressed his back against the wall and stared at his father hoping to see his face in the moonlight. His mother walked through the living room and into the kitchen. "Daddy," Henry said as Daryl flipped on the light and saw his father's cracked and raw cowboy face grow red. Henry stepped toward his father and again said, "Daddy."

Then Daryl Bolen raised his arm across his chest. The backhanded blow caught Henry on the side of his head and knocked him back against the wall. His knees buckled, and he slid down the wall into a sitting position, rubbed his face, and looked up at his father, whose mass of wrinkles seemed to sag. When Henry's butt hit the carpet, the dust that you just couldn't keep out of a home in West Texas rose up around him. He could taste blood. Though he was seventeen, he couldn't help but to cry as Daryl Bolen bent over, gently took his elbow in one arm, and helped him to his feet. His father turned away from him and said, "Now it's all done. You been punished. It's all over." His father turned to face him and then slowly backed away from him and said, "Don't do that no more. Go see your mother."

"But what I done?" Henry asked his father.

"Just don't do it no more," Daryl said.

When Henry walked into the kitchen, he saw his mother sitting in the dark with her hands folded on top of the kitchen table. She dipped her head toward a chair opposite her, and Henry sat down. She reached toward him to grab his hands and pulled them slowly to her until Henry's palms rested flat against her shoulders, just above her breasts, and his stomach pressed against the edge of the table. She closed her eyes and began to pray, and between the prayers, she begged Henry to pray with her.

As he had before, Henry tried repentance and prayer, but there was too much of his father in him. He couldn't get scared of the West Texas God. He couldn't know in his heart that he could repent for what he had done to Melinda Sue Wengler. He didn't even understand what he had done to Melinda Sue Wengler. Henry faked a prayer as best he could and told his mother he felt better. Clara Bolen pulled him farther across the table and folded her arms around his head, pulling him to her breast, and said, "Praise be to sweet Jesus."

Henry waited a week to decide that the best way to treat humiliation was to run away from it. He snuck out of the house with a duffle bag over his shoulder and ran for the tracks. He knew the Missouri Pacific railroad ran from Odessa to Pecos, and he knew that, for years, bored Odessa boys, stuck in the age of earned sex, jumped the late night trains for Pecos, an old cow town where they could find open bars and cheap women, a town that catered to cowboys with no religion. He ran for the tracks as he heard the chugging of the train, knew nothing about hopping a train, but saw an open box car. He flung his duffle bag into the box, and hooked his elbows over the edge of the box car as the train gained speed. His feet got tangled, and as he slid down, he dug his fingers into the wood of the box car's floor and felt his fingernails seemingly rip as he slid closer and closer toward the wheels below him.

Then, a pair of hands hooked under his armpits and started to weakly pull him across the box car floor. At first, he thought that God himself was saving him, started to praise Jesus, but then knew the tremors shaking the hands pulling him to safety were not the tremors of God. He looked up to see a dark figure in a loose fitting jacket and a ragged hat holding his arms and straining to back across the box car. When Henry's shins scraped over the edge of the floor, the man stopped pulling him and walked over to Henry's duffle bag. Henry pushed himself up then sat in a corner to watch the ragged man paw through his duffle bag. "That's mine," Henry said.

"Not too goddamn grateful, are you pup?" The man dropped the duffle bag, grunted, and dropped to his knees when the train bounced. He held his hand out to Henry. "Lucien," he said, and Henry grabbed his hand

and thanked him for saving his life. "Got any liquor?" Lucien asked. "Prohibition's over. No more grain alcohol."

* * *

Four years later, Henry's head again bounced against the wall of a railroad car, this one a cattle car being pulled toward Odessa. From the drying cow shit that filled the cattle car, Henry knew cattle had probably been unloaded just before he jumped on. He had company, a wetback sitting in the corner. The slats of the cattle car made wide stripes of light and dark across the wetback's body. The wetback wouldn't keep his glassy eyes adjusted on any one thing too long; his eyes just shifted in his head. Henry stared at him and became amused by him.

The wetback reached into his back pocket and pulled out a switchblade. He twirled the knife around in his hands, then quickly flicked his wrist to lock the blade into place. Henry looked straight at him, having learned most tough acts aren't really dares. The wetback lowered his head and folded his blade into the handle, then looked back at Henry, his glassy eyes starting to water, and he snapped the blade open in front of his face. He was younger than Henry.

"Crap," Henry had muttered to himself and looked away from the wetback. Henry had seen men like the wetback before, flashing switchblades to hide a fear that would force them to use the knife sooner or later. After a robbery or murder, this wetback would be a real tough guy, for a while. Then, he'd be dead or in jail. Henry closed his eyes and leaned against the slat in the cattle car. He would rather smell the cow shit than watch the wetback. Young, stuck in the Depression, Henry heard his mother's hymns ringing in his ears and felt a need for forgiveness, a straight and narrow path, not because he believed in a West Texas God anymore than when he was seventeen, but because he was scared to death that unless he changed his life, he would be dead.

Lucien and Henry had ridden the train to El Paso and, when Lucien jumped off in the El Paso train yard, Henry could think of nothing better to do than jump out after him. As they walked beside the tracks, Lucien continued his lecture to Henry about how to be a good bum. "We're going to go to Juarez," Lucien told Henry. "This country ain't worth a good goddamn anymore." Henry now knew what Lucien meant. In Juarez, poverty was normal; bums could find some pride, even associate with people other than other bums. But, the place to beg, steal, or panhandle was across the river in El Paso.

Lucien took Henry to a whorehouse. Freddy, a black-haired, red faced Irishmen, who must have found himself drawn to the Catholic Mexicans, was the pimp and manager of the El Gallo bar. Freddy eyed seventeen-year-old Henry and said, "No free samples, gringo." When teenaged Consuela strutted into the bar and smiled at Henry, Lucien said, "That's who he means." But they stayed several months in the El Gallo, and Henry watched her every day.

Henry opened his eyes when he heard, "Hey man," and felt a tapping on his shoulders. And he smelled the peculiar smell of marijuana, an odor he was only slightly familiar with, mixing with the smell of the cow shit. The wetback held a lit joint in front of Henry. And, Henry the adapter hesitated at first but then took the joint and sucked in on it.

At a liquor store in El Paso, Henry had watched from across the street, through the large window as Lucien pointed an unloaded, rusty pistol at the store owner. Henry saw the owner give Lucien a few bills from the cash register and Lucien stuff the bills into his tattered coat pocket. Then Lucien, always the drunk, ordered two pints of bourbon. Lucien didn't slowly lower his gun and back out of the liquor store as any good stick-up man would have done, as even seventeen-year-old

Henry could have guessed to do. But, Lucien dropped his gun hand to his side, put his gun in his coat pocket, turned his back to the owner, and ran like hell. He came out of the door of the liquor store smiling, a happy drunk, glad for his small heist. But, as Lucien clomped across the street in his slow gait that was barely faster than walking, Henry saw the store owner appear in the doorway and raise a gun. "Lucien," Henry had screamed. Lucien just smiled and held the two bottles of bourbon out in front of him where Henry could see them. The first shot hit him in the neck, and the second squarely between the shoulder blades.

Lucien held his pint bottles out in front of him as he hit his knees, and he protected the bottles as he fell face forward on to his forehead. Henry ran to him and grabbed the two bottles. Lucien raised his head, a knot above one eye, and squeezed out of his blood clogged throat, "my pocket." But Henry was too scared to grab anything other than the bottles and ran as fast as he could, stiff legged, flat footed in his heavy, thick-soled boots.

Henry, at that time, was learning to run well. He ran back to the El Gallo, then ran with Consuela to a flop house in Phoenix, Arizona. When Irish Freddy caught up with them, he twisted Consuela's arm so hard that he dislocated it from her shoulder. He threatened to shoot Henry.

So, Henry ran to Los Angeles, where he met Wild Jack, a World War I vet with one hand and a hook. Wild Jack found Henry roaming the streets in Los Angeles with Barefoot George. His first night in Los Angeles, Henry slept in an alley next to George. George gave Henry two sips of his wine, rolled over, and started to snore. A black man, George had come to Los Angeles from New Jersey for the warm winters. When Henry met him, his last pair of shoes had dissolved off his feet, his kinky hair was clotted with mud from the alleys where he slept, and his breath stunk. Wild Jack found them in the alley and hired them to smuggle leather goods and dope across from Mexico. They sold the leather goods on the Venice boardwalk to tourists, and they sold the dope to Jack's friends. When George died from drinking too much, and Jack's woman got pregnant, Henry got scared again. He kissed Jack's woman good-bye because he wasn't sure that the baby in her belly was not his. He got drunk and jumped a train heading east for Texas.

As that train pulled into the Odessa train yard, Henry jumped out of the door before any yard cops could see him. The wetback jumped out after him. They both ran until they got past the tracks and on to a street. Henry headed for downtown. "Where you going, man?" the wetback asked.

"Here," Henry said.

"Me to," the wetback said.

"Not with me."

Henry turned his back to the wetback and started walking down the road. Glancing over his shoulder, he saw the wetback following him. Henry turned around. The wetback froze. "Get out of here," Henry told him.

"Want some more dope?"

"Goddamn, don't show no dope here."

Henry turned his back to him and walked down the street. The wetback crossed to the other side of the street and followed him to downtown.

It was Saturday in Odessa, and Henry wandered around town looking for things to remember while the wetback walked behind him. Finally, softening or realizing his debt to strangers met on trains, Henry looked over at the man and jerked his chin, and the wetback ran up to him. Both had a few cents but neither wanted to spend their money for a drink, so they looked in store windows and watched the traffic. They looked into the Sears catalog house, almost pressing their noses against the glass; then they walked across the street to

Perry's five and dime, where they could roam the store aisles without buying anything. They ended up at the building that used to be Slick Tom's Billiards Hall.

Henry stood in front of it and looked at its new sign: The L & M pharmacy. The wetback stood beside him, tapped him on the shoulder, and said, "Let's go." Henry shook his head and sat down on the curb. The wetback sat beside him, then looked across the street, then ran across it to the small grocery store. While Henry sat on the curb in front of the L & M pharmacy and looked for landmarks or friends, the wetback ran into the grocery and came back with two oranges. He gave one to Henry. Henry peeled the orange, pulled loose a slice, and bit into it. He felt the spray of orange juice from his bite hit him in his face. He looked back at the wetback. "I don't need no wetback following me all over town," he said.

The wetback looked at him, the sticky orange juice clinging to the thin hairs that he used for a mustache. Henry knew he couldn't easily get rid of the wetback. He pressed his palms against his aching forehead, then opened his eyes to see a woman holding a baby and getting out of a car. Henry watched her knees slip out from under the hem of her dress, and he admired the way she held the slumped baby in one cradled arm. She walked straight toward him then stopped in front of him.

Melinda Sue, the poor Baptist girl stuck in the age of earned sex with a baby not enough younger than she was, looked down at Henry and must have recognized him—or so Henry thought—because she smiled. But as Henry rose and she turned to look back at the car that had just dropped her off, her smile disappeared. She looked down at the wetback, then at Henry. She tightened her grip on the baby and, with her free hand, pushed the baby's face into her shoulder and stuck her chin over the baby's head. Henry felt his rough beard and pushed up the brim of his hat that had lost all shape and just drooped. And, he must have wanted even more dearly to be something other than what he then was. And, he knew he had to get rid of the wetback.

So Henry took the wetback to the train yard and told him to stay low and wait for him; then he went to his old house beside Monahans draw. Now, due to the lucky genes that he and his father shared, the house was bigger. Without any effort from Daryl, Clara's parents bubbled up a few barrels of oil, and Daryl and Clara were able to add on. When he rang the doorbell, he kept his chin almost to his chest and looked out from under the brim of his drooping hat. His mother answered the door, put one hand to her throat, then smiled. "I thought I would drop by since I'm back," Henry said.

"Praise Jesus," she said, "I prayed you'd come back. Lord, I prayed you back." She opened the door, and Henry stepped in, and she hugged him. "Praise Jesus," she uttered again and again. Then she turned away from him and matter of factly said, "Dinner's ready. Clean up, Henry." His mother went into the kitchen, and Henry looked around the house that he barely recognized. The floor was a shiny golden with new wooden slats and a new rug, not the old rug with frayed edges. The furniture was re-upholstered. His mother came back in to look at him, and he hung his head. "Praise God," she said and hugged him. Henry followed her into the kitchen. She pointed at a new gas oven. "A wonderful thing. Praise God."

Then, Daryl—dressed in an undershirt, khaki pants, and an old pair of boots—came through the backdoor. Daryl Bolen had gotten fat. His belly stretched out his undershirt and hung over his pants. Loose flesh that used to be muscle hung down from his arms. He stared at Henry and stepped back as Henry stepped toward him. "I'll be . . ." his father said, his words trailing off before he took God's name in vain.

"Daddy," Henry said and nodded his head.

"So you come back," Daryl said and looked first and Henry then at his wife.

"So what you do for a living nowdays?" Henry asked his father and smiled.

"Nothing," his father replied. "I live off your mother's parents' oil money."

"It's a blessed miracle," Clara said as she opened the door to her new gas oven. Henry didn't know if she meant his return or the oil money.

At dinner, Clara prayed for Henry and thanked the Lord for sending him back. Henry sat at the head of the table across from his mother, and Clara looked at him, almost never dipping her head toward her plate. Her gaze annoyed Henry. His cowboy father, now with a big belly and loose flesh hanging from his arms, said nothing, and Henry poked chunks of roast beef, the best dinner he had had in years, into his mouth to keep from talking to his father.

After dinner, Henry washed as his mother dried dishes. Often, their hands brushed together so that Henry could feel the rough back of her hand, the rising veins, and the twisted joints of her long fingers. And once, in the soapy dishwater, his mother pressed her finger tips to his palm. While they washed dishes, never really talking, his father walked through the kitchen to the backyard that faced Monahans draw. Henry watched as his father walked down the slopping backyard to the drainage ditch. His mother grabbed his soapy hands in her own and led him away from the sink.

Their hands clasped together in dual prayer, Clara Bolen started, "Pray to Jesus with me, Henry, and show me that you've changed." Henry closed his eyes but couldn't get a word of prayer out of his mouth. His mother sunk to her knees and pulled him with her. "God sent you back. I prayed, and the Lord sent you back. Now you pray with me." Henry stood slowly and gently pulled himself away from his mother. He turned his back to her and walked out the backdoor to his father.

He walked down the backyard slope to Monahans draw, the sun setting in front of his eyes. Daryl threw rocks and dirt clods toward the draw. Like all cowboys, he looked comfortable without a chair, looked natural in his squat, even with his belly hanging over his belt. Henry squatted beside him and threw a rock toward the draw himself. Then slowly, pushing his hands against his knees, Daryl stood. Henry rose with him. "You saw your mother. I can't pray with her no more than you could. Matter of fact, I can't stand her praying anymore."

"I know you can't, Daddy. I figured that out."

Daryl Bolen looked at his son, then stuck his hands into his back pockets the way cowboys would. "You should never of gone," he said.

"I didn't mean to," Henry said.

"And, you should never of come back."

"I got no place else."

"You just got no place, then. You can't find nothing here. You're mother's damn near lost to us now. You come back, you'll make her Jesus crazy."

"Daddy, I got nothing," Henry said.

"And the hard truth is you got nothing here."

Henry saw his father squint, and a vein in his forehead, just under his receding hairline, filled with blood and stood out.

"I'm scared. What am I going to do?" Henry asked his father. Daryl Bolen pulled his arm across his chest. And as his loose-fleshed, flabby arm came toward Henry. Henry raised his hand, palm out, and grabbed his father's wrist before the back handed slap could reach his face. He held on to his father's wrist and watched the loose flesh on his arm quiver. His father had tears in his eyes, but he wouldn't cry.

"I can't whip you," Daryl said. "Ain't much either of us can do," he said. Henry backed slowly away from him then turned toward the house. He jerked open the screen door to the kitchen, then put his hand behind him to catch it and let it bounce quietly in its frame. His mother was sleeping. She was sitting in a chair, her arms folded on the kitchen table, her head resting on her arms. She had set the chair so she could see out to the yard, but she had fallen asleep and was snoring. Henry walked straight through the house and outside.

Then, on the front porch of his parent's house, Henry's instinctual urge that had become the first great conviction of his life took over. He ran. Change and distance could erase memory. He put one heavy-booted foot in front of the other, until he got to the train station. He heard a voice behind him, "Where to, man?"

"Huh?" Henry said and remembered the wetback.

"Where we going to go?"

Here was something, Henry thought, just a wetback, but he was something. And, he thought about what his father had said, about the legends he had heard from those men just a bit older than his daddy, about the rumors of wild nights in Pecos. He said, with some degree of conviction in his voice, "We're gonna be cowboys."

After I heard Henry's story about his early difficulties with Consuela and Melinda Sue Wengler, I thought that Henry just had the bad luck of being born at the wrong time—the age of earned sex. At the time, in love with Victoria, with a joint and a few beers, I fancied myself some crusader for the new age of enlightenment. Now I don't know. Like the rest of us, Henry got what he wanted, not what he needed. Mick Jagger had it backwards.

Chapter 3:
Shorty and Emma

When the "wetback" Henry had gone to cowboy with got cut up in a bar fight and then got deported, Shorty Martins had become Henry's best friend. In 1943, somewhere around Pecos, Texas, Shorty Martins and Henry Bolen sat in a cold bunk house with nothing but bed rolls, a poorly working heater, and a bottle of bourbon to keep them warm and talked about Henry's agricultural deferment from World War II and his future. Shorty was too crippled and too short to get into the service. And, at the time, Shorty had just glimpsed over the edge of fifty to see his future. Alcoholic, displaced, with no hope of ever being more than what he was, Shorty had only death as the next great event in his life. Shorty, like Henry's father, knew the sad truth that over-worked, under-paid cowboys, if they weren't lucky enough to find a wife and get into some other business or get real lucky and manage a ranch, became crippled-up old men in their fifties who lived in cold bunkhouses off a rancher's sense of social responsibility.

So small he often had to buy a boy's saddle, Shorty was too abnormal or ugly to ever find a woman, but he could make a horse do anything. Henry told everybody about the way Shorty rocked in the saddle and moved with the rhythm of the horse and how "pretty" the horse looked with his muscles working "fluid-like" beneath its skin. Henry told me that once, with his reins in his teeth, a pistol in each hand, guiding the horse with his knees, Shorty had ridden through the West Texas prairie and blasted at jack rabbits to show the cowboys how the old Texas Rangers had scared the hell out of Mexicans, Indians, and Yankees.

That night, Shorty lay on his bunk, took a long swig at the bottle of Old Crow bourbon, then passed the bottle to Henry. Henry sat in his bunk with his sleeping bag wrapped around him, listened to the whir of the kerosene lantern, and watched the shifting shadows as the wind, not just a draft, blew in through the cracks in the cabin's lumber to shake the lantern. He took the bourbon that he was just learning to drink and appreciate and took a long swig from the bottle.

"For a young man like yourself," Shorty said, "This war might be a good thing."

"What sense is quitting a job and a deferment to go get killed?" Henry asked. Shorty reached for the bottle and shook his fingers for it.

"What you think you gonna become here?"

"It's a job. A cowboy is better than what I once was."

"Yeah, but you join the service and make it through a war, you are a hero."

"So what good is a hero?"

"So what good is a cowboy? Ain't been a real cowboy, let alone a useful one, in fifty years. We ain't nothing more than heirlooms." Shorty took a drink from the bottle, lay his head down, and looked up at the ceiling. "The worst that could happen is you get killed. But war has to end, and if you ain't dead, you're a hero. You stay in the army, you become a sergeant or something, and you got a roof and three squares assured to you. Can some fat ass rancher offer you that?"

"I could be a sergeant," Henry said to confirm Shorty. Shorty raised his head up just a bit, stuck the bottle between his lips, and sucked out the last of the bourbon just as Henry reached for the bottle. "Jesus, Shorty, I got hardly none of that to keep me warm." Henry looked at Shorty to see him silently staring at the ceiling on the verge of screaming or shaking. "You okay?" Henry asked.

"This war is a big thing and is gonna give a lot a people a lot of chance. It is going to shake things all up."

Henry stared at his friend whom he had thought too mean and too by-God proud to be on the verge of crying, and then, looking closely at his friend for maybe the first time, Henry saw his future. "You want to enlist with me?"

"They already refused me." An alcoholic tremor went through Shorty's body. "Goddamn it is cold," he said. "It bites into your bones." Henry knew what Shorty meant. The bourbon didn't really help against the cold; the warm tingle it left in your throat, chest, and stomach just took your mind off the cold.

"I got this blanket stuffed into my bag. You want it?"

"It's yours," Shorty said, and Henry watched him shake from the alcohol or the cold chills that ran through him. He reached above his head to turn off the kerosene lantern, so he wouldn't have to listen to its whir, or watch its shadows, or see Shorty.

* * *

Henry got trained just in time for the Normandy invasion. He got mad when Travis Lilly, a fellow Texan from Houston, only twenty-two years old, was made corporal over him and put in charge of Henry's squad. Henry thought his five years of varied experience gave him more common sense ability. He began to fear that rungs on his career ladder were slipping out of his fingers and from under his feet.

Travis Lilly, for his part, must have doubted his own ability to lead men. He had been in the army no longer than Henry and now had a minor part in waging the most important battle in history. But he must have gained confidence in his own ability when he and Henry hit the beach side by side. They dove head first into the sand and came up coughing and spitting it out. He turned to Henry and was the first one to see the former cowboy staring dumbly at the shattered wood of his rifle's stock, then at his own finger tip—the one that had pulled Melinda Sue Wengler's panties down to her thighs—lying in the sand.

As Henry had raised his rifle to fire, a lucky German bullet or a stray American bullet had hit his trigger finger then shattered the stock of the rifle, sending splinters of wood into Henry's chin and cheek. Travis Lilly must have at least thought himself less shocked and disoriented than the poor cowboy. "I didn't even fire," Henry said. He held up his broken rifle. "What do I do now?"

"Jesus fucking Christ," Travis said. Since Travis Lilly was the corporal, Henry figured Travis should give him some advice, should order him to do something, but Travis said, "I guess you should pick up your finger." Then they heard a lieutenant or someone who sounded important shouting to advance. Travis Lilly got to his knees and elbows, then to his feet, and ran forward. Henry followed him.

When they dove into the sand again, just next to a barbed wire fence, Henry borrowed a handkerchief from Travis Lilly and wrapped it around the shreaded knuckle of his trigger finger. Henry also tried to cock his head and to hold his tongue just right to pray like his mother prayed so he could pick up the Lord's transmissions, but everything was going too fast, like in the movies of World War I, so Henry again failed to contact the Lord.

Henry followed Travis Lilly on into France. He followed him and the rest of his squad for three days, right off the beach and into the hedgerow country of northern France. His rifle was useless. He was afraid it might go off and shoot somebody, so he pulled out the clip as best he could with his one hand and dragged the rifle behind him by the barrel, the splintered stock scraping against the ground. He figured since it was the only weapon he had other than his bayonet that he should keep it; maybe he could use it as a club.

On his third night in France, Henry tried to follow Travis over a brick wall. As he grabbed the edge of the wall with his right hand, he screamed from the pain that shot through his trigger finger all the way into his shoulder. He fell backward and tried to twist in mid-air to regain his feet. When he hit the ground, he broke an ankle. Travis and a Georgian minister named Wesley Zirkel felt along Henry's ankle and listened to him scream. They decided the ankle was broken. "Guess now you just can't go with us no more," Travis said to Henry, shook Henry's left hand, then led his squad over the wall.

Henry was unconscious when another squad with a medic found him and sent him to the rear. He was carried back to the beach in an ambulance and put on a ship, just like a hero. And when he was recovering in a hospital in London, a colonel came by and gave him a purple heart and a citation for bravery for stumbling after his squad for three days with a shot-off finger.

The finger had gotten infected and the doctors had to trim it down below the second knuckle of the forefinger, nearly to the knuckle on his hand. The compound fracture of his ankle was worse. The doctors cut into it and put it in a cast, then took the cast off and cut again. He got a letter from Travis congratulating him on his million dollar wound, the kind all the draftees prayed for. Henry, the desperate cowboy, immediately volunteered to go back to the front. His doctors and the colonel who gave him his purple heart mistook him for a hero because he wanted to stay a soldier, but they said his missing trigger finger would keep him out of combat.

Nearly one year after he enlisted in the army, two days before he was to be released from the London hospital, the colonel who gave him his medal told him Travis Lilly had been killed. And then, on his last day in the hospital, the colonel shook Henry's hand (the one without the trigger finger), told him the army needed more like him, and gave him an honorable discharge. "I'll re-enlist," Henry said. The colonel cocked his head at Henry's remark and said, "No, son. You've done your time. Your country owes you. You are disabled now. Go home. You have a pension coming."

* * *

A cedar chopper, according to Sam Penschorn and Pete Proctor, was the lowest form of human life in the Hill Country. Too ignorant or stupid to find work, cedar choppers settled on chopping down the cedar and clearing the brush off land that ranchers or farmers were trying to develop. Shipped to Fort Sam Houston in San Antonio, Texas, Henry drifted toward the Hill Country and became a cedar chopper. He worked with a large woman who had a red face with her gray hair always pasted to her forehead by sweat, Emma, and her semi-retarded son, Bud. Emma had supported herself for years as a cedar chopper and was known to all the Hill Country ranchers and farmers as a cheap hand. "Used to have some good men work for me," she had said when she hired Henry, "Now they are all off at war."

Almost a year after Emma had hired him, during a warm spring day, Henry was working with her and Bud clearing brush away from a creek and cutting cedars for the owner of the property who wanted to turn his useless land into pasture. Like most cedar choppers, Henry had welts across his face, hands, and arms from the slaps of tree limbs and brush. Though his right hand with its missing finger didn't always hold an ax or a scythe very well in those pre-chainsaw days, Henry developed his own way to chop and saw; he got used to his sweat dripping into the cuts on his face and arms and making them sting like hell, the gnats and horseflies buzzing around his head, and the taste of saw dust and grit sticking to his teeth and lips. Cedar chopping, he learned, was no easier than cowboying.

After working until they nearly gave out, they quit at four o'clock and drove to the nearest town for a beer: Fischer. When he walked into Marie's, Henry got his first view of Sam Penschorn and Pete Proctor bellied up to the bar and talking about their peach crops. He saw black-haired Evelyn without a trace of a gray hair. And Emma introduced him to the owner of the land they were clearing, a doctor in Fischer named Jack Hillier. Other people from around town were in the bar, and by five o'clock, more began pushing in to hear a politician who was going speak. The area representative to the U.S. Congress, a Lyndon Johnson, was going to come by and talk up some votes. A lot of people knew him. Most just used him as an excuse to take off work early.

A native of the Hill Country, Johnson gave Henry hope. He promised to make life as easy as possible for the returning G.I.'s, to make sure they had money for college and loans to start businesses and buy property. Nothing was too much for the men who had whipped ass in Europe and the Pacific. And Johnson promised to improve life for the common man in the Hill Country. The army corps of engineers would be building dams to bring electricity and irrigation to the entire Hill Country, he promised. After he was through speaking, Johnson walked through the small crowd to shake hands. As Henry stuck out his hand for Johnson to shake, the congressman looked down at the missing trigger finger. Henry smiled, and Johnson seemed to know Henry lost it in the war. To Henry, that handshake was his personal guarantee from the congressman and future senator and president that, though he was out of the army, his service had been rewarded. As Henry saw it, Lyndon Johnson was in Marie's tavern in Fischer, Texas to make good on Shorty Martins' speculation.

The next morning as they started a new day of

clearing Dr. Jack Hillier's land, Henry paced off a barb wire boundary at the back of the property. The overcast sky would keep the heat down until about noon when the sun would come through. Henry heard the cicadas in the trees, noticing their rhythm for the first time. Though he had never heard them in West Texas, their sound was a natural part of summer and spring days in the Hill Country. He looked around him at the cedars, some tall enough to provide decent shade (no shade in west Texas, he thought). The live oaks gave even more shade. He stared at the shadows of the trees on the ground and thought of what a pretty and cool thing shade was. At night, he noticed, the gulf breeze would blow through the trees and cool down the heat of the day.

He started to climb up the highest hill on Doc Hillier's property, slipping over the limestone rocks, his ankles rolling inside his boots. He bent over to look at the yellow, orange, and green moss that clung to some of the rocks where the water from springs dripped almost year round. He felt the moss and the cool spring water and stuck his fingers in his mouth to taste the water— sweet, clear, cold. He continued to climb, and as he came over the top and stopped on the ground that begin to level out, he looked south and saw Emma and her retarded son taking axes to cedars; and beyond them, he saw the gravel road they came on, Ranch Road 12; and still farther on, he saw two peaks higher than his own stretch into the low haze of a sky. And between the peaks, he saw fields of bluebonnets, Indian pinks, and sun flowers looking like waves of color.

He turned west and walked across the gently sloping part of the property that formed a nearly level green pasture. Green, he thought; in West Texas, pastures were brown. He continued until he came to tall grass. He pushed through the grass toward the sound of water falling on rocks, spitting against the gnats that flew into his teeth and lips, then saw the headwater of Fischer creek form a mossy pool, spill over the limestone rocks that acted as filters to purify the water; then he saw the water slow down to again make a green pool. As he got closer to the pool and stuck first his arm then his face into the water, he saw that the green came not from the clear spring water but from the mossy green rocks on the bottom.

As he walked back to Emma and looked at their work, he tried to remember what had been the most beautiful thing he had seen in West Texas. Horses! Shorty on a running horse, its muscles working smoothly under its skin and Shorty rocking with the gait of the horse. When he got back to Emma, she yelled at him, "Where the hell you been?"

"Looking," he said.

"Stop looking and start working," she said.

As he pulled on gloves and picked up an ax, he yelled over the noise of axes biting into trees to Emma: "You think that Doctor would want to sell this land?"

Emma cracked a smile. "He ain't like these hard-headed square heads, hold on to something just cause it's theirs. This land is worthless and he ain't got enough of it. Price is good, he'd sell in a minute." She laughed and swung her ax into a tree.

And a thought, as straight and as quick as a Kraut bullet, hit Henry between the eyes. He and Emma and her retarded son would clear off the land; Lyndon Johnson would give him a loan; Jack Hillier would sell him the land. And then, in the natural pasture above him and in the land he was now clearing, he would raise horses and watch them run across his property. Here it was. One year short of thirty, Henry could stop running. Emma, an angel of the Lord, bearing His message, had shown Henry how.

Two years later, with his own land, a new stallion, a Stetson hat, and money in his pocket; Henry had a banana split at a downtown San Antonio five and dime with a young girl more beautiful than Consuela or Wild Jack's woman. So in the age of earned sex, in a clear, spring-fed pool on his own property, Henry initiated his marriage contract.

When he married Rebecca, Henry saw the perfection of life, the promise of America, and some proof, maybe just some, of a God that didn't hate him. With Rebecca, his land, and his horses, he was no longer running against time. He and time had stopped. Emma and her retarded son, like God's very own angels out to do His will (or like cedar choppers), just disappeared. When he yelled out Emma's name when he died, he must have been conscious, and if he was conscious then he knew that I was listening. Only I fully knew about Emma. Or maybe, shouting out Emma's name when he died was the only prayer Henry ever said without his Mamma's coercion.

* * *

I wait outside Buck Cronin's office, my legs crossed, the photos of Kay Menger in a manila folder resting on my lap, my hat on top of the folder. Buck's secretary, an older lady wearing half-rimmed glasses with a gold chain connected to their arms and running around her neck, lowers her head to peer at me. She smiles. I pull the photos out from under the hat and raise them, "Someday, I'm going to catch you, Betty," I say. And Betty lets a sly smile slip into one corner of her mouth. She drops her head as I lower the photos back into my lap.

"If I were foolin' around, I wouldn't get caught, and I'd make damn sure my husband didn't get Buck Cronin for a lawyer," Betty said, her head still down. She sorts through the mail and keeps her stoic, straight face on. I am glad that Betty is in Buck's office. Sometimes I think that Buck keeps her as his only secretary so that he isn't tempted by more innocent, malleable, or amiable women.

The door to Buck Cronin's office opens, and a well dressed brunette steps out. Buck is right behind her. She turns her head to look at me, and I stand and nod my head. I am trying to relearn or retrigger the nearly inbred courtesy that my mother pounded into me ("graciousness") so that I too can have the manners of a lawyer.

As I smile at her, I let my eyes linger. She wears a navy blue business suit, the classy and sexless uniform of a professional woman. But this professional's blouse plunges lower than a man's shirt, to reveal cleavage. The tight skirt stretches over rounded butt. Dark eyes under the lighter hair and a slightly up-turned nose make her pretty and almost girlish. Buck will probably tell her to keep the cleavage and the tight skirt out of court. When she turns back to Buck, I notice that the mascara and rouge under one eye is slightly smeared. She had probably started to cry, and Buck had probably consoled her with his "gracious" manner that he learned not from law school but from fifteen years as a divorce lawyer.

Buck shakes her hand, says "goodbye," but does not introduce her to me. What I now do for a living surrounds me with women, many real stunners, all lonely and hoping for or *susceptible* to anybody willing to show some "graciousness." But what I do for a living only lets me watch. I can't touch them; I can't talk to them; I never see the results of my work.

Buck and I watch as she walks out the front door. Betty lifts her head to watch us watching. I wink at her. She returns to her work. Buck lightly slaps me with the back of his hand and jerks his head toward his office. I grab my photos and my hat. We go into his office, and Buck sits down and leans back in his high, plush office chair. Buck's cream colored chair matches his peach colored walls, which is a good color to highlight Buck's rounded ceramic sculptures and shiny split rocks. The interior decorator who bought the sculptures, painted the walls, and moved the furniture around says so.

"Jesus," Buck says and lets his cream colored chair spring him forward, "I can smoke with you." He quickly reaches into his desk drawer and pulls out his pack of cigarettes. He pulls one out and illegally lights up. Since Buck's building adopted a no-smoking policy, Buck is having hell not smoking around his clients. He could get kicked out for filling other peoples' lungs with his smoke. According to Buck, the earth mothers and health freaks of the sixties turned into health fascists.

Buck inhales and smiles at me. "Jesus fucking Christ," he says, "you're not in college anymore, you don't live on a ranch. Get a pair of slacks. And if you have to wear a hat, get something besides that thing." Buck inhales and holds in the smoke.

I hold up Henry's so that both Buck and I can see it, and say, "This is a good hat, broken in, distinct." I prop one foot on Buck's desk. "These 'sneakers' cost me $80."

"Get some class, Roger," Buck says with smoke coming out of his nostrils.

"I left all my class in college." I throw the manila folder on his desk. "This should prove I got no class."

"You get a pair of slacks, couple of sportcoats, a business suit, and I might make you a partner." Buck starts to open the envelope.

"Why the hell would I want to give up this great job? I set my own hours, get to look at nasty pictures, spy on pillars of the community."

"Well yeah," Buck says as he dangles his cigarette out of his mouth and looks at the first 5 x 7 glossy. "Somebody's got to do it." He looks at me, "That's why I hire you." He chuckles while a cloud of smoke wraps around his head.

"So what do you think? Am I getting better with the camera?"

Buck stands, "You're a goddamn artist. Keep your sneakers. You're genius. Look at the well placed shadows adding drama. Look at the stark beams of lights, evoking the work of Walker Evans. Look at the emotion in those faces." Buck slaps the back of his hand against the glossy.

I rise and put my hat on. "Well, I've got some more 'art' to do. Some other lawyers like my pictures. And I've got some of my own cases."

Buck lowers the photos for a moment, "You've got your own cases?"

"Mostly U.T. students."

"Shit," Buck says and looks back at the photo, "So you're writing nasty letters to landlords at $40 a pop."

"Some of the student-exploiting, bourgeois pigs might actually go to court."

"For a $75 property deposit that the student probably doesn't deserve back anyway? Who is going to take the trouble? Keep writing your letters."

"Weirder things have happened."

"Well, be sure to give me credit for inspiration and understanding in your memoirs."

"Thanks, Buck," I say as I reach for the door to his office.

"Roger," Buck says as I step into his doorway. I turn to listen, "You really are good at this, seriously. I've never seen anybody catch on so quick, build up so many contacts so fast." Then a smile came back to Buck's mouth. He slapped his hands together, "We've got Kay Menger by the short hairs."

"Great Buck, give her a tug for me," I say.

"And hey, Roger," Buck says as I turn back toward his door. I turn to face him. "I've seen your date. Great gonzongas." Buck holds his cupped hands in front of his chest.

I smile. "I'd just as soon she had a 'nice personality.'"

"Pervert," Buck says and sits down. "Go make us some money."

Chapter 4:
Clayton Tanner

When I met Clayton Tanner, he was a mystic, an ascetic, or a lunatic. After I listened to him talk, his voice rattled around in my head for years. He told me how Rebecca Bolen became Becky Bolen, Ph.D. By my calculations, Becky left him in 1971.

Sixteen years before Becky Bolen left him, Clayton Tanner had moved from Dallas to Taos. In Dallas, his clients were worried about their failures—failures in business, marriage, ambition, talent, or sex. In Taos, his clients were worried about their souls. Both brother Dave with his spiritual transformation and Tanner with his degrees were still in Taos. Shamans, magicians, priests, and psychologists of various sorts lived all across northern Mexico. Not all of them had the proper license like Tanner did.

But even with a license, Tanner couldn't support himself solely on the rich clients who drifted into his office during the 50's and 60's. So he worked for The Bureau Of Indian Affairs as a counselor to the Jemez, Taos, Tesuque, Pojoaque, Cochiti, all the pueblo people that Tanner told me about. He took field trips to supposedly treat the alcoholism and frustration and mentality that contributed to the poverty. But mostly he just talked to the Indians. He talked about their secrets, their views of the whites, their customs, and their religion (which they never fully revealed). An old story teller once told him that the whites have a worthless religion because they are so quick to give it away. "We want to keep ours," he said. The old man had showed him Kivas and explained the ceremony to Tanner. He invited Tanner to one of the dances, in which the women, their hair dragging the ground behind them, taking tiny steps, barely moving, suggested both movement and stillness. Tanner never thought of the Indians as clients, but he liked them as well as his clients. He made enough money to buy his house on 223 Maestas street. Then he met Becky.

Tanner told me all of this and more. In fact, you couldn't keep him from talking, and most of his talking spiraled, like smoke, above his head and mine. What he always came back to and made him stare off, as though looking a great distance, was his memory of the day that Becky left him.

The morning she left, he had wakened and propped himself on one elbow to see her at the foot of his bed. In her bra and slip, Becky was looking intently in a full length mirror. She grabbed and bundled her slip on either side of her waist, the hem of her slip rising to her thighs. Then she let go, and the slip slid back to its proper position just above her knees. She was looking at the weight that had padded her hips in the ten years since Tanner had known her. Tanner saw her looking in the mirror often these days. Some primitive peoples believed that mirrors and photographs were entrances into other worlds, the past, or the future. And Tanner thought perhaps Becky did not now look in the mirror to see her youth passing but to see her future coming.

The one lamp with its soft white bulb made the slip a cloudy mist that just did cover her body. Tanner remembered when she first came into his bedroom some ten years before. She had slipped her translucent white dress over her head, and he could see her thin and sun golden body in the soft light of the lamp. He had thought then she that might be a shape shifter or one of the tricksters the Indians talked about and not a lover.

But the morning she left him, she had stepped into

a wool skirt and slid a green sweater with pink trim around the neck over her head. Her hair had made a golden halo around her head. She was dressing up for her last day of work before going off to Oklahoma. She turned and saw Tanner staring. "I could stay home today. Call in sick. We both could."

"No, let's stick to routines," Tanner said.

Tanner felt her breath on his cheek as she bent over him; then her lips, moist with lipstick, kissed his own. He opened his eyes to see her walk out of the bedroom door, then closed them to keep her in his mind longer.

After a steamy shower, while pulling on his boots and jeans, Tanner looked out his north window and, in the bright morning light, saw sagebrush shake and juniper bend to the wind and the dark matted clouds roll over Blue Lake Peak. The Taos Peoples' ancestors, Tanner told me, crawled out from their heaven in the earth's womb and swam up through Blue Lake Peak to come out to live on the land.

The window in the Maestas house rattled in the stuccoed adobe bricks, and the wind seeped through the caulked seams. The north window made the upstairs bedroom cold. Downstairs, he started coffee in the percolator and put an English muffin in the toaster. Molly, already his second black lab, crawled out of her doghouse, stretched—seemingly pulling her large black body at both ends with her neck and her tail—then scratched at the sliding door, smearing it with the mud on her nose and paws. Tanner went to the refrigerator, scooped three spoonfuls of Alpo into Molly's bowl.

When he slid the door open, the cold northwest wind shot through him and brought the smell of dog shit into his house. Molly put her muddy paws into his stomach, leaving prints. As soon as he set the bowl down, Molly started gobbling. Tanner sniffed at the dog shit and looked across the sagebrush at the mountains.

Inside the house, he closed the door against the wind,

felt the warmth in the sunbeams, and sipped the last of his coffee. Back upstairs, he opened the medicine chest, saw their toothbrushes next to a sloppily squeezed tube of Colgate. He rolled the tubes from the bottom, but Becky grabbed and squeezed. He saw the package of tampons next to his shaving cream and knew that in the cabinet under the sink both their dirty clothes mingled in a hamper. He walked back through his house, pulled his sheepskin-lined coat and hat off the hanger, and drove his four-wheel drive pickup to his office.

Tanner's office was imitation adobe—stuccoed cinder blocks—but it held the windows in place, so they didn't rattle like the ones in his house. From this office window, he could look out over several roof tops and see the southwest corner of Taos plaza. Spinning to his left, he could look out of his other window and see the narrow alley behind Ledoux Street and his parked pickup. From his window, he could see the spot where the Taos Pueblo people, incited by the last Mexican officials, killed Governor Bent.

Mid-morning, on the day that Becky left, the door to his office slowly opened. He could see a long, dark nose and high cheekbones through the crack of the door. "Rita?" he said. Rita Gomez opened the door and stepped in.

"I'm sorry, I know I'm not scheduled, but I thought that I could slip in before your first patient."

Tanner smiled, "I have clients, Rita. You and the rest of the people whom I see are clients, not patients. Have a seat, Rita."

Rita sat in the chair in front of Tanner's desk. She had a tightly rolled purple bandanna around her forehead. She wore a turquoise and silver necklace and matching belt, fur-lined snow boots, and a leather vest. "My second ex-husband called last night."

She stopped and looked down her long slender nose at Tanner. Tanner, expecting more, hesitated. "And?" he asked.

"Well, what about the call?" Rita asked.

"Is it important to you?" Tanner asked.

"Is it supposed to be?"

"What do you think?"

Rita slammed her fist into her open hand. "Do you ever say anything that doesn't end with a question mark?" Tanner laughed. Rita was aristocratic, Spanish, middle-aged; she was adept at finding and divorcing husbands. So far, she had tried pottery and printmaking, but found she had no artistic talent. She tried buying and managing a shoe shop, but found she had no business sense. She seemed to live gracefully off her trust fund, but married shallow men. "Maybe if you tell me what your first ex-husband said."

"My second ex," she corrected Tanner and smiled.

"He wants me to start seeing him again." She looked at Tanner, but Tanner kept his hands folded in front of him, forcing her to go on. "I mean this is pretty startling news," she said as she swung one knee over the arm of the chair.

"Do you think you could live with him?"

Rita doubled her fist and lightly hit her knee, "Another question!" Tanner wished he could say, "Yes, Rita, marry the poor bastard."

"I'm sorry, Rita, but you're going to have to do most of the talking."

"Cush job. You get paid to sit and listen." Her eyes smiled for a moment, making her crow's feet more pronounced; then her eyes grew frantic and scared as her crow's feet disappeared. "What do I do?"

"Could you live with him?"

"Yes."

"Do you love him?"

"Jesus, who knows. What do I do?"

"Some people have indeed, Rita, remarried. And have lived as contentedly as, as possible. But it's tough; you have to decide for yourself. It may not be a very good idea for you at this time." Rita's crow's feet reappeared as her eyes smiled. Tanner hoped that in giving her an answer rather than letting her discover that answer, thus altering his usual method, he had been kind to her.

At lunchtime, Tanner turned the collar of his sheepskin coat up against the back of his neck, pulled his felt hat tight onto his head, walked to the plaza, and sat on one of the long cement benches. After awhile, the cold bench warmed up. Tanner crossed his legs, and looked at the toe of his boot, then at the aspen leaves waving and rolling in the wind so that the two trees shimmered and looked like the cheaper paintings displayed in some the galleries. Soon, Billy Crossing walked up to him, slapped him on the shoulder, shook his hand, and sat on the opposite end of the bench. Billy swooshed his braids over his shoulders with the backs of his hands, reached into the pocket of his Levi Jacket, and pulled out a bottle wrapped in a paper bag. Billy stuck the bottle between his lips and took a long drink. When he brought the bottle down, he said to Tanner, "Hear your old lady is leaving."

Tanner nodded. Billy continued, "You know, you gotta brutalize them ever once in awhile or they get that way. They want to leave or some shit." Billy scooted to Tanner and offered him a drink. As he shook his head, Tanner looked at the long ugly scar down Billy's forearm. Billy had made it himself when his woman left him to go to Albuquerque. Billy was a Kiowa from Oklahoma who had drifted west, and like most of the plains peoples, he practiced scarring. The theory was that, when the pink tissue scabbed over, then became a dull red scar, the grief or guilt would be there to see but the pain would be gone. Tanner had never prescribed a scar, but he wondered if he should. The salve he rubbed on emotional scars didn't always work.

Tanner stuck his hands into his coat pockets and

looked across the street at the Mexican Import Shop and Cafe. An old, gray-braided Indian wearing a navy pea coat walked out of the cafe. An old woman followed him. The Indian had on black flannel pants and moccasins, and slung through and over his belt and hanging nearly to his knees, loin cloth style, was a terrycloth towel decorated with bead designs. The old man was the storyteller.

The old, gray-braided storyteller stopped, scratched himself up under the terrycloth loin cloth, and spit. He walked on. Then Tanner watched the tiny old woman who was his wife follow him. She pulled her Indian blanket over her head and bent over slowly to pull up her stockings that were rolled down almost to her ankles. She pulled one stocking higher then the other. The old man never stopped walking. Slightly crippled, the old lady, who looked like a bundle of laundry, gimped after him.

The Indians weren't like the misfit expatriates who couldn't adjust, so came to Taos and called themselves free souls, still unable to escape psychological maladies, thus becoming Tanner's clients. The Indians and Hispanics threw beer cans at and made money off Tanner's clients and the tourists who came to ski in winter or to see the galleries and scenery in summer. The Indians and Hispanics were misfit expatriates everywhere but in Taos.

Tanner got up from the bench and walked across the plaza and through the alley to Bent Street, then to the Queen Bee Print Shop. He stood in the cul-de-sac, too narrow for a car to turn around in without backing up, and stared through the front window of the Queen Bee. Becky had her back to the wall. He could tell her by her green sweater with the white and pink trim around the neck and the way she stood slumped on one hip. Since it was her last day, employees and friends of the Queen Bee Print Shop were throwing her a lunch party. Becky turned around. She had a tamale half into her mouth. When she saw Tanner, she hesitated before biting into the tamale. She bit, chewed, and smiled only with her eyes. Tanner crossed his arms and stamped his feet because of a sudden but slight chill. Donna, Becky's colleague, saw Tanner and motioned with her arm for Tanner to come in. Tanner shook his head. Becky took another bite of her tamale. Tanner waved good-bye to her. She waved with her hand out straight and moving side to side, like Porky Pig saying "That's all, folks."

The summer before, Tanner had pulled a letter out of the mailbox with Oklahoma State University, Stillwater, Oklahoma, as the return address. He was tempted at first to open it and read it, then tempted just to throw it away. But he gave it to Becky and watched her read it, as he had watched her read over fifty others, and then hugged her and congratulated her when she read that she had been accepted as an instructor at Oklahoma State University. It was a rare mid-year appointment. She would replace a professor on leave for the spring semester. And then, she had a chance to stay on. Through ten years, she had left, then come back, going to school in Los Angeles to pick up the graduate degree, working for one year as a photographer, but always swallowing ambition and coming back for the light, or for the ambiance, or for Tanner. But this time, Tanner and she knew it was for good.

In September, just before the weather turned cool, Becky had asked Tanner to go with her. She had just bought a pair of sandals at a summer closeout sale and was painting her toenails a bright red so that she could wear the sandals the next morning. She bent both legs over the arm of the sofa and held one foot up as she brushed at each nail with three smooth, even strokes. Tanner stared at her strong but graceful-looking feet sticking out of her faded, ironed jeans and thought about how attractive she was.

"Tanner, why don't you go with me?" she asked, and stared at her small toe, and dabbed rather than stroked the nail.

Tanner thought for a moment. "I can't go."

"Why?" She looked up from her toe and at him.

Tanner just knew at the time that he couldn't yet leave Taos. "My business."

"You sold one business."

"My clients."

"Come on," she said, "You know better than to get dependent on them."

"I'm not dependent. I'm used to them. I like them. I'm happy here. Some people think this is paradise."

Becky arched her back, stretched, yawned, then frowned at Tanner. "We can be just as happy anywhere we go. You're the one who says that you take your environment with you."

"You could stay," Tanner dared to say.

Becky looked over her shoulder from painting her big toe. "We've discussed that. You're the one who can stay or go. I can only go. Taos is a dead end for me."

Tanner had sat beside her and put his arm around her back. "I'm not ready to go yet."

Tanner walked into the wind and back toward his office for his appointment with Gilbert Hutchins. Gilbert Hutchins had lived in a suburb of St. Louis until his wife drove herself and the Hutchins kids into a pylon on a free-way overpass. Gilbert escaped to Taos. Tanner thought sometimes that Gilbert needed a psychiatrist. But Tanner was all Gilbert had.

Gilbert always wore a coat and tie to the discussions, so unable to shuff off suburban businessman manner, so unaccustomed to Taos. He was waiting at Tanner's door when Tanner came back from lunch. That day, he didn't talk much because he tried to keep from crying. "I don't sleep, but I have dreams," he said.

"About what?"

"You're supposed to find an answer in the dreams, right?"

"Freudians do that, I just give advice." Gilbert tried to chuckle, but snorted, then coughed.

"The Indians say that dreams are another world."

"The Real World?"

"No just another one. And if somebody wakes you before you finish your dream, you'll be stuck in another world."

Tanner had heard the stories. "Who tells you this?"

"I like to go to the pueblo. An old man tells me stories. He's the guy you see at the Old Mexico Imports Cafe."

"The one with the crippled wife."

"Yeah, he said he talks to you."

"Do you believe him?"

Gilbert hesitated, too afraid perhaps of getting stuck in his nightmares if he admitted to belief. Tanner liked the idea though. He felt himself a guide with a flashlight, ready to lead poor Gilbert and the others out of the dark. Yes, he was a guide through the wilderness—like Brother Dave, like the penitents, like the old Indian, like Lamy. He sat by his fever-sweated patients and, to exorcize the psychological demons, ran rosary beads through his fingers while uttering Hail Marys. Or he danced and chanted, wearing an ugly mask to scare the evil spirit. And, afterwards, in an effort to keep them well, he threw bone fragments across the floor, squatted beside them and read the future, which always held some miserable fact, like Becky leaving.

* * *

Before he met the Indians and felt significance in the world, before Becky came to the land of expatriates and made him feel loved, Tanner felt happy in the bars and cafes of Taos. He could eat or drink beer with Mexicans, Mexicans who called themselves Spanish, Indians, tourists, and cowboys wearing work shirts with the sleeves rolled up to their biceps. So late in the afternoon on Becky's last day, he went to Andy's Fiesta Saloon to find T and see if he could feel happy.

T was at his usual table, sitting by himself, his cowboy hat cocked to one side of his head, a Budweiser bottle and a small glass sitting in front of him—T liked to drink his beer from a glass rather than a bottle. His name was Tyrone but, in the 30's in the West Texas oil patch, nobody liked the name, so the crews started calling him T. Before he retired and moved from Hobbs to Taos, a chain had cut into his gut; a pipe was dropped on his back; most of his teeth were missing. His breath whistled through the holes in his mouth when he talked so that you could barely understand him. "I be goddamned, if it ain't ol Tanner," T said when he saw Tanner. "Jonelle," he yelled to the bartendress/waitress, "Quit dog-earing the sexy pages of them soap opera books and bring ol' Tanner a beer."

"Hello, T," Tanner said as he walked up to T's table and sat down.

He slid his arms out of the sleeves of his jacket and let it drop across the back of the chair. He lay his hat, crown down, on the table.

Jonelle was at Tanner's side as he sat down. She had forgotten what Tanner drank. Tanner had to remind her: "Coors in a long neck." Jonelle patted his back and left.

"Been a long time," she said.

T cackled, the way Gabby Hayes and other old men laughed. "Nobody comes here this time of day much no more. I hear you got so pussy-whipped since that woman come back that you was worthless."

"You jealous, T?"

T cackled, "Momma'd kill me I chase skirts like you." T called his wife Momma. "You goddamn fancy ass lawyers and doctors and such got nothing to do but chase them young girls always touristing through here. I think it makes you crazy."

Jonelle brought Tanner's beer, and he gave her thirty-five cents. "I never did half of what I said." Tanner remembered the skiers and the tourists and the students he would meet at restaurants, bars, or lounges and date a week or two, but then he remembered how long ago that was and how lonely he was then.

"That may be, but it don't mean that I can't like listening to it," T said.

"How's Momma?" Tanner asked, looking at T.

T stopped cackling. The lines in his face no longer pulled up toward his forehead but dropped toward his chin. T could see why Tanner was in Andy's. "Momma ain't too good. She still has to hobble around in that damn ol' walker. I got to do all the cooking and cleaning cause she just can't get around. We got to live with all those other old people, too." The wrinkles in T's face pulled up as he smiled. "And half of 'em is crazy. One old fart in a wheel chair pokes his finger through his pants zipper and waves it at the poor old ladies." T put his fist in his lap, then waved his forefinger to show Tanner what he meant and started to giggle again.

"How long you been with Momma?" Tanner asked.

T stopped waving his finger and stopped giggling. The lines in his face dropped again. "Long enough, forty-four, no, no, it's forty-six years."

"You stop counting?"

"Yeah, nobody counts years that much when they been married to one old woman for so long. Nobody counts years when you get this old."

"T, you're good therapy," Tanner said.

"Ain't nothing of the kind," T said and started to cackle.

* * *

Late that night, Tanner felt beery and bloated. His stomach pushed against his belt, and his head felt as though his brain pushed against his skull. He knew he shouldn't have drunk so much on his last date with Becky, but for a while drinking made him see more clearly. He had once taken some peyote with two young, hippie-like Cochiti boys to purify himself. One boy claimed that he flew. Tanner just threw up. No, the liquor, like dope, didn't help. So he sat in his kitchen drinking glassfuls of water out of a large plastic tumbler, the best way to prevent a hangover. Becky was upstairs getting ready for bed.

Tanner thought of himself in a Kiva ceremony. He would climb into the kiva to be whipped by the ugly gods of nature, whose faces looked like the kochina dolls that scared the hell out of Taos children; then the gods would take their masks off to reveal themselves to be Rita, Billy, and Becky. He would thus be purged of fear like the young men of the Pueblo people. He would be initiated into manhood.

Becky came down the stairs in her nightgown. Tanner couldn't see her face, only the outline of her body highlighted by a silver aura made by what dim lights shone through his plate glass sliding door. She shivered slightly in the cold house and felt along the wall until she got to the kitchen table. Tanner still couldn't see the features on her face, so he closed his eyes to see blonde Becky in her translucent nightgown, her body sun golden in his mind. He opened his eyes again and saw her body but still not her face across the table from him. "Aren't you cold?" Tanner asked.

"Aren't you coming to bed?"

"I'm drinking some water."

"I want an early start." She hugged herself against the cold.

Tanner sprang up, knocking the chair over behind him. He held the tumbler in his hand like it was a grenade and thought about throwing it through the plate glass window. He closed his eyes to see her face, and when he couldn't, he opened them again. She let go of her shoulders and raised her arms in an exaggerated shrug—that looked, to Tanner, like the first movement for casting a spell. He took a step forward and got his feet tangled in the chair that he had just knocked over then kicked at it, sending it sliding across the floor to strike a wall.

"Clayton?" Becky asked

Tanner sat down in another chair. The point was at hand and not liquor or anger or T could help. He could easily have said the words, could have easily have pleaded with Becky to please let him go with her, but what he actually said was, "Don't go."

"Oh, Tanner." Becky looked up at the ceiling. She shrugged again, circled one hand and looked at the ceiling, the continuing incantations of her spell. "We discussed this. We decided not to argue. We decided what was best."

"Goddamn, don't go." Tanner chanted.

"Why?"

"Because I can't leave."

"Jesus, Clayton. This place is so goddamn quaint. I want to join the Twentieth Century. You don't have to, just go with me. Hell, these Indians, they leave, but they never change. They're so damn incorruptible." Tanner listened intently to her prayer, and closed his eyes to try to see Billy anywhere but Taos.

"But the Indians always come back."

"Have some faith in yourself." Tanner had more than faith. He knew. He knew he was not strong enough to leave Taos and still have it.

Becky sat across the table from him and said, "Let's go to the real world, Clayton."

Tanner put the tumbler mouth-down on the table. Then he put his hand out in front of him on the table, fingers spread, palm down. Becky stretched across the table and lay her hand over his. They sat in the dark until Becky asked him to go up to the bedroom with her. He told her to go ahead. She went upstairs without him so she could get some sleep for the long drive to Stillwater, Oklahoma.

Tanner whispered a chant to himself that he had heard from the old storyteller. He had the rhythm and few of the sounds, but at the time, he didn't know what any of the words meant. Ten years before he had seen Becky at the Taos bus stop, a cardboard suitcase by her feet. She looked poor and disoriented when she asked Tanner for directions. He gave her a ride and a tour. She wanted to look at the galleries. Even then, Tanner could read her entrails; he knew the diagnosis. She had left a husband after marrying too young. Working as a waitress and with some money from Tanner, she commuted to a few classes at St. Michael's in Santa Fe, found something in education she had lost and so left for more education. She came back a left-over hippie, a neo-beatnik, left again but came back again, all the while thinking that trees and mountains could take the place of people; but in each excursion she became less frightened, realized she couldn't use the trees and mountains and Indians and Spanish descendants and a laid-back atmosphere as Tanner could. She had cured herself and so was leaving for the last time.

He got up and walked unsteadily to the kitchen drainboard and opened the top drawer. In the dark, he felt until he touched his butcher knife, grabbed it, and walked back to his chair. After he sat down, he lay his left forearm out in front of him. With the handle of the knife in his fist, blade down, he put the point of the knife against the skin of his forearm and begin to press down.

Then he heard a scratching at the door and turned to see Molly awake and pawing at the sliding plate-glass door. He thought ahead to daylight when he could sit in the sunbeams and eat breakfast, then go into his backyard that smelled of dog shit and feed Molly her Alpo. He could go to work and talk to Rita Gomez, a neurotic movie producer who had nothing to produce, a homosexual movie agent who saw him when he was in town and called him from Los Angeles when he was not, and a retired, alcoholic faith healer. He could have a beer with Billy in the plaza, drive out to check on the people in the reservations, talk to the old storyteller, have a beer with T.

Tanner stood, his knife still in his fist. He looked at Molly. He threw the knife as hard as he could at the plate glass door. The glass didn't shatter; the knife bounced off. Molly yelped and ran into the dark. Tanner knew his therapy, but he needed salvation.

Chapter 5:
Kyle

My ex-brother-in-law, Kyle, never talked to me much, but he had told me, more than once, about the summer after his mother left. It was in the middle of the fifties' drought, when the ground split open, when Fischer Creek dried first into several muddy puddles then just flaked dirt, when Henry's horses started dying. Left without a wife, Henry cussed his luck and tried to raise his horses and his kids as best he could. Both horses and kids were too tender in his opinion.

In the summer evenings, when the Gulf breeze blew in and cooled his property, Henry would put his two kids in the cab of his pickup truck and bounce over his homemade roads. Kyle, once he was old enough, wanted to help his father. Victoria was too young to leave by herself, and after staying around the house all day with her older brother watching her and bossing her, she liked to get out in the evenings. So Henry took his kids with him for his evening drives. Kyle, because he was older and the boy, got to ride next to the passenger door. Though she complained that she never got the door and open window, five-year-old Victoria always rode between the two boys.

On a hot August day, a weak mare had wandered out of the high pasture and into the brush at mid-morning and hadn't come back to the stables. That evening Henry, as usual, loaded his kids into his pickup and drove around looking for the horse he guessed had died of heat or disease. Kyle sat down and held on to the door handle. Victoria stood up in the middle of the seat and giggled as she bounced nearly to the roof of the cab. "Sit down," Henry told her. Kyle took her arm and pulled her down into the seat. She whimpered a bit, but then started giggling again.

Just where the road curved around a stand of cedar trees and brush, Kyle spotted a horse lying on its side with its head in the road. "Daddy," he said, pointed, and smiled. Henry drove up to the mare and stopped the truck. Kyle could see her head on the road, but the rest of her body was hidden in the brush. He could also see the spray of blood and foam soaking into the rocks in front of the mare's nostrils. Flies buzzed around and landed on her eyes. Kyle opened his door and started to get out, but Henry was out first and walking toward the horse.

As Kyle walked toward his father, Henry turned to the boy and said, "Your sister." They could see Victoria's tiny hand on the door of the pickup and her one leg dangling beneath the door, lowering slowly, trying to touch the ground. "Get her back in the truck," Henry said. Kyle took another step toward the horse. "Kyle!" Henry said.

"But Daddy," Kyle said.

Henry walked to Kyle, put a hand on his back, and gently pushed him toward the truck. "You watch your sister."

"I can do what's got to be done," Kyle said.

"You don't know what's got to be done," Henry said.

"I can watch it be done,"

"You can watch your sister."

Just as Victoria hit the ground, Henry walked back to her, picked her up, and put her back in the cab of the pickup. "I wanna see," she said and slapped at Henry's hand. Kyle had followed Henry, and he grumbled as he got into the seat beside Victoria. Henry shut the door and looked at them through the open window.

Henry went to the bed of the pickup, slung a tarp over his shoulder, and grabbed a chainsaw, which he now used for cutting cedar. He came back to the pickup and looked in at his kids. "Victoria," he said, and Victoria looked at him. "Kyle," he then added but still looked at Victoria. "What I am going to do, I got to do. I got to find out if this horse died of disease. I got to take its head to a vet."

"Is he dead?" Victoria asked.

"Yes, dummy," Kyle said.

"You watch her, Kyle," Henry said and walked to the horse.

Victoria stood up in the cab to watch her daddy as he started the chain saw, but Kyle grabbed her and turned her around. "Let go," she said. "I want to see."

But Kyle held her tight and said, "Don't look," then watched out the truck door's window as Henry lowered the chain saw until it bit into the neck of the mare.

"What's that?" Victoria asked.

"Daddy's got to cut that horse's head off," Kyle said, and Victoria started to cry. Kyle saw the mare's blood splatter and spray across the rocks and onto Henry's face, arms, and chest. Still he watched everything his father did and patted his sister's back.

Henry walked back to the truck with the mare's head in the tarp. He slung the tarp over the side of the truck and into the bed, and Kyle, as well as his little sister, heard the plop the horse's head made on the wooden slats of the truck bed. Victoria had stopped crying but still whimpered.

Henry climbed back into the truck. Spots of blood dotted his face and chest. "Ruined this damn shirt," he said, then looked at his kids. "Are you okay, Victoria?" he asked. He looked at Kyle, "Did you explain to her why we had to do that?"

"Yes, Daddy,"

"Thank you for helping me, Kyle," Henry said and

drove his kids back home for a late dinner of baloney and macaroni and cheese, their favorite.

* * *

When Kyle got out of high school, he joined the army and went to Vietnam. "I'm gonna fight just like my father," he had said. Before he left, he began to plan for coming back. He proposed to Darlene, a high school sweetheart, and she promised to marry him when he came back from the war. He served in the Quartermaster Corp, never saw combat, and sent half of every check home so Henry could put it in a growing savings account. When he came back to marry Darlene, she was in college and refused to give up college life for a country boy. So Kyle found Suzy, married her, went to college himself for five years, bitched about taking courses like history and English that had no practical use, got a realtor's license, and started to make money on Austin real estate. He delayed having kids until he had enough money to support them in the right way. Then he and Suzy had two, a boy (Bobby) and then a girl (Kristen).

* * *

I first met Victoria on a hot, still October night at a dance in Gruene Hall. She was a sophomore, and I was a radical. I had spent a year flunking out of Southwest Texas State University in San Marcos, another year dodging the draft, two more at Southwest Texas, and another year as the editor of *The Other News*, "an alternative newspaper." When the local rednecks firebombed my car and kicked the shit out of my newspaper office, and the draftboard started threatening, I went back to school for the deferment. As my luck would have it, the year before I met Victoria, the deferments ended, and I watched on TV as I got a high draft number in the lottery. A miracle. I didn't like the idea of Vernon and Faye Jackson's only boy being shipped home to them in a zip-lock plastic baggy. Nor did I like the idea of his coming home and growing into one of those old men who told war stories about the way it really was. I decided to stay in school, become a lawyer, and do something about the mess this country was in. I also salvaged the equipment from *The Other News* and started *Rumors*, an "entertainment magazine, with political commentary," for the area. If I hustled for ads, it paid my bills.

Gruene Hall was an old, historic dance hall that got popular with the students of Southwest Texas State and the residents of New Braunfels and San Antonio. The night I met Victoria, Guy Clark was playing progressive country music. In the early seventies, around Austin, his type of music had become our anthem. I really couldn't afford the three dollar cover charge, but Richard Nixon had pulled out of the Vietnam War "with honor," my newspaper was making a meager profit, and I was doing well in school. I had things to celebrate. So I listened to Guy, sipped my beer, and sweated in the crowded dance hall.

As I sat in a folding chair parked under a short table, I saw her come in and walk past me. She wore tight jeans: Wranglers, the jeans of country girls. She had a red sash as a belt, maroon boots with rounded toes, and a sheer white blouse, her blonde hair made something of an aura around a pink, nordic face. Her blue eyes, squared features, and rounded nose gave away her German blood. I had seen her before: across from me in my honors class, "Utopian and Dystopian Thought in American History." She came in with a couple of her sorority sisters, who looked like geese, stretching their necks to see if they could spot other sorority sisters or boys they could talk to or dance with. Victoria, though, looked at me.

I drank several beers and watched her dance with some yokel in a straw cowboy hat that could have made shade over them both. He could dance, though. He moved her smoothly across the floor and held his body in a rigid but poised fashion. When the dance was over, she walked to me.

"I know you," she said. She sat down beside me, and I wondered if I had enough money to buy her a beer. "You're kind of a legend at Southwest aren't you?"

I chuckled, "I don't know if I'd call myself a legend. Most people call me a . . . a . . . an asshole."

She chuckled and slapped at my arm. "Come on. All the hippie and dope stuff is over," she said. "Nobody cares what you are now."

"Is that why you're in a sorority?"

Her smile disappeared, but she didn't get up and leave me. "So what's wrong with a sorority?"

"Aw, come on," I said and took a drink of beer. "'Look yes, but say no,' and all that shit."

"It's no more fake than long hair and an earring."

I smiled, "You like my earring?"

She smiled, "I have two just like it. Where do you keep the other one?"

"Home in an earring box."

She reached across the table, grabbed my arm, and pulled me up. "Let's dance," she said. I pulled back and sat down.

"No." I said.

"Come on."

"I don't dance Country and Western."

She sat down beside me. "Then you can't dance?"

"No."

"Hell, most of those guys can't either."

"You looked pretty good with the guy in the ten gallon hat."

She smiled, said, "He's a prick," ducked her head, then looked up at me smiling. I laughed. She laughed. I stood and pulled her to the dance floor.

I pushed and pulled her in a couple of circles around

the dance floor and stepped on her toes. When the song mercifully ended, she grabbed my hand and pulled me out into the courtyard outside of Gruene Hall. "You were right," she said, "You can't dance." I shrugged my shoulders.

Then she pulled my arm around her and lay her other arm on my shoulder, and said, "I'll teach you. It's easy. Two steps are all you have to know." So in the courtyard outside of Gruene Hall, with the Japanese lanterns making soft yellow light, with a few drunk students easing their queasy stomachs, Victoria taught me to two-step. We slid our feet through the loosely packed dirt, her boots and my tennis shoes kicking up chalk colored clouds of dust.

When she thought I had learned well enough, Victoria took me inside to join the rest of the crowd and meet her friends. We danced, me stiff and nervous, preferring the loose dirt to the slick floor, and drank up what money I had, then Victoria bought the beer. As the lights came on and the bartenders starting yelling at us to leave, I hugged Victoria in the middle of the dance floor as her friends watched. She whispered into my ear. "Can you take me home?"

"Sure," I whispered back.

"Ya'll go on," she yelled to her two friends.

One scrunched up her face, and the other smiled and said, "Victoria Bolen, what would your Daddy say?"

Victoria waved her hand at them and said, "He'd ask if I had a good time."

I held her hand and walked outside with her. Once through the door and in the street in front of Gruene Hall, congested with traffic, we kissed for the first time, breathing in each other's beer-soured breath. We walked to my '64 Chevy pick up truck, not even ten years old then, and kissed some more. When she scooted away from me, I said, "Now let me show you what I can do."

She gasped and scooted away from me toward the

opposite side of the cab. "No, No," I said and held up a joint and a bottle of tequila. She smiled, slapped at me, then kissed me. We watched the crowd leave as we took tequila shots and smoked the joint. "Where do you live?" I asked.

She giggled, "Fischer."

I coughed up some smoke from my joint, "Goddamn."

"We better get started," she said seriously. "I ought to get home. My father's expecting me."

"Your father?"

"Yeah."

"You live at home?"

"Yeah."

"Goddamn."

* * *

As I drove to Fischer, Victoria passed out across my lap. Unlike most college sophomores, though, she didn't throw up in my lap. Once we got to Fischer, I had to gently slap her face and shake her to wake her up, so she could tell me where in Fischer to go, but I couldn't get her up. I dug into her purse and found a check book with her telephone number and address. At the Fischer Sac & Pac convenience store, I called her number and asked Henry Bolen how to get Victoria home.

As I drove up the long gravel road toward Henry's house, I saw a rectangular light appear, then a tall man stepped into the light coming from the doorway of the house and leaned against the door frame. "Jesus," I mumbled. "Victoria get up. Please, for God's sake wake up." I pulled in front of the house and hoped for Victoria to wake. I again slapped her and shook her, but she wouldn't budge. I got out of my side of the cab and rounded the front end to the passenger side. As I opened her door, I looked over my shoulder and saw Henry Bolen taking long strides toward me.

I pulled Victoria out of the cab and cradled her in my

arms, then turned to face Henry. "Need any help, son?" he asked.

"Uh, no," I said.

"Okay, but she's heavier than what she looks," he said. He curled so he could look at Victoria in my outstretched arms. "She drunk a little, huh?" Then he walked up the steps to the veranda that ran around his house.

Far from being sober myself, I stumbled up Henry's steps and almost dropped Victoria on his veranda. Henry pushed the front door open and turned to look at me. "You need some help with her, now?" I nodded, and he reached out and plucked Victoria out from my hands, hefting her across his chest. The light hit his face, and I saw the stern look the sun had baked into his eyes, his white hair, and his white, stubbly beard. He smelled like ivory soap. From under Victoria, he stuck out his hand and said, "Henry Bolen."

"Roger Jackson," I said and watched Victoria's lifeless head wobble as we shook hands. I noticed he was missing a finger.

He turned away from me and said over his shoulder, "Sure do appreciate it, son." I took a step out of the door way, and as I pulled the front door shut, I watched Henry Bolen carry his daughter across the living room.

* * *

The following Saturday, I drove back to Henry Bolen's horse ranch in the Hill Country's clear autumn daylight. I passed by Fischer and saw Marie's Drive Inn standing guard at Wimberly Avenue where it intersected Ranch Road 12. Marie's was Henry's beer joint, the place where he met the old Germans, his neighbors, and judged good and ill of the world over frosty bottles of beer. Henry's friends were Sam Penschorn and Pete Proctor, who had lived in the Hill Country far longer than Henry, and Doc Jack Hillier, the most educated and imperturbable man in the county. In time they were to become my friends as Marie's became my beer joint.

I crested the small hill past Fischer and looked down at the first gate. As directed, I got out, pulled the gate open, and closed it behind me after I drove through it. I turned into it and drove up Henry's road toward his house. I had to shift down into first a couple of times to climb the hill. As it flattened, I looked to my right and saw his lower horse pasture. It still had some green. A dark brown horse with sun reflecting off his rump and making his hide look silver lifted its head up from the grass and stared at me. He must have seen that I was a stranger because he trotted with the truck but kept his distance and looked warily at me. Then I looked up at the house to see Victoria standing on the veranda looking down the road at me. Henry came out behind her.

I pulled up alongside the veranda and slowly walked up the steps of the wide front porch. Victoria hugged me, and I looked over her shoulder at Henry in his weathered Stetson. When Victoria let go of my neck, she said, "You two met." I wanted to brush my hair back behind my shoulders (at least I hadn't put it in a pony tail), and I wished I had left my earring at home. I stuck out my hand.

Henry stuck out his hand and smiled. "I got deer chili going. You like chili?"

"Sure," I said.

"Venison?" he added.

He walked back into his living room, and Victoria took my hand and pulled me into his house. "How about a beer?" he asked as he went into the kitchen.

"A bit early, yet," I said.

"Good time to start," he said and came back with two cans of Lone Star. "Besides, Victoria tells me you're a good drinker." He handed me one, and we pulled our ring tops in unison. I sat down on the sofa, and Victoria sat beside me. Henry sat in his easy chair and pushed his hat farther back on his head. "Victoria has some idea that she needs to be on a diet, so she don't drink beer–until evening, that is," Henry said.

"Beer goes straight to my hips," Victoria said.

"Hell, so you give up beer cause of a natural phenomenon," Henry said. I chuckled and patted Victoria on the knee.

Henry glanced at me. He raised his right hand for me to see his missing trigger finger. "I lost that in World War II, the Normandy Invasion," he said.

"Daddy!" Victoria said, and Henry put his hand down. "People do not want to see or hear about your old finger."

Henry looked at me again, then squinted to see me better. "So, why do you wear your hair long?" he asked, and I knew the argument was coming.

"Daddy!" Victoria said.

"Just curious," Henry said.

Victoria looked at him crossly. But then her brows knitted, and she asked, "Why do you?"

"It's a protest against social propriety," I said with an angry tone. "I do it to show I'm fed up with all the bullshit forced down our throats by silly people with silly rules."

"Don't it get hot? Make your head warm?" Henry asked.

"I don't believe so," Victoria said. "That's a myth. It just makes your neck hot."

"Now that I think about it, women never seem to get any hotter than men," Henry said. "My wife used to sweat worse than a mule. Hair down to her shoulders, too. But she never bitched about getting hot. Chopped cedar, tended the horses, had a baby. Sweated a lot, but didn't get hot." Henry took a long drink from his beer. "I still don't understand the protest stuff, though. Far as I can see hair is just hair."

I felt myself smile, "Well, maybe you're right."

Henry pulled off his hat and rubbed the sides of his close-cropped haircut, and said, "Maybe I ought grow my hair a little longer. LBJ did. Course, I couldn't get a earring—Pete and Sam would tease me merciless."

After we drank our beers, Victoria took my hand and led me outside. On the veranda, she hooked her arms around my neck and kissed me. Then she led me across the road to the horse barn. In it, two horses were saddled and tied to their stalls. "What's going on?"

"We're going to ride."

"You're going to ride," I said.

"You scared?"

"You kidding?" I asked. "I'm terrified." And just as she had taught me to dance the week before, Victoria taught me to ride a horse–or at least the rudiments. I started to learn to use my knees to dig into the horses shoulders. I felt the motion of the horse's muscles beneath my butt and between my legs, the pounding and the rhythm of the horse's running that my own body absorbed. As we tried galloping and trotting around the pasture, Henry came out of his house to look out at us. He stared for a moment, then walked past his barn toward us. Victoria reined up beside him, and I clumsily stopped my horse. "Mind if I try him there, Roger?" Henry asked

"Sure," I said and started to get off the horse.

"Other side," Victoria said, "Get off on the other side."

When I got off, Henry easily slipped his foot into the stirrup and hoisted himself into the saddle, grinning at me and Victoria. Victoria smiled back at him. Henry delicately held the reins in front of him between two whole fingers of his left hand. He held the other arm bent out to one side of his body to balance him in the saddle. Then he kicked the horse into a trot, and his body bounced in perfect time to the horse's hoof beats. When he reached the end of the pasture, he put the reins into his teeth, kicked the horse into a full gallop, and steered with his knees. He looked to be the most perfect and romantic imitation of a nineteenth century cowboy. "Daddy's showing off now," Victoria said.

"Oh, my God," I mumbled and took a step back as he got close to me. But before the horse could trample me, he grabbed the reins with his left hand and jerked with the horse to a stop. Henry swung a leg over the saddle and jumped off the horse. He handed the reins to me and said, "The old Texas Rangers used to ride like that. An old cowboy named Shorty Martins taught me how."

When Henry left us, we rode over several trails cutting through the hills to look at the property. By mid afternoon, we were hot and sweaty and resting beside the part of Fischer Creek that Henry owned. The horses were tied up, the cicadas were buzzing in the trees, the shade from the trees and the breeze made light shows around us, and Victoria lay across my arm. She looked at the green pool that Fischer creek formed, got up, and stepped toward the pool. "Let's go skinny dipping," she said.

I immediately started to pull off my clothes, then stopped to watch as she pulled her T-shirt over her head, unfastened her bra, stepped out of her pants, and slid her panties down. She stood straight up, naked in front of me, and I saw her rounded, soft, white body with the dimples on the sides of her thighs and around her curved belly. She turned around in a circle as if to show herself to me. She didn't have a sun tan, as was the fashion, but delicate white skin with tiny traces of blue veins in her cheeks and behind her knees. It was a body full of youth.

She turned and ran for the creek, her breasts and dimpled butt jiggling. I stripped and ran after her. She dove in and started swimming. The cool water shocked me, but I swam after her. Midway across the pool, she stopped and tread water. She swam on her back, her breasts barely raising above the level of the water. I grabbed at her feet. When she got to shallower water, she stood up to look at me, her hair curled into ringlets around her forehead and neck and shoulders. I stood beside her. We lunged toward each other, the water swishing behind us, and met with a long, open-mouthed kiss.

Pawing at each other, kissing, coughing from breathing in a little water, we swam back to our clothes for the sex we had anticipated for a week. In the just arrived age of unearned sex, when the difference between lust and love seemed irrelevant, and you could heed your hormones, Victoria and I explored each other's bodies for the first time.

Afterwards, with Victoria again lying across my outstretched arm, with the shadows of leaves dancing across our naked bodies, we heard Henry banging a heavy wooden spoon against a pot. Then we heard his faint shout, "Chili's on." We dressed and went back for dinner. As we walked into his house, Henry cocked one eyebrow to study the two of us, guessing what we had done in his creek.

* * *

We studied together the rest of the semester. The following spring semester and summer, I spent a good portion of my money driving out to Fischer. Victoria quit her sorority and started taking the pill, causing her butt to spread out a little. She worried about it, but I could throw away the condoms. During the fall semester, Victoria packed up most of her room in Henry's house and moved in with me. Toward the end of the next semester, as I began to think about law school, Victoria got pregnant. We blamed the doctor for a bad prescription. She moved back in with Henry, "for a while," she said, to think about what she wanted to do. Then her brother Kyle came to see me.

At the time, we lived in a small one bedroom apartment

above a bar that I cleaned in the mornings and tended on some afternoons. On the weekend nights, the noise was tolerable; we were able to get used to it. But on the weekends, we usually went down to join the noise instead of trying to sleep through it. After a morning working at my newspaper, I heard a knock on my door and pulled it open to see Kyle Bolen. I waited for an introduction. He peeked inside the door at the shabby apartment. Then he stuck out his hand for me to shake, "My name's Kyle Bolen. Victoria's brother."

"Come in," I said and held the door open for him.

He came in, stared at my hair. "Doesn't it get hot?" he asked.

The apartment was too small for two people. Victoria and I had notes and books stacked in all the corners. An expanding pile of laundry had spread out beyond the bedroom and into the living room/kitchen. I had a typewriter on the coffee table with the stories for my magazine lying beside it. An ashtray with the remains of several joints was also on the coffee table. Since we had no kitchen table, nor a kitchen large enough to put one in, I ate my Safeway frozen dinners on the coffee table, next to my typewriter. Last night's aluminum tray with the hardening beef gravy sat by the typewriter. "It ain't much," I said, "But I call it home."

"I had forgotten what college is like," Kyle said, shook his head and said, "what a pain. Glad I'm out."

"Victoria's talked about you. She said you're a real crackerjack realtor." Kyle shrugged his shoulders.

"What are you planning to do when you get out?"

"Law school," I said. Kyle looked at my hair.

"What type?"

"Contractual, I think."

"You ought to get an M.B.A.; it's a lot more marketable, and there's less of 'em running around. There's a lawyer under every rock in Austin."

"You want to sit down?" I cleared several books off

the couch, and Kyle sat down. I sat on the other end of the couch. "Want a beer?"

"No, thank you," he said. "You look a little older than most students. Been in the service?"

"No." He looked at me as though expecting an explanation. "I was busy dodging the draft and running a newspaper." I reached beside me and held up a copy of *Rumors*. "One kind of like this. It stirred up a lot of people around here." He looked at me and patted the back of the couch.

He stared at his feet and mumbled, "I've heard about Victoria."

"What have you heard?'

"Come on," he said and looked sternly at me, then dropped his head to look at his feet. "I want to know what you intend to do."

"About what?"

"Come on, now you know what," Kyle said, looked quickly at me, then looked away.

"She's at home now with your father, thinking about what to do."

"What has my father said to you?"

"Not a thing."

"You been to see him?"

"No."

"You ought to go see him."

I got up, "Look man," I said and gestured with my hands, "this whole affair is between Victoria and me. What you or your father have to say is of no concern to us."

"It is to her. And it should be to you."

"And I disagree."

Kyle stood up, and I was afraid he would take a swing at me. "Look here, I'm not meaning to piss you off, but it's time to grow up now."

"What?" I was thinking of taking a swing at Kyle.

"Cut your hair, get a job, quit writing for radical

newspapers, and face up to responsibility."

"And marry Victoria?"

"Not necessarily," he said and sat as if backing down.

"The way I see it, you can get married or, if you'd rather, just get out."

"What do you mean?"

"Put some distance between you and Victoria. Move away. Let her forget you. It'd be easier for her to deal with the whole thing if you just left."

"That's it. Those are the only two alternatives, I have?" I chuckled.

"The only realistic ways to look at this."

"Kyle, there are other answers."

"If you love her, I want to encourage you to marry her. As you probably know, she's a real good girl. And I think you could be happy with her. Hell, you could learn to love her."

"I do love her, but I won't be pushed into marriage."

"I know how you feel," Kyle said. "I was younger than you are now when I married. Marriage changed my life for the better. I never want to be single again. Don't even miss it. I've got a lovely wife."

"Do you love her?" I asked sarcastically.

Kyle thought a moment then said, "Sure." He reached into his back pocket and pulled out a fat envelope, held it over the table and dropped it. "I'm not gonna push you. You can marry her or leave. Either way, there's five hundred dollars in that envelope. Enough to get you out of town or to start you off in marriage."

I picked up the envelope and turned it around in my hands. I opened it and looked in at the twenties wrapped with rubber bands. "This is a pay-off, a bribe."

Kyle looked away, "I didn't give it with that attitude."

I threw the money down on the table, said, "Get your money out of here," walked out the door, and slammed it behind me. I walked to the bar downstairs and had two stiff drinks while Kyle sat upstairs in my apartment.

Victoria and I didn't want "a marriage." Kyle had a "marriage."

I left the bar and walked around the Hays County courthouse on the town square. When I went back to my apartment, Kyle was gone, but the envelope was still on the coffee table. I picked it up to tear up his money, but the money was gone. A note was inside the envelope. "If you change your mind, give me a call," it said and gave his telephone number. I tore up the envelope.

* * *

Henry suggested the most realistic and obvious solution. He talked to Doc Hillier privately down at Marie's. Roe vs. Wade had just passed; Texas wasn't sure what it would do, but discreet Doc Hillier agreed to help Henry out and not to tell anybody about the abortion. I stayed overnight on a Friday evening. Henry and I eyed each other over dinner Friday night but didn't speak. After dinner, Victoria and I took a walk to Fischer creek. We came back and watched TV. She went to bed early, and Henry and I watched Johnny Carson. About midnight Henry went to his room, and I slept on the couch. At breakfast on Saturday morning, as Henry leaned against the kitchen door frame and watched Victoria and I eat, she urged me to let Henry go along.

Victoria wore a yellow dress with ruffled sleeves and a ribbon at the waist. She sat between us as I drove to Doc Hillier's office in my pickup. Doc Hillier was waiting for us, had in fact opened up especially for us. In the waiting room, Victoria kissed me, then her father, then followed Doc Hillier into his office.

While we waited, Henry thumbed through two issues of *Newsweek*, and I avoided looking at him. "Nice of ol' Jack, isn't it?" he finally said.

"I appreciate it. I'll help you pay."

He waved his hand at me, "No," he said.

"Please."

"Consider it an apology for Kyle. He's a good boy, but he sometimes gets real funny ideas about things."

"He's good at making money."

"Yeah, must of got that from somebody other than me."

"Look, I'll help pay."

"No," Henry said and looked back into a *Newsweek*.

I got up walked to the door to the office, looked at the secretary's desk, then walked back to Henry. He looked at me and said, "Calm down. Jack knows what he's doing."

"I know," I said, cleared my throat and said, "Look, I'm sorry, okay. I am sorry. Not much I could do, but I'm sorry this all happened. "

Henry patted the seat beside him. "Sit down and don't worry; I ain't gonna do nothing to you." I sat down beside him. "I hold nothing against you. Things like this happen. I know it best not to let them worry you any long amount of time. What happened is happened, and what we're doing is for the best. Women, whether they're your wife, mother, or daughter, are just meant to cause you trouble."

"Thank you," I said and hung my head.

"I wish you'd cut your hair, though. Sam and Pete are teasing me about the long-hair my daughter's running with." I laughed with him.

Victoria came out of the examination room smiling. Doc Hillier was patting her on the back. Henry stood up and shook Doc Hillier's hand as Victoria walked to me and put her arm around my back. Doc Hillier then came to me and shook my hand and patted my back.

That night, with Henry's approval, Victoria and I slept in the same bed in her room. She held on to me tightly for an hour, then rolled away from me. "It hurt," she said

I rolled around her and squeezed her tightly. I proposed to her. Then, because I couldn't sleep, I snuck outside and tried to smoke a joint, but Henry caught me, and I had a beer with him, and he told me about his parents and Consuela the whore who still haunted him.

Two months later, Victoria accepted my proposal. I cut my hair, married her in Fischer Lutheran church, applied to law school, then fell in love with her.

Chapter 6:
Vern and Faye

I pull off my new $80 New Balance jogging shoes, the type Buck Cronin calls sneakers, and my sweaty ankle high socks, stuff them into my shoes, put the shoes under a picnic table, and take a running dive into the chilly spring water of Deep Eddy Pool. I surface and feel my heart thump from being first hot then chilly. The lifeguard, a UT student, blows his whistle at me, yells, "Don't run," then smiles. From the water, I wave, nod my head, and he smiles and waves back. It is a routine that we go through when I take my dip at Deep Eddy's. The admonition is mainly for show, for the early morning kids and his boss.

I start a breast stroke and then change into a crawl as I get halfway across the pool. Why do I jog then dive into this pool? Because it feels good? Because I can still do it? Because I can do it in this part of the country? I catch up with the older lady in the baggy black swimming suit and bathing cap. She is finishing her daily morning laps. She does a few more in the evening. She hits the bank, expertly curls, and starts back across the pool. I have yet to perfect the curl. I get water up my nose and come up coughing. So I grab the cement lip, tuck my feet up under me, and push off from the side of the pool. I start swimming as fast as I can, and the older lady, used to our game, sensing I'm gaining on her, starts to stroke harder. I ease up as I get to the opposite bank to let her win. She hoists herself up on to the bank and smiles at me. "You should race someone your own age."

"They're no competition," I say. Someday we should introduce ourselves to each other.

She pulls off her bathing cap and starts to towel off. I have no towel so I walk back to the picnic table, my feet getting muddy once I step off the cement that surrounds the pool. The young lifeguard yells again, "No more running, or we'll kick you out." The threat sounds good. The children stare up at him with their wide eyes. Their mothers point up to him and whisper to their children: "See there." The lifeguard turns his attention away from me and returns his attention to the pool, but he holds his chin a little higher. I like my role as the bad guy. In running to the pool and diving in, nearly everyday, I perform a social function; I am fulfilling my civic duty.

I lie down on the picnic table in the shade of a pecan tree and look up through the branches of the pecan tree at the blue sky and the sun's glare. I squint to make the sun hazy. I close my eyes to stare at the orange backsides of my eyelids. Why do I jog?

While I jog, I think. The increased motion increases thought, and I seem to work through so much. I do my wondering about Kay Menger. I do my planning for my rounds for the day. I remember my wife and in-laws, retrace our history, ponder my decisions and actions, punish myself for my mistakes, question myself about what was a mistake and what was not, suggest to myself that the whole outcome was inevitable. My thought for the day: transcendence, idealism, doing the right thing, and solutions all belong back in the sixties. But now we are in the existential, give-a-shit, less innocent, wiser, conservative, Christian intoxicated eighties. Get used to it.

* * *

It didn't take much to be a sixties radical in Texas. The sixties didn't even come to Texas until the early seventies. So when I was in college at Southwest Texas

State University in San Marcos, I became a part-time, luke-warm, Texas-style radical. Southwest was a state school where middle income parents sent their kids rather than risk sending them to the University of Texas thirty miles up the road in Austin where they might become hippies or liberals. The radicals at Southwest were nothing compared to the radicals at The University of Texas, and the radicals at the University of Texas couldn't hold the black arm bands of the students at Berkeley. But, to the conservative Baptists and Germans who lived in San Marcos, I was one of those long-haired, earring-wearing, trouble-making, filthy, hippie types. Then in the mid-seventies, everybody at the school, even college administrators and Sunday School teachers, started smoking pot, growing long hair and beards, and wearing diamond earrings. I understand that, even today, a few non-descript students want more out of college than a B.M.W., an attractive mate, and a career. But no one seems authentically pissed off anymore. In the sixties and early seventies, I pissed people off because I was pissed off. I was pissed off because I wanted to be noble.

But I had no artistic talent, was bored by science and math, couldn't write all that well, wasn't into dry academic research, and wasn't about to study business or accounting. I stayed noble and poor for seven years. Law was to make my life somewhat useful, and somewhat noble. So when I got accepted into the UT law school, I had my chance to be both noble and, if not rich, at least not poor. I gave up nobility somewhere in law school.

The local working people of San Marcos had a different explanation for me: I was the spoiled rich kid who didn't know about life or work. They were partially right. I spent a lot of time being poor either despite or because of my parents' money.

My parents weren't really rich, but they never had to worry about money, unlike most of the world's population. My father had the good fortune and the foresight to buy a house on the edge of the River Oaks section of Houston. The property values zoomed. The location was appropriate for my father. He got close to a six digit salary before he retired as an accountant for Texaco, but he never made the big, fast money to entitle him to the privilege of a River Oaks estate. He remained on the periphery of the Houston social elite, often a guest in the homes or offices of the residents of River Oaks. He was high-class hired help. He figured their taxes, got their money out of sticky legal jams, and kept their investments and financial schemes legal.

In World War II, my father was a lieutenant. Fresh out of the corp at Texas A&M, he went to Europe in time for the March across France. He was behind the frontlines, requisitioning gas, sort of like what he would do the rest of live. Maybe he saw Henry Bolen being shipped in the opposite direction. He returned to find my mother and the American dream that eluded Henry.

I enjoyed growing up in our house. I liked its ivy covered, manicured back yard, its ferns, roses, mockingbirds, hummingbirds, crows, and its white gazebo that made a great fort or spaceship. But when I started college, I began to resent the people who enabled my father to buy that house. What my parents were seemed to be what was wrong with America, and their choice seemed a moral fault. I thought that I could correct a portion of that moral fault caused by the River Oakses of Texas if I could become the right kind of lawyer.

But my parents remained interested in me and offered me money whenever I came home, whenever we talked over the telephone, especially after I married Victoria. It was time for me to grow up, they figured, and take advantage of my advantages. I refused their money. My mother offered to send us to California or Acapulco for our honeymoon, but I refused to let them. On our way to our honeymoon in Corpus Christi, though, we spent two nights in their house. Used to the wild, drug smoking hippie girls I had begun to date, my parents looked relieved when they saw Victoria. My mother told me she was glad I had married such an attractive and gracious girl. Graciousness was my mother's favorite attribute; *gracious* was her favorite word.

They also wanted to meet my in-laws. We promised to bring the others after we got back to Fischer. Kyle, my brother-in-law, didn't want to go, but Henry liked the idea of a free meal in Houston. My parents planned a late lunch, the kind my mother would have had for her bridge club.

On a clear fall day, the kind of day everybody in Texas dreams about all summer, we drove from Fischer to Houston in Henry's ten-year-old, convertible Lincoln. After he married off his daughter, he decided to live a little, so he bought the used convertible. He especially liked the automatic windows and locks. He had to take care of everything from his cockpit, so only he got to lock and roll down the windows. We drove east on I-10 past the Czech and Bohemian towns—Schulenberg, Weimar, Columbus—with the top down. Henry ever so often clamped his hand on to the top of his old Stetson to keep it planted on his head, while Victoria tried to hold her hair behind her head in a bun so it wouldn't blow around in front of her face. And the whole way the stereo blasted out country music above the sound of the wind.

When we pulled in front of the house, the stereo still blasting, Henry took off his hat and held it in his hands even before we walked to the front door, "Jesus," he said, "You're rich, Roger."

"My *father*," I said, "isn't hurting."

We walked down the sidewalk toward the front door, and Henry twirled in a circle to look at the other houses in the neighborhood. Victoria and I held hands, and she kissed me on the cheek as I rang the doorbell. Henry stood at the base of the steps, his back to the door, and looked across the street. My mother, wearing a purple velour warm up suit, answered the door, immediately hugged me, and stood back to look at Victoria. She held out her hand and said, "So nice to see you again, Victoria." The charms on her bracelet clinked, and the diamond in her wedding ring emphasized the cheapness of Victoria's own wedding ring when she shook Victoria's hand.

My mother had the money to keep herself tanned and her hair tinted, to make weekly visits to a health spa, to join weight watchers. Still she was never extravagant; she bought her clothes on sale. She looked past Victoria to Henry standing below us, his hat in his hand, looking like a peon. She stepped past us down the first step, and Henry took another step up, then reached to grab her hand. "Mr. Bolen, I'd guess?" my mother said.

"Right," Henry said and shook her hand.

"Come in, come in," my mother said and led us into the house. Henry looked at the shiny polished wood, silver vases and serving sets, and oriental rugs, all kept spotless by my mother's Mexican maid. I remembered the days before the maid, my mother scrubbing the walls herself to get my muddy handprints off. She tried to scrub then patch the charred spot in the old carpet where I accidentally lit a match then dropped it on the floor. After twelve years of looking at the charred spot that she could never remove or cover up, she got the idea of oriental throw rugs on the brightly waxed wooden floors.

As we went through the living room and to the kitchen, Henry studied the house, seemed to sniff at the apparent wealth, leaned close to me, and said, "By god, you *are* rich. You said you didn't *have* big money."

"I don't have *any* money," I whispered back to Henry, "and my parents *don't have big* money."

My mother held the back door open, and we stepped into the backyard. Since I had left for college, my mother had hired a landscaper to plant shrubbery and exotic grass around the white gazebo in the center of the yard. The high green hedges kept the neighbors eyes out of our yard. Henry looked up at the trees to watch the squirrels that played above our heads, lowered his head to look at my mother. "I like this," he said. "I like to watch squirrels and animals and stuff."

"Mr. Bolen," my mother said, "You're welcome to come watch our squirrels whenever you want." Henry nodded his head and took another quick look up in the tree branches. He put his old Stetson back on his head.

My father stood in the gazebo by the table and mixed a pitcher of martinis. He had several ice chests below him. He wore tennis shorts and a soft cotton sweater; we could see his knotty but well tanned legs. He had a gold chain around his neck and had grown a neatly trimmed gray mustache. "Roger," he said, walked down from the gazebo, and shook my hand. He looked at Victoria, "My god, she is beautiful," he said to me, then shook Victoria's hand. "I had forgotten what a beautiful girl you had married," he said. Then he turned to Henry and said, "Mr. Bolen," shook Henry's hand, then added, "Vernon Jackson. I'm glad to meet you."

"Likewise," Henry said.

"A drink before lunch?" my father asked

"Sure," I said, and we all sat around the table in the gazebo.

"Wine? Martini?" my father asked.

Victoria decided for the white wine, and my father poured Henry and me a martini (over ice, at Henry's insistence). My mother drank a glass of apple juice. Henry took the martini from my father, swirled the gin around, then smelled it. He took a sip and wrinkled his nose. "Stout," he said.

My father sipped his and said, "A beer instead,

maybe?"

Henry weakly smiled and said, "Since you already poured this. . . "

My father immediately flipped open the top of an ice chest and pulled out a long neck bottle of Lone Star and jerked the cap off with a can opener. Henry's smile broadened. He took the bottle, pulled off his hat, and held the bottle against the top of his forehead. "I like the cool feel of the bottle." He took a gulp from the beer, set the bottle in front of him, and put his hat back on.

My mother sat by Victoria and said, "So how was the honeymoon in Corpus Christi?" The remark was meant for me.

"It was fun," Victoria said.

I turned to face them. "Good as anywhere else," I said so my mother could hear me. She grimaced at me.

"It is a beautiful city," my mother said.

"I never really been to Corpus," Henry said, "but I seen the Atlantic, during the war."

My father sat by him. "I was in the War, too," he said. It occurred to me that my father and Henry had both joined up to go to their war while I ran away from mine.

Like a mathematical truth, Henry raised his hand and showed my father his trigger finger. "Got my finger shot off," he said.

"Daddy," Victoria said sternly. "Daddy!" Victoria said again and pinched me lightly. "No one wants to see your old finger." But my mother leaned across the table to look, and Henry stretched his hand across the table for her to see. My mother took his hand in her own and looked at Henry's stub. Henry had a serious look in his eyes and a grim, tight mouth.

Henry took his hand away. My mother eased back into her chair. My father clinked his ice cubes against the side of his glass. Victoria scowled across the table at Henry.

"Roger tells me you are a cowboy," my father said.

Victoria ducked her head. Henry smiled. Henry began to tell us about his adventures with wetback cowboys, the horse riding feats of Shorty Martins, rattlesnake bites, and a hundred mile trail drive through the Trans Pecos country.

After Henry ended his stories, or rather after my father steered him into a different discussion, my mother excused herself to go to the kitchen to fetch lunch. I went with her to help her. The maid had prepared finger sandwiches the night before and left them covered in the refrigerator. My mother pulled the plate of sandwiches out as well as a large bowl of chilled cucumber soup. We dished the soup into smaller bowls and stacked the sandwiches onto a large silver platter.

"Now, Roger, I know you get upset about our asking," my mother said, "but do you need money?"

"No," I said.

"You're going to need it for law school," she said.

"Then I'll wait until I need it to take it."

"We want you to take our money. We can afford it."

"That's not the point," I said.

"I won't argue anymore," she said, "but it is the point."

She picked up the tray loaded with the soup, and I picked up the silver platter with the sandwiches. She turned her back to the screen door and began to back into it.

"Mother," I said before she could get out, "You don't have to try so hard to please Henry."

"He's a pleasant man," she said.

"Come on, mother," I said. "You normally would never meet or talk to anyone like him."

My mother frowned, "We didn't raise you to be so snobbish and so graceless." She pushed the door open and took the sandwiches out to both sides of my family.

We set the silver trays on the table, and everyone hesitated while we looked at the food. "Go ahead,

Henry," my father said. Henry grabbed one of the dainty sandwiches and stuck the whole thing in his mouth. Victoria, who had her sorority training, took small bites.

"And this is Charlotta's best cucumber soup," my mother said and placed a bowl of soup in front of each of us. Henry looked at his, sniffed it, then lifted a spoonful to his mouth. He sucked it up without slurping. He made a sour face. "It's not hot," he said.

After lunch, we all had another drink. Victoria and my mother drank wine, and my father, Henry, and I had a beer. We heard a couple of squirrels chattering, and Henry stood and walked out from under the gazebo to look up in the trees. He cocked his head and looked up like a hungry dog. "I see them," he said and pointed.

"We have quite a few squirrels," my father said.

"They're almost tame," my mother said. "They always play in the yard. They chase each other and tease our cat."

Henry still peered up into the tree, "I like squirrels, but I'm like a kid. I'd be tempted to shoot at them, just to see if I could hit 'em. Have you ever eaten squirrel?"

No one answered, but Henry didn't tell us about eating squirrels. He did something of a pirouette in his boot heels and looked around the backyard. It was as though he were taking a movie camera pan of my parents' property to assess it. "I sure do like this place," he finally said. Then Henry added, "but ya'll gonna have to come see my place sometime. See my horses. How pretty they are." He looked back at us, smiled, and took a long gulp from his beer.

Two years later, when his horse farm again began to fail, Henry drove to Houston to see my father in his office and walked out with a five-thousand dollar loan. He tried, but I don't think he ever paid it back.

My father's loan to Henry is only half a mystery. Knowing Henry and my father, you'd never think it possible. But knowing about Henry and the way he could ingratiate himself and knowing about my parents' weakness for me, you can imagine it. I figured that half-mystery out. The half-mystery that I wonder about on long nights is how my parents stayed so happy with each other.

* * *

The flames from the candles on the table flicker in the cool, gentle breeze coming off the Colorado River. The River shines with the soft reflections of Japanese lanterns. The pigeons coo up in the trees. The mood is all just right, but I can't get interested in my date.

I look at the silver medallion resting in her cleavage, take another bite of my veal, and try to think about sex with her. But my mind betrays me and makes me wish for just one more night with Victoria.

The breeze tosses my hair and gives me a whiff of my date's perfume. I squint at her cleavage. She is a friend of a friend of Buck Cronin's wife. While Buck and I work to put asunder, Buck's wife helps to join together. Maybe, Buck and Shelly should become partners. Buck could split them, Shelly match them with someone else.

"I love Italian," my date says and sucks up a short tail of spaghetti. Had she not been on a diet and trying to shed some of the natural pounds that attach to a mature lady's butt and thighs, she would have left a smear of sauce across her lip. But my date ordered the spaghetti sans sauce. She sucks up bare pasta.

I push myself back from the table and say, "Why don't we get something to drink?" I had a glass of wine, but my date drank only water.

"I don't really drink alcohol," my date says. "Alcohol is really bad for you."

"How about if I get a drink," I say. I desperately want a beer, a whiskey, some prop to stare into as I talk to this woman.

"Do you need a drink?" She smiles sweetly, then her

brows pull together as she thinks about the way she said what she said; then she adds, "but if you want a drink?"

"I just drink to soothe my nerves," I say and force myself to smile at her.

"Oh, do I make you nervous? I'm sorry."

"No, no, let's just get a drink. You can have some ice cream or something."

"I'm trying to cut down on sweets. They're worse than alcohol."

"Iced tea, then," I say, and my date's eyes flicker at the mention of something that she could eat or drink.

I get up, drop my napkin on the table, and help my date out of her chair. "But, if I make you nervous, you just tell me, and I'll stop talking," my date says. "I can just talk your head off if you let me." I think about thin Victoria. How does she keep her weight off? Was it from watching her father die? Living with me? Maybe, my date should try misery and stress as a diet plan.

* * *

As we walk along the jogging path on the bank of the Colorado, we can feel the cool summer breeze blowing across the water. It is time that I try something like this. I should thank Shelly for her insistence. I should phone her in the morning and tell her how much I enjoyed myself. Right now, I want only for this date to be over. My hands in my pants' pockets, I feel my date's fingers on my wrist. I look down at the pocket of my new slacks. My date gently lifts my hand out of my pocket, and we hold hands as we walk along the river. Then she stops walking. I smile at her, and she puts her head against my arm and reaches across her voluminous chest to grab my forearm with her other hand. Again, I catch a whiff of her perfume, and I feel her stiff, sprayed hair on my arm. Sam Penschorn, Pete Proctor, and Doc Hillier would be impressed with her great knockers and soft, cushy butt. Even Henry would be impressed with her. So why can't I kiss her? Some drinks would help, and I hope that she will drop her diet or her convictions and have a drink. My new slacks chafe my crotch. My new cordovan shoes rub a blister on my heel.

* * *

As my date climbs out of my Toyota pickup, she tries to hold her skirt in place. But I am still given a glimpse of her panties. I could not convince her to have a drink. I take her arm and lead her toward her apartment. She stoops over to open the door. Then she turns around to me. I prepare to kiss her, but she says, "Would you like to come in?"

I could not say "no" without upsetting her, making her wonder why I wouldn't act like any other man. I wonder if I have lost the urge, forgotten how, learned to be a celibate, become like Clayton Tanner. Perhaps my last tense meeting with Victoria, where I could have pounced on her, only several weeks before, have left me impotent? Perhaps, like Sam and Pete, I am getting old.

We walk in. A teenage babysitter, her hair in curlers, is sitting on the couch under the painting of waves falling on a beach with storm clouds gathered behind. There are a few Norman Rockwell prints on the other walls. I spot a couple of plates with inscriptions on them. One says, "God is bigger than any of my problems." A plate underneath it says, "God does not play dice with the universe-A. Einstein." The baby sitter doesn't say anything to either of us but keeps her eyes on the TV set. *Saturday Night Live* is just ending.

As the show ends, my date digs into her purse for money for the baby sitter. I know that this is a cue. I don't want to be out any more money, but I quickly pull ten bucks out of my billfold. "Will this help?" I say.

"Oh, really," my date says. "You don't need to. You shouldn't." The baby sitter shifts her weight on to one foot, crosses her arm, and slouches into the posture that only teenage girls can affect.

"I'd like to," I say. My date smiles. The babysitter, who is probably a veteran at sitting for divorced mothers and has thus seen this ritual time and again, rolls her eyes.

"But then just five dollars would be fine," my date says.

"But he probably doesn't have change," the baby sitter says and snatches the bill out of my hand. "Thanks Mrs. Adcock," she says as she walks to the door.

When the babysitter steps out, my date curls her index finger toward me. "Come here," she says. I suck in some air, smile, and prepare to kiss her.

When I get close to her, as I am about to wrap my arms around her, she says, "I want you to see my sweet, little girl." I wonder if "little girl" is some kind of crazy personal nickname for one of her private parts.

She takes my hand and leads me down the narrow hallway of her cramped apartment. "Shh," she says. She opens a bedroom door, "look," she says, and I step beside her to look at a sleeping girl. "That's my little baby."

"She's sweet," is all I can think to say.

"Ohhh," my date says. "You're sweet to say so."

She takes my hand and leads me back down the dark hallway and back into the living room. I stand until she says, "Please sit where you would like."

When I take a seat on her sofa, she dims all of her lights and says, "Oh, let's listen to something." She sticks a tape into her cassette player, and I hear waves splashing and elevator music. She comes back to me and sits beside me.

"This is soothing," my date says and rubs the back of her neck. "Waves are therapeutic. They're symbols of our peaceful existence in the wombs." She looks at me as though she wants me to take her seriously. "And there is a subliminal message on this tape. It tells you things that make you confident. I'm working on my confidence."

I listen for a moment then ask, "What does it say?"

"I don't know. It's subliminal."

I turn to look at her, and I wonder what kind of casualty she is. I cannot resist saying, "Well, then how do you know it isn't saying something to make you unconfident? Something like, you slime sucking moron? Or something like that?"

I smile and wait for her to giggle, but she says, "They wouldn't do that."

I want to say, "Fooled you didn't they;" or "Are they the ones who make you eat spaghetti with no sauce?" But I cannot be that cruel. It would not be "gracious." So I say instead, "No, I guess not."

She turns her head and smiles at me. She says, "You really are a sweet man. You are not like all the others." I know that this is an invitation to be like all the others and make my move. I slowly lean toward her until she gets the hint and leans toward me.

We start kissing. Then we slide down the sofa until we lie side by side, nose to nose. I begin to think about Victoria. But after awhile, I discover that I am not too old. I'm not like Sam and Pete or Clayton Tanner. My eyes are still blue, and my peter is still red. Unlike Pete Proctor's joke, my date will not have to play pool with a rope.

After some heavy breathing, she takes me by the hand and leads me down the dark hall, past the "sweet, little baby girl's" room, and into her bedroom. She lets go of my hand and sits on the edge of the bed. Some streaks of light come in from the window by the bed and show dark shapes. The small bedroom seems crowded. The bulging closet is open; a rack holding nothing but shoes hangs on the closet door. The small apartment cannot accommodate what used to fit into the three-bedroom, ranch style house that she lived in before her divorce. I step on clothes and move toward her. And she, like a school girl, looks at me with puppy eyes and cocks her head to one side. There is not a whole lot of difference between her and her baby sitter.

When I sit beside her, she undoes the clasp on her watch and leans across me to put her watch on the nightstand; then she turns her attention to herself. She reaches behind her back and goes into some contortions as she pulls the zipper down the back of her dress. This is too methodical. We ought to be rolling on the floor. I think of Victoria. And, as I am wishing, hoping, and regretting, an image of Kay Menger in her nightgown, kissing her boyfriend good night flickers in front of my eyes.

I force my attention back to my date. We should be lunging, sucking tongues, rolling across the floor, crying. But, instead, I wait while she lowers her blouse.

With her blouse down, she stands and steps out of her skirt. She neatly folds it, and I start unbuttoning my shirt. In the dark, I can see more of her cleavage. Her breasts fight against the tight, low cut bra. Two folds of skin overlap the rim of the bra. I look down her trunk and see why she had been dieting. She is pudgy but soft. Victoria is thin, hard. . .wasted? But gaining weight.

My date sits beside me and pulls me with her as she lays back on the bed. I get my arm caught behind my back and wiggle to get it free. I close my eyes and feel her breath on my face, her perfume filling my nose, her hair stiff against my arm. I clamp my eyes shut even tighter and think of all the women whom I feel sorrow for, the women for whom I have regrets. And I stroke my date's cheek as though she is the embodiment of all these women. Tears seem to float behind my eyelids. I could cry if I let myself.

Then my date whispers to me, "Did you bring the raincoat for your little soldier?"

"What?" I say. I open my eyes. No tears roll down my cheeks. The images of Victoira leave my my head, and I am with just my date looking at me with bulbous eyes.

"Did you bring a raincoat?"

"Huh?"

"A wrap?"

"What?"

"A condom?"

I roll away from date and sit on the edge of the bed. "No," I say. "To tell you the truth, I didn't think we'd get this far tonight." I lied. I was hoping we would get this far. But now that the age of unearned sex was slipping into the age of AIDS, I had forgotten to bring a rubber. The old Germans and Baptist who burned my car and taunted me in San Marcos would say that I am getting what I deserve, that fright of AIDS was God's punishment for my loose morality. Instead I know that irony, which always sucks when it happens to you, caught up with me and my generation once again in our era of unearned sex.

Suddenly, I feel my date's breath on my neck and her arms around me, "Oh, I'm so sorry. So sorry. You must think I'm terrible. I'm sorry."

"No, don't be," was all that I was able to say before she went on.

"You know with all the scares about disease and all the advice that you get. Did you see Phil Donahue's show?"

"No."

"Well, you're a clean guy aren't you. I mean, I trust you."

"Are you clean?" I let slip before I realize what I had said.

She pulls away from me, then curls up like a doodle bug. She raises her hands to her head, "Oh, I've made a fool of both us. I must have made myself seem like I was a dirty girl."

"No, I didn't mean that. . ."

"I'm so sorry. I'm so sorry. You must want me to go."

"We're in your apartment," I say and stand and catch my feet on some clothes as I inch toward her bedroom door.

"I guess, I'm just a fool," my date says, but I do not say, "Yes, yes that is right." I hear sniffles.

"No, No. It's all my fault. I'm sorry."

"No, No, No," she wails and her shoulders convulse with crying. "I just always do something dumb like this." She pulls her head out of her hands, and from the light coming in through the window, I could see the tears running down her face. "You see I have a confidence problem."

"Yeah, I really should go," I say. She needs to be alone with her problem. "I'll show myself out." I hear a wail from the woman again.. But, as I take a step forward to go back to her, I suddenly imagine myself lying alone with my date "afterwards." What would we talk about? Would I have to listen to waves? So, I back to the bedroom door, forget any concern that I have for her, and walk rapidly out of her apartment.

* * *

I hope for a second wind, but one does not come. It is the day after a rain and the weather is clear but humid. I ought to move west to a drier climate, another place booming with yuppie discoverers–Albuquerque, Phoenix, Denver. Sweat pastes my shorts to my legs today. Beads of it run down from my forehead and into my eyes and mouth. I blink against the salty sting and blow the bitter taste out of my mouth. I retrace my steps along the Colorado river bank that I made the night before with my date. At least my feet feel better in jogging shoes. At least the date is over. I can still feel the blister on my heel.

The night was still reasonably young when I left my

date last night. So, I drove around town looking for a drink. I ended up at Studebaker's, which was so named because the club had a sliced up '53 Studebaker in the middle of a circular dance floor. It was one of those places that played 50's, 60's, and early 70's music so that the people my age, who would have more money than the present youngsters, would come in and drink and dance while they grew sentimental about the youth that they were losing. My new cordovan loafers had rubbed blisters on the back of my heels. My new slacks itched. But I watched balding men and sagging women dance and drink and try to remember their youth. I sat there, just drinking, and tried to forget my youth. So when I got home, I phoned Becky and got her up out of bed. It is a habit of mine she has come to accept. She started laughing and never stopped as I told her about my night.

The woman whom I recognize as the "oriental coed" chugs by me in her choppy, studied jogging style. She nods her head, and I smile as best I can. In the past, I have thought about changing directions and joining her, striking up a conversation, but she wears a Walkman, and I doubt if she would pull the plugs out of her ears just for a conversation with an aging hippie jogger.

Later today, I'll have to go to a bank and try to con a teller who knows Buck Cronin into letting me see the deposits that Terry Delouche has made over the past six months. Mrs. Delouche thinks that her husband is lying about just how much money he has coming in from his computer consultancy firm and wants her fair share, which is all she can get. From the bank, I must drive to Bonham junior high and find Jennifer and Billy Sandoval as they walk home from school. Mrs. Sandoval hired some other lawyer than Buck Cronin when she got her divorce, so she lost her two kids. Now she wants them back. So she hired Buck Cronin and told him that she suspects Mr. Sandoval of child abuse. I must ask

Jennifer and Billy delicate questions about their lives with their dad. I will give each kid $20 and charge Buck Cronin.

I chug up the steps to get to the First Street bridge and cross to the other side. If I don't cross here, I'll jog too far. I stride across the bridge and accelerate my pace because I want to look good for the drivers. Some stare at me. Others giggle at my silliness. Fellow enthusiasts nod. Why do I jog? Why does the question keep coming up when I jog? In the sixties, we wanted to be in good intellectual and spiritual shape. Now, we want to boast that we still have the same size waists that we had back when we wanted a spiritual workout.

I stop and look at the drivers. I look over the bridge at the Colorado. I wonder about the etiquette involved with a bad blind date. What should I say to Shelly? What should I say to my date? Should I apologize? Ask her out again? Forget the whole affair and be content not to ever see her? Roxanne was her name.

Chapter 7:
Doc Hillier

Henry spent most of his life after Rebecca left lonely and horny, but he wasn't completely celibate. After they got old enough to be left on their own, Kyle and Victoria remembered "lady friends" whom he took to dances or occasionally brought home. Mostly the lady friends were failed attempts at hormonal relief. After Victoria and I married, Henry began driving his Lincoln into San Marcos. He meant to make up for lost time and chances. Henry, pushing sixty, started to chase young women.

On Friday or Saturday nights, he drove to area night spots to drink and dance in the bars that played progressive, Austin-style country music. He always wore his fading, cracked old Stetson, a freshly ironed white or blue shirt, wrinkled jeans, and his work boots. The students at Southwest Texas State began to recognize him, talk to him, buy him drinks. He even let a few come out to his place, and go swimming in the pool that Fischer Creek formed. Some coeds referred to him as that lecherous old man, and others talked about the cute old cowboy. For a sorority "woman" to be seen with the white haired man became a status symbol. Some fraternity boys started wanting to get older faster.

Victoria was glad when we graduated and moved to Austin, not only because I was starting law school, but because she was getting embarrassed seeing friends or sorority sisters riding around town with her father in his Lincoln. To me, the suspicion that Henry had slept with several of Victoria's former sorority sisters was a delicious scandal, but Victoria found that it gnawed at her liver.

When we moved to Austin, though, we didn't have time to worry about Henry's hormones. We were poor. Austin was always a haven for what intellectuals or liberals there were in Texas. But because there were so many, most stayed unemployed or underemployed. They gave Austin its slow, beer sipping, conversational pace. Victoria tried to get a job with her brand new secondary teaching certificate in history. But any teaching job in Austin was hard to get.

I considered asking my parents for money. Instead, I worked part-time bartending, and Victoria got a job as a waitress at Green Pastures, the classiest restaurant in Austin, because she could pronounce the names of the French foods. She could pull in sometimes fifty dollars a night just from tips.

By mid-October of my first year in law school, we decided to spend a little of what little money we had at the annual Chili Cook-off in San Marcos. We roamed around the Hays County Convention Center grounds tasting chili and drinking beer, and we spent ten dollars on the cover charge to go to the dance in the large convention hall. The hall was an aluminum building with a cement floor. Willie Nelson's band played country music, and the students, locals, Houstonians, San Antonioans, and Austinites pushed into the hall, shoulder to shoulder, and danced and drank. Victoria and I sat at one end of a very large table next to a beer booth and the backdoor, the V.I.P. entrance. A couple of Victoria's younger girlfriends joined us. Each wore a short shag hairdo, a sleeveless blouse, jeans, and high top tennis shoes. I took turns dancing with Victoria and then with each of them, until they found two boys and brought them to our end of the table.

Toward the end of the night, one of the girls looked at the V.I.P. entrance then immediately poked Victoria. All the women turned to look. "That's Marilynn Katz with him," one of them said. "I know her."

"Oh, my God," Victoria said. I turned around to see Henry standing in the doorway with a young blonde dressed like Victoria's two friends hanging on his arm. A college boy hired to guard the door came up to him and told him that he couldn't come in that entrance, that he had to go to the front gate. But Henry stuck his thumb into his shirt pocket and held out an honorary Chili Cook-off Marshall's badge. I wondered how he had gotten it, whom he had conned.

Victoria looked at me. "Should we say hello to him or hide?"

"Say hello," I said. "Hell, he's a celebrity."

"God, look at her, she's younger than I am."

I turned to look at Henry, and he saw me. We simultaneously waved at each other. While the men at the beer booth weren't looking, he reached into one of the large ice-filled trashcans and pulled out two beers. Then he walked toward us with the girl still holding on to his arm, and the college kid following him. "Sir," the kid said, "really. You need a pass not a badge to get in. I'm supposed to make sure you have a pass."

Henry walked up to the table, and Marilynn held her hand up and, dipping her fingers, waved at Victoria's two friends. "How ya'll," Henry said. I could tell from the red streaks in the whites of his eyes that he had been stealing a lot of beers.

"Sir, if you don't give the beer back, I'm going to have to call the law," the college kid said. His red, acne-scarred face showed no authority. He was the wrong guy to guard Chilimpiad from the likes of Henry Bolen and other beer rustling cowpokes.

"I am the law," Henry said, put his thumb in his shirt pocket, and poked the badge at the kid.

"Okay, Okay," the kid said and ran off. Henry sat across from Victoria by one of her friends, and Marilynn squeezed in beside him.

"Victoria, Roger, this is Marilynn," he said, then pulled open his two cans of beer and gave one to his date.

"Daddy, what are you doing . . . here?" Victoria said.

"I'm an honorary Marshall. Some guy at Cheatham Street Saloon gave this to me and said it could get me in free."

"You're gonna get thrown in jail," Victoria said.

"Let's dance," Henry said to Marilynn.

"He's your father?" Marilynn asked Victoria. But before Victoria could answer, Henry pulled Marilynn up to dance.

"He's precious," one of Victoria's girlfriend's said.

"That bimbo," Victoria whispered to me.

"Come on what harm can he do them?" I asked.

"That's not the point," she said. "Look what they are doing to him."

"Come on. He's having a great time."

"They parade him around. They use him. I can't believe I once liked these people."

"Victoria," I said. Her shoulder vibrated with the tension that gathered at the base of her neck. "Relax," I told her, and myself, as I witnessed, for the first time, the concern and shame for her father—and her terrible allegiance to him.

Before the dance ended, the college kid with the pimples, who had failed at guarding the door, came back with an off-duty San Marcos policeman moonlighting as a security guard. The kid pointed Henry out, and Victoria and I got up and walked up to the policeman. "We'll take care of him," Victoria said. "I'm his daughter." The policeman looked at her with a curious smile. And Henry took Marilynn's hand and led her off the dance floor and to the back door. The kid pointed at him, just as he and Marilynn slipped out.

"Good job," the policeman said drily and patted the

kid on the shoulder.

Victoria and I walked out the door and saw Henry and Marilynn getting into his top-down Continental. He had parked it in a loading zone reserved for officials and beer trucks. "Daddy," Victoria said as Henry held the driver's door open, and Marilynn scooted just to the other side of the wheel. "Are you okay?"

"Fine," Henry said.

I walked up to him and patted his back, "Can you drive home?"

"Sure," he said.

"Henry," I said, "you gotta be careful with young women."

"Roger!" Victoria said.

Henry got in his car. Marilynn reached into an ice chest on the passenger's side, popped the top of a can, and handed it to Henry, and as he backed out, Marilynn grabbed him around the neck with both arms and kissed his cheek. "Jesus," Victoria said to me as Henry drove away with his hand waving a frantic good-bye.

"He'll be all right," I said and put my hand around Victoria's shoulders.

*   *   *

Doc Hillier called us just as we got back to our apartment in Austin. Henry was in the Hays County Hospital, "laid up pretty bad." We went right back to the car and drove the thirty miles back to San Marcos and the Hays County hospital.

Doc Hillier met us at the entrance and walked with us to the waiting room. "They got him doped up now. But it'll a wear off in about an hour. Then they'll let you see him before they give him something to put him to sleep for awhile."

I put my arm around Victoria, but she rolled out from under it and said, "Goddamn that bitch."

"Victoria, it's not her fault," I said.

Doc Hillier hung his head down and said, "Don't say anything about her to Henry, not just yet."

"What can we do?" Victoria asked.

"Nothing," Jack said.

Victoria turned away from him and me and said over her shoulder, "So how bad is he?"

I walked to her to touch her, but she again stepped away from me to look at Jack. "You tell me now, what happened to him?"

"His backbone's chipped in three places," Jack said matter-of-factly. "But he's lucky."

"So what's that mean?"

"He's not paralyzed, but he's gonna hurt, and he's gonna have to be tied up in a back brace for about nine months, the first few months, though, he's gonna be here in the hospital." Doc Hillier dropped his head, then pulled it up like he was growing tired of all of us. "Should I call Kyle?"

"No," Victoria answered quickly. "We'll tell him tomorrow. He'd just come down and piss somebody off." Victoria's voice dropped. "Thank you Dr. Hillier, thank you for taking such good care of him. If you'd just let us know what we owe you when. . ."

Jack straightened up and held up his hand to cut her off. "I'm here as a friend not his doctor. I just happened to be the first one the sheriff called after he got to the accident. You could hear the crash from Fischer. Henry didn't make a curve ."

"Was he drunk?" I asked.

"And she was hanging all over him," Victoria butted in.

"The sheriff ain't gonna say nothing about Henry drinking or about her," Doc Hillier said nervously.

I got worried. "What about her?" I asked.

Doc Hillier sat down and stared at his boots. "Sheriff found her hitch hiking down Ranch Road 12." He looked down to keep from grinning at us. "Something Henry said or did pissed her off." We both bit our lips to keep from laughing.

"I can imagine," I said. Victoria poked me with an elbow, but then she was the one who started laughing.

* * *

Late at night, when the first beams of sun started making the horizon edge orange and pink, they let us in to see Henry. He was still in intensive care in a bed by himself. Doc Hillier pushed the door open, and Victoria and I walked into the dark room with the one dim night light shining over Henry's head. Jack shut the door behind us.

Henry had a tube in his nose and another one in his arm. He was taped to a wooden plank resting between his back and the bed. With a bandage around his forehead and another around his chin and two swollen black eyes, his face looked like a mummified raccoon's. He couldn't move his head, but he shifted his eyes to see us. He spoke, but the words made no sense. He tried again. "Sorry to get ya'll out of bed."

Victoria stepped toward him and said, "Oh Daddy. You all right?" I almost laughed at the absurdity of her question. Henry gurgled trying to laugh; his eyes watered. Victoria put her hand over her mouth and started to giggle. Even Dr. Hillier could laugh. Laughing still, Victoria sat on the bed beside him, touched the battered knuckles of his left hand, and rubbed his fingers and the back of hand, right around the needle of the I.V.

Henry swallowed hard, getting the spit caught in his throat, choked, then gasped and closed his eyes as a pain shot through him. Doc Hillier said, "Maybe we better leave."

"No, No," Henry said. "It's lonesome as hell in here, and I can't sleep on this goddamn two by four."

"We were just supposed to see you, not talk to you,"

Jack said and held the door open for us.

I walked to the door, held it for Victoria, and, as she let her arm slide down Henry's and backed toward the door, I said, "Good night, Henry."

Henry said, "Roger, you stay for a minute." Hillier looked at me, shrugged his shoulders, then left. "Please," Henry said. I let the door go, and it gently swooshed shut behind me. I walked to Henry's bed, looked down at his raccoon eyes, the tubes in his arms, the battered knuckles the emergency ward crew might not have even noticed, then looked down at the floor. "I want to talk to you cause you always been honest with me."

"That's because I haven't really talked to you that much."

"See there, you're honest."

"Please Henry, just forget this," I said and wondered why he didn't want Victoria to stay.

"Coming down toward my place from Fischer, she was hugging and kissing all over me, just kinda clinging, like she was sucking an armpit or something." He sucked in for some air. "So I pulled off the road. And I started to unzip her pants to get to her panties. She does the same to me. But all I got is memories."

"Oh Henry, you had a lot to drink."

"But that's not the bad part." He swallowed hard. "She slapped me and took off walking. I followed behind her making a traffic hazard of myself, but she's got nothing to do with me. I wasn't thinking right, so I just sped out of there."

"Maybe she deserved it."

"She didn't deserve the hike. But she's Melissa Sue Wengler all over again."

"Who is that?"

"I'll tell you later. And maybe you can help me figure women out. You saw, though. You saw her at the dance," Henry said.

"You're right. She was hanging on you," I said and

put my hand over Henry's battered knuckle.

"No, no, no. That's not what I want. I want you to tell me, tell me honest. Victoria would take my side, and Jack'd be sneaky and not tell me honest." He hesitated to suck up some more air.

"What, Henry?"

"I want to know if I was foolish. I want to know was I foolish-looking chasing the young women around. Were they hanging around me and my now wrecked convertible car just to amuse themselves?"

"Henry . . ." I started.

"You see, I knew no women my age. And honestly, since Rebecca left me, I been almost scared of women. But these young ones were something new. You be honest. You say if I am a foolish old man."

"Who can figure 'em, Henry? I'd have thought for sure you were going to get some."

"If I could have done something about it," Henry smiled underneath his blackened, raccoon eyes. Later that night, when Victoria and I were in bed and away from Henry, and we started laughing, Victoria's laughter turned to crying—for Henry's foolishness and damaged pride.

* * *

The cracked pieces of Henry's spine didn't grow together in a proper weld. "Not much you can do with a backbone injury," Doc Hillier told Henry. "Can't put a cast or sling on it. Just have to grit your teeth." Henry gritted his teeth through some long nights of recovery. He would roll over a healing vertebrae, scream, then grit his teeth. On the nights when she stayed with him, Victoria would run to his room at the sound of his scream, try to inch him into a comfortable position, then wipe the sweat off his forehead. He would shake in her arms until the pain went away then breathe heavily. Victoria learned not to hold his hand while he gritted his teeth because he would squeeze her hand so hard that she thought her knuckles would pop off. There were drugs, Doc Hillier said, but Henry said that this was why there was booze and not drugs. He said that he could do the pain.

Victoria learned how to endure Henry's pain, but sometimes at night, in bed with me, when she told me about her nights with him, she would cry about his pain.

Henry got better, though, and he begin to hobble around in his back brace and walker. He could get around in his house and out onto his veranda, but he fell several times trying to get to his horse barn. Kyle scolded him, and Victoria laughed at him when he showed his skinned elbows and knees during a Sunday dinner. After that, Kyle gave Sam Penschorn and Pete Proctor a couple of bucks each week to keep an eye on Henry.

During our Sunday meals in the long summer of his recovery, I hated to sit next to Henry. He had a tough time getting into or out of a shower or bath tub, so he didn't bathe. And because the back brace made him hot, he wore only a sweaty undershirt under it. We could see the scales of dirt, dried skin, and B.O on his arms and chest. Kyle offered to hire a nurse to give Henry a sponge bath, but Henry refused to let her into his house.

But if not as good as new, Henry did mend. His back straightened, though it never grew as rigid as it had before the accident. He bathed more but not as much as before the accident. He talked about riding his horses again. We had sold all but three. And Victoria got pregnant.

Victoria and I decided to keep this child because we were happy and because I could see an income ahead. I had one more year of law school before I could become self sufficient. We lived moderately well from the tips Victoria made at the Green Pastures Restaurant. My parents, when they heard about the baby, sent me three hundred dollars and a promise to send two hundred dollars a month once the baby arrived. I accepted their money.

During her sixth month, we spent a Saturday night with Henry. He tried to stand on his head to show us his back was okay. Victoria and I both tried to talk him out of it. But he got down on all fours, and some tiny shiver of pain Doc Hillier said would always be with him shot up into his shoulder blades. We helped him to bed, and Victoria massaged his back. When she finished, we sat in the living room watching *Saturday Night Live*, and I lifted the bottom of her maternity blouse to peek at her bulging belly and kissed it.

The next morning, I woke up to see Victoria awake beside me and rubbing her naked belly. Her brows were wrinkled and sweat beaded on her forehead. "Victoria?" I asked.

"Nothing," she said. "Just the usual morning sickness."

"Can I get you anything?"

"No. Damn. It's starting earlier."

"A glass of water, maybe?"

"No, why don't you help me up. We're already both awake. We might as well get up."

"Is it that bad?"

"No," she said, but as I pulled her arms, she groaned. And about mid morning, when she went into the kitchen for a cup of coffee, leaving Henry and me in the living room, Henry telling me about which vertebrae cracked, she screamed. I ran into the kitchen, and Henry limped in after me. Victoria lay on the kitchen floor biting into her knuckles and kicking at the bottom cabinets. Her cup lay broken beside her. The spilled coffee stained her white blouse and scalded her belly and the top of her thighs. As I cradled her head, Henry ran for the telephone. I saw blood seeping from the white knuckles she was biting, so I pulled her fist from her mouth. She screamed again.

Henry called Jack Hillier at home. "I'm retired now," was the first thing he said to Henry. But Jack called the Hays County sheriff and asked for a helicopter. "You kidding?" the dispatcher said. But an ambulance showed up at the house, and two hours later, Henry and I sat in the waiting room of Hays County Hospital in San Marcos.

Henry rubbed his back then looked at me and said, "You should have done something."

"Done what?"

"Should have sent her to a doctor," he said.

"She's been going to a specialist in Austin."

"Still," Henry said. He folded his arms and stared at me, then looked ahead. "Maybe I should have done something," he added and looked at me with heavy lidded eyes.

"All that could, has been done," I said.

Kyle walked into the room with a nurse following him. He had on jeans and a T shirt but had forgotten to take his house slippers off. The loose shoes slapped at his heels. He looked at us and said, "Where is she?"

"You cannot see her," the nurse said.

"To hell you say," he said. "She's my sister."

"No one can see her yet," the nurse said. Kyle turned away from her and saw Henry and me sitting down.

"Nothing to do but sit down," I said.

"We don't know no more than you do," Henry said.

Kyle sat down, looked angrily at the nurse, then looked at me. "So why can't we see her?"

"Would you want to see somebody in the middle of surgery?" I asked.

After ten minutes, Kyle said, "I hate this waiting."

Back where my head joins my neck, a nerve seemed to snap, making me jerk. I got up, fumbled in my pocket for some change, and walked toward the Coke machine.

I dropped one quarter, then threw the other one at the machine. I turned around to look at the other two. "She's my goddamn wife. How do you think I feel? Jesus Christ. You bastards think . . ."

But before I could go on or they could answer, Doc Hillier walked into the room looking ridiculous in a surgical robe and hat. I couldn't imagine him a doctor at all. He sat by Henry and patted his knee. He looked at me, then Kyle, then turned to look at Henry eye to eye. Kyle rubber-necked to see Doc Hillier, and I shouted, "I'm her husband, talk to me."

Doc Hillier turned around to look at me. "Slow down, there. I ain't the surgeon. They just sort of let me in there to watch." He patted Henry's shoulder again without looking at him, stood, and walked to me. "I figure I know you fellas. And I figure you can take it." He breathed deeply. "It's a miscarriage, if you hadn't guessed already." He hesitated. "Some women just have trouble. Her mother did."

"Shit," Kyle said.

"How is she?" I asked.

"She's cut up a little inside, doped up, and gonna be sore and depressed."

"Can I see her?" I asked.

"No," Doc Hillier said and shook his head. "I wouldn't recommend it. Let her come to."

"Shit," Kyle said again.

He patted me on the shoulder and stepped back so he could look at me and Henry. "Excuse me now, fellas. I'm getting old. Can't hold my bladder like a doctor should. Ain't been since I got here. My condolences."

* * *

Victoria and I improved. After three years of classes, part-time bartending, some borrowing from my parents, Victoria working as a waitress, I graduated from UT law school. To me, with a law degree in hand, it finally seemed that I had a few options in my life. I joined two classmates (we all worked for the Democratic party while in law school but were probably all closet socialists) and opened a law office in Austin, just off Lamar, on the bottom floor of a fifty-year old stucco bungalow. Victoria helped us pull out some walls and chose the interior paint color. Life holds promise for you when your new partners and your wife help you paint your new business.

At first, the Howard, Jackson, and Schmidt law firm threatened large apartment complex owners and student ghetto landlords with suits from cheated college students. Then we represented several environmentalist groups who wanted to stop the construction on the hills above Barton Springs. We dedicated a lot of our services to this cause and eventually lost. A mall appeared above Barton Springs, and its drainage still closes the old Austin landmark about four times a year. We got involved in the real estate wars. We'd oppose anybody with money.

But we finally got a chance to make some real money for ourselves when Schmidt's uncle, Walter Newberry, a grand-old-style Texas lawyer who liked white suits without ties, straw fedoras, and shoes without socks, got elected for a term as a state senator. We learned very quickly that friends and relatives have a relation to eating well. We wrote a bill for uncle Walter that then became a law. Uncle Walt got the lieutenant governor to let us write the two hundred and eighty-seventh amendment to the Texas Constitution, something about voting districts. I, personally, developed a talent in writing archaic, rambling, redundant, and wordy state laws. For awhile, if the legislature needed a law written or if Austin needed an ordinance rewritten and interpreted; Howard, Jackson, and Schmidt was the firm to hire. A lawyer with a partnership, several state laws under his belt, and a connection in the state senate could count on becoming a stud duck in Austin. I kept my old pickup truck, which still ran perfectly, to remind myself and others from whence I came. And I hardly ever wore a tie. Jeans and tennis shoes were good enough for Howard, Jackson, and Schmidt's office.

This was not enough for Victoria. She still felt bad. She lost weight. Her face became gaunt and shallow. The roundness of her belly and butt firmed up. And Henry started to get old. His stomach became uneasy, and he could eat only certain things. As though his backbone, weakened by his accident, went limp, Henry started to curl forward. Rather than walk, stretching his legs in front of him, he begin to shuffle his feet. A turkey wattle begin to hang down between his neck and his chin. At a Sunday dinner, he said, "I feel bad."

"You'll get to feeling better," Kyle said. And Victoria looked at him intently.

"It's not just I feel bad," he said to Kyle then turned to Victoria. "I am dying," he said to her. She lay down her fork and stared into her plate. Suzy, not yet even pregnant with Christen, calmly fed Bobby in his high chair.

"Come on, Henry," I said. "You're just scaring yourself and everybody else." Bobby spit out some peach-smelling baby food. Suzy scooped it with her spoon and pushed it back into his mouth.

"That's foolish talk, Daddy," Kyle said. "It's just a touch of flu or something."

Victoria looked at Henry and cocked one eye like she was a nurse. "What does it feel like?"

"I just feel it."

"What's it feel like?" I asked.

"Like I'm gonna die."

"Come on, Daddy," Kyle said. "Don't talk like that. You're just getting old. Hell, you're pushing seventy. What do you expect?"

"He's only sixty-three," Victoria said

Kyle and I went right on eating, never pausing. But

Victoria got up and went to the kitchen, and Henry's head swung around to watch her, then returned to his eating, but every once in awhile looking up from his food, he glanced at Kyle and me.

"This whole sickness stuff is in your head. Hell, we ought to send you to a psychiatrist." Kyle smiled at his wife and kids. Henry looked at Victoria, and she walked behind him and rubbed his shoulders.

We spent the night at Henry's, and I woke that night and felt the cold, empty side of bed that was Victoria's side. I got up and felt my way in the dark down the hall, across the dining room, and into the doorway of the kitchen. I saw Victoria outlined in silver by the moonlight shining in through the open kitchen doorway and staring at Henry's upper pasture. "Look at him," she said. "He knows. Something is wrong with him."

Doc Hillier called Breckenridge Hospital and scheduled some tests. After two days in the hospital, Henry had his results. Though he was retired, Doc Hillier held on to his office because he couldn't get a reasonable price for it in a dying town. He had the results from the hospital sent to his office.

Kyle, Victoria, Henry, and I went through Doc Hillier's unlocked door and saw him waiting for us. He shook my hand, then Kyle's, then patted Henry on the back. He sat behind the secretary's desk and brushed some of the dust off it with the palm of his hand. "This place is going to shit," he said.

The three of us sat on the couch in front of the desk and dust rose up between us and the man we kept so busy. Doc Hillier folded his hands together and put them on the desk. "I'm gonna tell you straight out, Henry, face to face, without sneaking around your back to relatives." Victoria raised her hands over her face. I put my arm around her, and he stopped to look at her.

Henry looked at her, then said, "You were saying."

Doc Hillier looked Henry in the eye and said, "You

got a cancer. It's prostate. They think it's spread around some. But they think in Austin you can get some chemotherapy and have a chance."

"No operation?" Henry said.

"They'll have to open you up and take a look. And then the drugs'll make you sick," Jack Hillier said.

Henry nodded his head. "That's just one opinion," Kyle said. Doc Hillier gave him a mean glance, telling him to shut up, so we didn't have to go further into this.

"I trust Jack," Henry said.

"But it's wise to get a second opinion," Kyle said.

"Save yourself the time and the money," Doc Hillier said.

"We got the money, Doc," Kyle said, patted Victoria's shoulder, and nodded to himself.

Doc Hillier looked at Henry with watery eyes but answered Kyle, "It's obvious, Kyle. Another doctor'll tell you the same."

"Thank you, Jack," Henry said, got up, and shook hands with Jack. Jack left without looking at us, opened the door to his examination room and office, went in, and closed the door behind him. I thought, at the time, it a dirty thing for Jack Hillier to leave his life-long friend alone with the news of his own death. But now, I think that those two old men, who grew up between world wars, who became mystified but amused at the way times had shaped them, were allowing each other a hard, cowboy dignity. Or they were just afraid of breaking down in front of each other.

* * *

Henry needed someone to drive him to the hospital for his chemotherapy, and he probably needed someone to watch out for him on his property. I didn't want to leave Howard, Jackson, and Schmidt and Uncle Walter Newberry. After suffering through a student's life for so many years, I finally had money enough to support myself and my wife without worrying about next month's rent. Victoria then suggested that she move in with Henry and that I stay in Austin with Schmidt and Howard. "You're going to have to decide between me and your father," I finally said to her. She just turned her back to me. She didn't have to tell me what her choice would be. The choice was mine.

I watched as Howard and Schmidt had my name taken off "our" door.

Victoria and I sold everything and moved to Henry's property. We could have moved into his house, but we wanted to give him and us some privacy. We got a loan, forcing us further into debt, and bought a used mobile home, parked it off of Henry's road, just off Ranch Road 12, at the base of his hill.

At first, rural poverty was romantic. I had gone back to nature, and once in awhile, I imagined myself a gentleman farmer. But then it became just poverty. I began to miss the world I had given up. I wanted to see movies, read books, have breakfast or lunch in out-of-the-way restaurants, go to the grocery store and not worry about what was on sale, see different faces around me, feel the rhythm of a city, think that I had done something useful, or just have something to do.

I rescued myself—for awhile—with politics. After seeing that most of the Chicanos in a three county region kept away from the polls and had no entry into county politics, I organized a local chapter of La Raza Unida. I drove around the county and shook the hands of people who were poorer than me and got them to the polls. I found a few people with the right attitudes and abilities to run for office, and the old white establishment lost a lot of their power. We won three county commissioner seats, and our state representative served two years. After three years, the Chicanos didn't need me any longer, and the old, white, red-neck Germans resented my interference.

Mostly, though, I waited for Henry to die. But he was tough. He took four years and a chunk of my life to die. Now, in my own way, spying on people, I hasten what is bound to happen. The people I hurt just can't see the hurt coming. So in a way, I am an agent of mercy. For most of us, it takes several years to see what I suspect only folks like Ol' Doc Hillier know. For all his honesty, he had the decency to keep his knowledge to himself.

* * *

Green Pastures is still the poshest eatery in Austin. Peacocks spread their tails and cry out, sounding like terrified or tortured infants. I push the old Stetson back on my head and absorb the shade as I walk under Green Pasture's tall oaks. My $80 NB's sink into the thick lawn. This is one of those side jobs that I mentioned to Buck. I must be getting good at this line of work. Several other lawyers have solicited my services. So now I have an assignment for Jim Sledge and his clients from Big Spring, Texas, a West Texas town with no springs. Jim Sledge hopes to run for state senator, so he wants me to watch the present state senator for Big Spring's district.

The restaurant itself is an old Edwardian mansion with a Texas style porch completely surrounding it. It is the type of high-ceilinged, spacious, shaded home that was built in Texas before air conditioning changed architecture and aesthetics. It too is now air-conditioned. Inside, during serving hours, young waiters don't hand out menus but write the day's servings in French on black slate boards, black not green like modern day "black" boards, with yellow and blue chalk. As they meticulously make the loops of their neat script, they pronounce the French dishes for you, so if you listen close, you can order without sounding like a Texan. It is all sort of intimidating. I've known the owner and the business manager since Victoria worked at The Green Pastures as a waitress. They've given me one free meal.

If they are around, I'll try to con them into another.

I go to the backdoor, as Dominique instructed, and knock. The beefy kitchen manager with the trim beard and coiffured hair opens the door and holds it open for me, "Can I help you?"

"Yes, I'm here to see Dominique," I say and take off my hat.

The manager steps back and says, "So you're the guy he mentioned." I shrug my shoulders. "Just as well you caught me; I'm the guy you really need to see. Why don't you come into the office."

"Well, it's sort of a private matter." I say.

"Hey, this is a classy joint. Lot of people wanting to work here. And cause you know Dominique . . ."

I interrupt, "No. You don't understand. I'm not here . . ."

The manager is just as determined to interrupt me. "You're gonna have to start out washing dishes. Your hair is a little long, but I don't think you'll need a net. Then we'll put you out on the floor. Course, you might need some better duds, but we've got an arrangement for that.

Why does every third person worry about the way I dress? Willie Nelson makes a fashion statement, and I'm labelled a bum. "No, I'm not here for a job." I try again. "Well, really I'm here to do my job."

The manager rubs his beard. "What is your job?"

"I'm an investigator," I say and step through the door.

The manager closes the door behind me and says, "A cop, huh?"

"A private investigator."

I continue to walk, and the manager sidesteps to keep up with me, "Like Spencer, Jim Rockford, Mannix, Magnum, right?"

"Just like them," I say.

"You don't look much like those guys."

"They don't look much like me." I enjoy our game,

but I'm in a hurry and want to get my business with Dominique over. "Where is Dominique?"

"Follow me, Marlow," the manager says, and I follow him into the dining area. It has clean walls with authentic-looking wallpaper and old portraits, lots of space and light, wooden tables with lace tablecloths, and gleaming silver forks, spoons, and knives.

Dominique sits at a table, his fingers curled, checking his nails. "Thank you," I say to the manager.

"You're welcome Kojak," he says, giggles, then adds, "No, he's a real cop."

"And I'm an unreal guy," I say.

I walk to Dominique's table, and he immediately hops up and gestures to a chair across the table from him. I pull the chair out from under the table and sit.

Dominique reaches across the table to shake my hand. I am careful not harm his manicure. Dominique, of course, is not his real name. He is a Chicano from Laredo, but after flunking out of UT, he purchased the clothes, the haircuts, and the cosmetics to pass himself off as European. From what I'd seen in the movies, I'd say he gives the place a hint of the Riviera. "Well, Mr. Jackson, so glad to meet you again."

"My pleasure," I say. This Laredo kid also worked on his pronunciation and his manners. He came to me because his landlord evicted him. I wrote a letter, which did him no good (he was guilty as hell of catching his landlord's sofa on fire—a dropped joint), but I got him an interview at Green Pastures because another "client" washed dishes. Dominique took to Green Pastures more than studying, so he became "Dominique" and worked his way up to Maitre'd. Reputedly, he took no notes, wrote nothing down, would remember every guest's name, their reservation time, and preferred table. He was a success story. He had put his intelligence to work for him and was doing something useful for his society.

Dominique puts his elbows on the table and leans

across it toward me. "Mr. Howard Bigelow was in here just last night."

"This is not top secret," I say to Dominique. "We can relax."

"Sure," Dominique says. "You want a Coke or something? I can even get you a beer."

"No thank you," I say. "Back to 'Senator' Bigelow."

"Wow, Jesus, the *vato* is a fucking senator?" the Laredo boy asks.

"A state senator, and some of his constituents back in West Texas want to know how he's spending their money and with whom. The legislature has been out of session for a month, and no one can account for Senator Bigelow."

"Yeah Rog, I see what you're getting at," Dominique says. "He was with a real fox. Thirty at the most. Jewelry. Boobs to here. My guess was first that she's some kind of society lady. But a waiter thinks maybe she's some kind of high class hooker. Good stuff, huh? Am I going to read about this in the papers?"

"How long was he here?"

"Three hours, man."

"Did he drink much?"

"A bottle of champagne an hour."

"How much was his bill?"

"Two hundred and nine dollars and seventy-six cents," Dominique says, proud of his memory.

I reach across the table and pat Dominique's shoulder. "Maybe you ought to go into partnership with me."

"Shit, Rog, you know what I make in tips?"

I reach into my pocket, pull out the crisp $50 bill that Jim Sledge gave me, and handed it to Dominique. "Tip for a tip," I say.

"Yeah, same as what Senator Bigelow tipped the waiter," he says.

I scoot my chair back and say, "If he makes another

reservation, why don't you give me a call and make me a reservation for the same time. Better yet, fifteen minutes later, but get me a table close by."

"You need a date too?" he asks.

"I'll try to get my own, but I may need the house coat and tie," I say. I stand, we shake hands, and Dominique shows me out the front door. I put on my hat and walk across the wooden porch.

"Nice hat," Dominique says.

"Thanks. It's old and authentic," I say over my shoulder as I go down the front steps.

I step into the cool shade of the oak trees. I turn to wave goodbye to Dominique. He returns my wave, smiles, then crosses his fingers. I stick my hands into the pockets of my Dickie khakis. I remember picking Victoria up after a hard night of waiting tables. We sat in the dark under the trees while she rubbed her bare feet in the soft grass. We kissed and fondled each other, and her manager yelled out at us to stop. "This is not goddamn lovers' lane," he said. Today though, is a good day for me. I've probably helped right a social wrong, have probably ruined another marriage (Mrs. Bigelow is one of the concerned constituents), and have probably gotten a free meal at Green Pastures (Jim Sledge, of course, will pick up my tab).

Chapter 8:
The Property

My feet slap the red-graveled, soggy running path and splatter pools of water. The drizzle hits me in the face and drips down from the visor of my cap to splash on the tip of my nose. My wet nylon shorts paste themselves to my bare legs, and my feet and socks are soggy. I like to jog in the summer drizzle. The rain and the exercise wakes you up.

As I jog, I recognize other joggers who run by me or, because of a stronger kick, pass me. When we meet, I raise my hand in a lazy wave, or nod my head. My soggy foot-falls join the chorus of running shoes hitting the pea gravel of the Austin Parks and Recreation Dept.'s jogging/hiking/biking trails.

We baby boomers, or yuppies, or whatever you might label us, aren't running away from anything or running toward something, we just run. If asked why we run, we would shrug our shoulders and say, "It helps me relax, clears my head, or feels good when I quit." In the summers, we swim laps in the clear water at Barton Springs or Deep Eddy Pool after we jog, except on rainy days. We spend our money in the theme bars and restaurants of Austin and rent or buy the over-priced condominiums. We have caused and will cause statistical swells in political, sociological, financial, and psychological charts all our lives. Because there are so many of us, we set the trends, get what we want, and determine marketing strategy. And because there are so many of us, we compete with each other for everything.

So we run and take pride in flattened bellies, tightened asses, and bulging calves.

My feet slap the running path, and an image from memory gets stuck in my head. In it, I sit on the curb in front of the deserted Alameda Saddle shop. It is night. The broken windows of the Alameda Saddle Shop make the building seem like it is yawning or screaming before it finally falls down. The image is a year old, but it comes into my head so often that it seems to have lost time.

* * *

That night, with nothing to do, wild, sex-charged teenagers cruised the main street, Wimberly Ave., in daddies' pickups, the richer ones in late model Camaros or Firebirds, and I sat at the deserted saddle shop and thought about where I could have been and what I could have been in Austin, Houston, or Dallas. A paper napkin from the Dairy Queen blew down the street and caught on my boot. Across the street, a stray dog pissed on the corner. Fast cars had made Austin and San Antonio, even New Braunfels or San Marcos or Kerrville, close enough for movies, dinner, drinking, or good times. Nothing was in Fischer except Marie's, a convenience store, and a Dairy Queen. The weekend tourists just drove by Fischer on their way to Canyon Lake. Maybe they commented about the beautiful view from Ranch Road 12. The cypress shaded the creeks; and cedar, pecan, and oak covered limestone hills made Ranch Road 12 appear as a scenic drive on Rand McNally road maps. I had bought a six pack from the only place open that time of night, the Sac & Pac convenience store, and drank most of the beer, while I waited for Dianne Natividad.

She pulled up to the curb in front of the Alameda in her '72 Chevy Impala with its rattling muffler. She leaned across the front seat and swung the passenger door open. I pushed the napkin off my boot, stood, looked down the street both ways, and got in the car with Dianne Natividad.

She took me to her place. We stripped and kissed and drank from the same bottle of beer. With Dianne Natividad's hot breath on my neck, I thought that maybe Victoria did love me, but I was not sure, so Dianne Natividad gave me what my wife wouldn't or couldn't.

I sweated into the mattress. Dianne Natividad's efficiency apartment was not air-conditioned. I could not see her, only her form, but I could feel the heat of her body next to me and smell her heavy perfume and the faint scent of the garlic laced fajita she must have had for dinner. I heard a loud *clack,* another *clack,* reminding me of the terrible booming tick of the clock in the living room of our mobile home. *Clack.* I squinted and focused until I saw Dianne Natividad sitting in bed and trimming her toenails. "You know, next week Eddie Sanchez is going to pick me up in his new convertible car, and we going to drive to his cousin's in San Antonio," she said.

"That's wonderful," I said.

"We going to put the top down and cruise West Commerce all the way to downtown. Go to a dance. Good times, man."

I rolled to my side and looked at a glint of light caught from somewhere and reflected by the nail clippers. *Clack.* The small reflection darted across the ceiling. *Clack.*

"You don't talk, Roger. Why don't you even talk? Eddie, he talks all the time. You ever seen Eddie? He's sharp, man. I mean he is a tough *vato.* But he is not like my boyfriend or nothing."

"Well, I'm glad he's so grand."

"*Grand,* huh, funny word, nobody says *grand.*" *Clack.* The reflection traced another fast path, like a shooting star, like a tracer, across the ceiling. "But you know, like I don't mean to put you down cause I talk about Eddie. You know. You just don't talk so much, so I got to."

"I like hearing about Eddie."

"He kind of likes you too." *Clack.*

"What do you tell him about me?" I rose on one elbow.

"Nothing." I lay back down. *Clack.* "Say man, you won't say nothing to Eddie, huh?"

"No, no. Let's keep this secret." I stared at the ceiling. *Clack.* It was Dianne Natividad's tenth toe. At least, I counted ten. I hoped she didn't do her fingers, so I could get some sleep.

I rolled away from her and heard splattering on her roof, rain. I knew that I would not get much sleep.

* * *

The next day, Saturday at noon, I kicked the toe of my boot against the bottom step of Marie's Drive Inn to knock chunks of drying mud off the sole and heel. I had just tromped across a field to show two deer hunters the land we leased each fall during deer season. I woke feeling sticky from the rain; I could smell Dianne Natividad. I had to peel the sheet off me and pull my back away from the mattress to get out of her bed. I kicked the other toe against the step and went into Marie's. Though Texas had passed liquor-by-the-drink, Marie's still sold only beer and set-ups. But Marie's customers were loyal.

Henry sat with Pete Proctor and Sam Penschorn at a card table and played dominoes. Doc Hillier wasn't in that day. Each old man stared intently at the dominoes in front of him. Henry looked up from his dominoes; since his treatment, he had lost weight and started to look old. The skin between his chin and throat quivered even more like a turkey's wattle when he moved his head. His worn, felt Stetson was pressed down on his head, which was bald from chemotherapy. His face looked jaundiced. He knew that I hadn't come home the night before.

I sat at a table in the corner next to the screened wall. Evelyn, Marie's spinster sister, brought me a beer. She didn't smile, didn't pat my back or kiss me on the cheek as she did to the old men and a few of her other regular customers. I took a long swig of beer, felt it cool my throat, and looked out the screen to the patio. The patio was the Mexicans' place. It had always been the Mexicans' place at Marie's. The old Germans no longer forced them to sit outside as they did years ago, but now the Mexicans preferred sitting outside; "heritage," they said. They drank beer, nibbled at jalepeño peppers, and ate Dairy Queen hamburgers. Evelyn even hugged some of them.

I turned around to see Henry stretch out his turkey wattle neck to see me. "Roger," he said, "Ol Doc Hillier didn't show up today. Why don't you come on take fourth seat so we can play partners." Pete shuffled the dominoes, and Sam, his fingers shaking, tried to pull a Pall Mall out of his pack of cigarettes. I held up my hands and shook my head. Henry turned back to the other two. "He don't want to play," Henry said. He looked at Sam, grabbed the pack away from him, pulled out a cigarette, and handed both the pack and cigarette back to Sam.

"Young hot shot too good for us or scared of us?" Sam said.

"Young men can't play dominoes, got other things on their minds," Pete said. "Minds are all crowded up thinking about sex. You are old, all you think about is dominoes." Henry looked at me. I turned away and glanced out at the Mexicans. Eddie Sanchez waved at me. I nodded my head, and he returned to his hamburger then laughed, a bulge of hamburger stuffed in his cheek. I turned back to the old domino players.

"Hell to be old," Sam said, and from deep in his lungs, coughed up some of the goo that had accumulated in his lungs from years of smoking.

Henry pounded the table with his thumb, the Nazi having shot off his trigger finger. "By damn when I was young my eyes were blue and my peter was red. Now my eyes are red and my poor ol' peter is blue."

"Goddamn, it's bad to be old, bad, bad," Pete said as he pulled his hands away from the thoroughly shuffled dominoes. "You heard about the one ol' whore who done so many old men she could play pool with a rope?" They didn't bother to laugh at this joke.

"Maybe we ought to ask one of the Mexican fellas to play," Henry said.

"Ain't seen a Mexican yet smart enough to play dominoes, don't think like a white man," Sam said.

"Hell, they're probably forming some activism, or rally, or co-op," Pete said. The comment was for my benefit. When I started the voting drives, Henry said to me, "Why the hell you want to be a radical Mexican, better practice some first as an ordinary Mexican."

"Stead of forming all kinds of co-ops, labor organizations, political coalitions, and all that kinda shit, Mexicans and all these other welfare people, ought just go out and work," Pete said loudly, coughed, then spat into a handkerchief.

"Hell, I had to enlist," Henry said, and I grimaced. "And get my finger shot off then work my ass off to get my property and horses." The old men picked dominoes out from the pile. Henry glanced at me then watched me as he placed his dominoes up in front of him. "One thing about Mexicans, though, " he said, "they're good to their dogs and families."

Henry was wrong. Now Victoria worked her ass off. She had become his nurse, secretary, cook, and field hand. She and I sold junk car parts, raised a few goats, chopped cedar, leased property to middle class bankers who wanted to shoot a deer, even occasionally sold a horse. At the time, I figured them to be ignorant, mean old men. At the time, I was glad that their times and what power they ever had were finished

Later that day, I turned my pickup into our road. Henry had made changes. I drove over the cattle guard that Henry bought so he wouldn't have to open a gate. A junked deteriorating '74 Comet marked Henry's property. Like a sentry, the old Comet guarded Henry's ninety-eight acres. The horse barn had only one decrepit occupant. Henry's house had a second mortgage. Henry still liked to sit on his veranda and look at the barn, the drive, our trailer, and a section of Ranch Road 12 curving out from between two hills.

As I pulled the pickup off the drive and in front of our trailer, I saw Victoria curled under the open hood and into the guts of the Comet. I stepped out of the truck and looked at her. She pulled her head out from under the hood of the Comet. Her sunburned face had deepening wrinkles, and her blonde hair looked like dirty barn straw. She pulled her forearm across her face and left a slash of grease mixed with sweat. She stared at me a moment, then ducked her head back under the hood of the Comet.

The mud was drying but was still wet enough to suck at the sole of my boot when I lifted my foot. I scraped my soles against the bottom step of the steps leading to my trailer door. I went inside through the screen door that bounced against the side of the trailer, then slammed shut. My home was like a boat—small, cramped, every space utilized. I sat on the sofa and listened to the wall clock tick miniature booms. Through the still vibrating screen door, I saw Victoria walking toward the trailer. She climbed the steps and came in and closed the screen door behind her. She stood with her weight on one hip, making her body angular; her jeans and work shirt with the tails tied in a knot just above her waist made her look slim and lithe. She rubbed at the black streak of grease across her face. Cleaned and made up for a dinner party, she would look far better than Dianne Natividad.

"Kyle, Suzy, and the kids are coming for dinner tonight. I'll start about four," she said. I slid the toe of my right boot under the heel of my left and pushed. The boot slipped off and fell to the floor, spreading a few small chunks of mud. Victoria watched.

"I'll clean it up," I said.

"No problem." She turned to go.

"Why don't you turn on the air?"

"The bills," she said.

"You can't live in goddamn trailer house without air." She shrugged her shoulders and started to leave. "Damn it," I said and stood up and took a step toward her, but I felt stupid hobbling around with one boot on and one off, so I sat back down on the sofa. She turned back to me. "Aren't you going to even ask?"

"Ask what?"

"Where I've been."

She swallowed hard, tried to go. I jumped up and hobbled to her in my one boot and grabbed her shoulders. I wanted to reach all the way around her, to hug her, maybe even kiss her, but I knew that she would just have been puzzled and would have turned right back damn around and left me for the Comet. "I don't want an argument," she said.

"Don't you think you have a right to know where I've been?"

"I don't want an argument."

"We never argue."

"I don't mind, Roger. I really don't. I understand."

"You mean you don't care."

She folded her arms across her chest, closed her eyes, then opened them. "All right, tell me where you were."

"Nowhere. I haven't been anywhere."

"God." She started to leave.

"We got to straighten us out," I said.

"I just don't have the time now."

"When?"

"Don't you know when? Can't you wait?" she said, her

back to me, and walked out the screen door. I watched the screen door bounce against the frame and looked at Victoria's back, the angular shape of her neck and shoulders. She was losing more than weight. I wanted her, but I wasn't sure if I was losing her or had already lost her.

* * *

At dinner, Kyle mentioned what he had come to talk about: money. But he was interrupted by his oldest child, Bobby, who was spitting creamed peas back on his plate.

"Kyle," his wife, Suzy, said and motioned toward Bobby.

"Bobby, don't spit your food out," Kyle said.

"I don't like it."

"He don't have to eat it," Henry said and smiled at his grandson. "I don't especially like peas either."

Victoria looked on, raising a fork to her mouth, occasionally smiling. "Someday ya'll are all going to have to come to our house for dinner," Kyle said, looking at Victoria. With a fork halfway to her mouth, Suzy looked up at Kyle, one corner of her mouth and an eyebrow raised.

After dinner, as Victoria, Suzy, and I cleared the dining room table (generally, Victoria, Henry, and I ate our meals together at the kitchen table), Henry went into the living room and sat on the sofa. Bobby jumped into Henry's lap, holding the 1895 model Colt revolver without a hammer that Henry gave him when they arrived. Henry groaned a bit as the child squirmed. Kyle followed Henry into the living room and sat on the sofa beside him. I stood over the kitchen sink with Victoria and Suzy to wash dishes. Then Henry yelled to me from in the living room. "Roger," he said, "Roger, let the women-folks clean up. Come in here and talk to me and Kyle for a minute or two."

"I'll help them," I said.

"No, now you come in here with the men," Henry said then patted Bobby on the head, "That's right, Bobby, us men got to talk."

"We can do it," Victoria said.

"Get out of our way," Suzy said with mock anger.

I walked into the living room and sat down in an easy chair across from Kyle and Henry. Kyle's current youngest child scooted by in a walker then stopped to stare at her brother in Henry's lap. Bobby turned the pistol in his hands.

I looked around the living room. I looked at the plastered cracks in the wall, caused by a shifting foundation. I inconspicuously sniffed. The house had that peculiar and pungent smell of old people, a mixture of stuffiness, infrequent bathing and medicine. It hung in the air, seeped through the plaster, and filled the cracks in the walls.

Henry looked at his grandson. He pulled on the barrel of the gun and said, "That belonged to Amos Fischer, the son of the man this town was named after. I bought it from Amos' son." Bobby, unimpressed, hopped out of Henry's lap and ran out the front screen door to shoot imaginary Indians or badmen. Henry reached toward the little girl in the walker. "Come here. Come on now. Let's let little Christen see *Opa*."

In his usual manner and with his usual talent, since moving to the Hill Country, Henry had adopted the prejudices, manner, and words of his German neighbors. He had learned so well that some of the old Germans even called him Heine. He lifted the child out of the walker, and she started to cry. Kyle scooted closer to Henry and said, "That's grandpa, Christen." Suzy appeared at the kitchen door, holding one hand under the other to catch dripping soap. She stretched her neck to see her child. I stood and stepped toward Henry. I put out my arms, and Henry, holding the child at full arm's length, handed her to me. I circled one arm under the little girl's butt and around her legs. I bounced her with my arm and patted her back with my other hand. She stopped crying but still frowned. I put her back into the walker, and she gurgled contentedly.

"Shoot," Henry said, "little kids, I mean the real little ones, before they can talk, never did like me."

"She knows who her Grandpa is," Kyle said.

"Yeah, but she don't like him. Victoria never would sit still for me to hold her. Always bawled for her mamma till she was walking and talking."

"She didn't know any better," Kyle said.

I got up, bored with the talk and started for the front door. "Now come on, you sit down, Roger. You're family too," Henry said. I stared at Henry, and he ducked his head. His bald head seemed to reflect some light at me.

"Come on, sit down," Kyle said. I sat. "I have this idea that I told Daddy about; he wants to see what you think." Henry looked up from the floor. His wattle shook. His eyes seemed watery, his stare softened.

"Kyle wants to change my property," Henry said.

I sat straight up in my chair. Then I placed my elbows on my knees and leaned toward Henry. Henry tried to mutter something but Kyle interrupted, "This acreage is worthless for raising or growing. Maybe you could get goats out of it, but you don't have enough of it. What it is good for is tourists. So we bulldoze a road from the main road here down to the river. We clear off the brush. Plant a lawn, just plain ol' Johnson grass would be fine. Then we build cabins with kitchenettes. We sell two of them and rent the others out. Hell, people in Houston willing to pay two hundred dollars a week for cabins like that. We could advertise in *Texas Monthly*: 'Hill Country acreage, pleasant surroundings, river front.' "

Henry looked at me, shifted his eyes away, then looked back at me. He looked old and desperate. "What you think, Roger? You lived here with me for a long time now. What you think?"

"Why don't you ask your daughter? Why don't you let her in here? She's the one who takes care of you and this place."

"I asked her," Henry said. He looked at me slyly. "This morning at breakfast." Then he smiled. "She says no."

"*No*," I said. "She says no because you say no."

"So I'm asking you," Henry said.

"Look," Kyle said, but neither Henry nor I looked at him; we remained staring at each other.

"No," Henry said and jammed his thumb into his knee; "Not going to have any goddamn tourists here. It's my property. Bought it so it would be mine. No goddamn tourists."

"Daddy, look, you don't even have to move. Stay right here. Watch after the place. Tell the people about your varied experiences," Kyle said.

"I ain't going to do that either. No, you tell him, Roger. You tell him what you think."

Henry had finally asked me for help. I had learned that Henry survived through the help of other people, even my father helped him. Then again, now, when I tilt my head just right, I see that Henry asked me for help all along, from the time we talked about Victoria's abortion, to the stories he told me, to the conversation about his escapades with poor Marilynn Katz. His subtlety was part of his talent for getting people to help him.

I stood, and again, I refused to help him. "To hell with developing it and turning it into Disneyland." Henry smiled. "Sell it," I said, and Henry's smile dropped. "Think about your daughter. Think about her, Henry." I looked up to see Victoria standing in the doorway. She dried her hands in a dish towel. She stepped into the dining room. She looked at me and shook her head. "She's in prison here. She lives to take care of you and this rotting place. You sell this place and you'll have enough to hire a nurse, or even to get into a nice nursing home. You do that and you set your daughter free." Kyle frowned, not knowing what I was talking about. Victoria closed her eyes, then backed toward the kitchen. "And you sell this place, and I can start a practice, support my wife and myself like I always wanted to, and maybe even think about children." I rested my hands on my hips.

Henry wiped his face with his open palm. Then he looked at me again, this time, a hard stare; his wattle did not quiver; his mouth was tightly clamped shut. He stood and said, "Thank you for your opinion." He walked down the hall toward his room.

As he left, Victoria came into the room and stared hard at both me and Kyle. "Damn, can't you wait?"

"I didn't start this," I answered.

"Oh, both of you. Don't you know better? Can't you see that he . . ."

"Okay," Kyle started to say, "It's over, dropped. I'm sorry."

"Kyle, it's just that he's irritable."

"He's always irritable," I said.

"Look, all I was doing was thinking of him and ya'll. Look, we won't discuss it with him. You and Victoria think about the deal . . ." Kyle was cut off as Henry came back into the living room.

He wore his weathered felt Stetson. He had his working pistol stuck in his belt. "I'm going for a ride," he said.

"In what?" Kyle asked.

"On my last horse," Henry said.

"No Daddy, don't," Kyle said.

I grabbed his arm as he passed by me and said, "Henry, you better not."

"Let go," he said. I let go.

He walked out of the front door, and Victoria, Kyle, and I followed him out. We stood on the veranda, watched as he walked to the barn, waited, and silently stared as though we could see him through the barn wall as he saddled his last, decrepit horse. He rode out.

Shoulders slumped, head bobbing with the horse's gait, Henry sat in the saddle, did not look at us as he rode toward us. "Daddy, please don't go," Victoria shouted.

"Just going for a ride," Henry said. The last, old horse had a slight limp; its eyes were sore.

"Daddy, don't!" Victoria shouted after him.

He paid no attention to her. He was a pathetic old man playing cowboy. He rode off the road and steered the horse between the clumps of cedar.

After Henry rode away, we sat on the veranda and watched the sun go down, hoping to see Henry ride back. He did not. Kyle and Victoria were scared, Victoria near panic. Suzy put the kids to sleep in one of the bedrooms. She stayed with them as much to watch them as to stay away from her in-laws. Victoria, Kyle, and I sat on the veranda, looked at the hills, trying to see a horse and a man in the twilight. "Why did the two of your bring up that whole can of worms?" Victoria asked. "Damn, I'll never understand."

"I was asked," I said.

"Like hell, you were just itching to—"

"It was my fault," Kyle said, trying to prevent the one argument Victoria and I did have.

"Why can't you two let him die in peace?" Victoria asked.

"Damn, Victoria," Kyle said, "Why do you have to be so morbid?"

"Because it's true. He knows it, and he expects us to."

"If you haven't noticed, he's been dying for years now," I said to Kyle.

Victoria looked at me, "And what good does his death do?" I didn't answer, but she knew what I would have said.

"God, would ya'll just shut up about dying."

"Face it, Kyle," Victoria said.

"You face it Victoria," I said. "What are you going to do when he's dead?"

"Look, goddamn it," Kyle said. "Forget this shit, we ought to do something."

* * *

Several hours into the night, Victoria drove Kyle's Buick Regal where it shouldn't go, and I drove the pickup, Kyle with me, going cross country, where the pickup shouldn't go, both of us hoping the pickup would not roll over or fall into a ravine. Kyle sat nervously beside me. I stopped the truck. "We're going on foot. We'll kill ourselves in this truck," I said. Kyle and I both got out and turned on our flashlights. Kyle walked over to me. I looked down at his Florsheim shoes, "You're gonna ruin those shoes," I said.

"That's okay," he said.

"It would serve him right if we just left him." The light of Kyle's flashlight blinded me. I felt its beam against my face.

"You'd like that wouldn't you? Just be rid of him."

"Yes, I would like that."

"How can you even say that?"

"Shut up, Kyle, and take that flashlight out of my face."

"No, No, you go back if you don't want to find him." He pointed the flashlight away from me.

"Jesus, Kyle, *you* clean his chemotherapy puke off the linoleum, *you* empty the bed pans! Try that instead of dreaming up real estate deals and having kids."

"Oh shut up, you're Rebecca all over again," Kyle said.

"You shouldn't talk nasty about your mother."

"I never claimed her. She deserted."

"She escaped, Kyle," I said. "She was the smart one."

"She was a bitch."

"You ought to thank her."

"To hell with you," Kyle said and walked into the woods.

I went into the woods and walked to the top of a small hill. I saw a tiny spark in a ravine and followed my flashlight beam; cedar limbs scraping my face; brush, cactus, and grass tugging at my legs; rocks rolling under my feet. I cussed him for making me scratch myself and risk snake bite and ankle sprains. I slid rather than walked into the ravine, and my flashlight revealed black shapes. The spark become a tiny camp fire, and Henry sat by it staring into the flames. He heard me, turned around, and squinted at the darkness. The surprised look on his face changed as I got closer. The muscles in his face sagged when he recognized me. He neither smiled nor frowned at me. His head dropped. He sat cross-legged, without his hat, his bald head reflecting some of the firelight. I pointed the beam into his face, and he showed his annoyance by blinking. I took the beam away and sat across from him. I turned off the flashlight and looked over the flames at him. I noticed that he held the pistol cradled in his lap.

"Where is your horse?" I said. He looked away from me and into his lap. "Your horse?"

"Threw me and ran off."

"Jesus, you okay?" I started to rise to help him up. He looked sternly at me, telling me to sit down.

"I can walk," he said.

I sat down, "Damn, you and that horse are both too old to be out riding . . . Jesus, let alone at night."

"Don't give me any shit. I've had enough shit," he said. The firelight enhanced the different shades and colors on his face and hands: browns, beiges, whites, yellows-the colors of sickness. He looked at the pistol in his lap. With one hand, he fondled it and turned it around in a circle in his lap.

"Come on, let's go back. You've given Victoria a heart attack." I stood.

He looked up at me, jaundiced, turkey wattle flapping, and I noticed, for the first time maybe, how really old and feeble he had grown. "I been trying to put a bullet in my head," he said.

"Goddamn it. Stop your jokes. You just upset people with that crap." I saw his disgust at me.

"I put my gun at my head, but I couldn't pull the trigger, no finger." He held up his hand to show me. "Then I turned the gun around, put the barrel in my mouth, and tried to squeeze the trigger with my thumbs. Again, I got no finger, and I can't exactly brace the gun, and my hands start to shaking, and I get scared that maybe I'll pull the trigger and because of my shaking hands I'll just cripple myself more."

"Come on, let's go. And don't say a thing about this to Victoria." His look told me to shut up.

"Next, I try with the gun in my left hand. And again I shake so bad I can't do it. Don't know whether it is real shaking or I am scared." He paused. I had nothing to say; I couldn't scold him; I couldn't be mad. He put his hands down by his sides, leaving the gun in his lap, and scooted closer to me, his butt scraping the ground. He picked up the pistol and held it toward me. "Here, you do it."

I jerked away from him. I stood and yelled, "Damn, damn, you are crazy."

"No, no. You shoot me; then just put the gun in my hand."

"I'm not going to listen to you."

"Nobody'll blame you. Won't even think you did it. You say you found me dead."

I surprised myself by saying, "What about fingerprints?"

"You could of handled the gun anytime. Sheriff here ain't going to raise no question. I thought it all out."

"Shut up. Shut up."

"No, I thought it all out. Kyle wouldn't. Victoria would but couldn't. You the only one could and would." He pushed himself up like a lazy, old dog; he stood and held the gun out to me. I turned my back to him. "It's the best way. This ain't no old man looking for sobs and tears. I'm just by-God better off dead now; ain't no use waiting." He paused. "I don't understand Kyle's talking about developing land and real estate tax and such stuff. And I never did figure that my property is standing in you and Victoria's way. And I think maybe I see I screwed up Victoria's life. You . . . you . . . know better. I see that now. I thank you for telling me. You've always been honest with me, Roger."

I turned around to face Henry and saw the pistol in his open hand. I grabbed the gun. Palmed the butt. Then I threw the pistol as far away as possible. It hit hard ground but didn't go off.

Henry squatted, the way only skinny old men can, and wrapped his arms around his knees. He dropped his head on to the top of his knees. Then he raised his head. "Let's get the hell out of here," I said through clenched teeth and noticed that I could taste tears.

"This property was supposed to be some of me after there was no more of me," Henry said. "That's why I got it, why I joined the army and lost my finger." Out of reflex he held his hand up. "And those horses were just so pretty against the green pasture. That's all . . . just didn't figure . . . a woman would have helped."

My hand shook as I reached out to grab his elbow. I grabbed the fleshy part of his arm just above his elbow and pulled him up. My hand squeezed through the limp flesh of the frail arm and tightened around the bone. "Let's go home," I said.

No longer talking to me or anyone who might have been in his mind, but mumbling about the nightmares that I helped give him, he said, "This Hill Country is the prettiest, best part of Texas, and I got some, you see. I got a view and a river, had a woman . . . just didn't figure."

I got scared and stopped to look at him. He focused on me, "Emma, Emma showed me this property. It was all Emma Shuler's doing. And Shorty Martins. It was Doc Hillier's, but now it's mine."

Chapter 9:
Letters

Kyle didn't have to wait for Henry to die before he started molding Henry's property into Bolen Resorts. First, he came out with a building contractor who looked over the land. I watched from the kitchen window as the contractor, sweating through his seersucker suit, pointed at stumps, trees, and rocks. Kyle stood beside him, looked where the man pointed, and grinned at the images the two of them conjured up. Within a week, a huge truck pulling a trailer with a bulldozer on it inched up our inclined road. A big bald-headed man stepped out of the truck, walked to our front door, and talked to Victoria to make sure that he was about to tear into Henry's land in the right place. In a six-hour day, he plowed through limestone and cedar to make a road to the creek. He left pried-up roots that looked like veiny fingers and dark, damp undersides of rocks reaching toward sky rather than into dirt. But he wasn't finished. Almost everyday, we heard the gurgling sound of his bulldozer and the ripping of the trees and rocks it tore out of Henry's property.

Victoria got the Comet started. Then, like her brother, not waiting for Henry to die, Victoria started moving into his house. She and I spent several days carrying, sometimes dragging, furniture and most of our clothes from the trailer to the house. She slept in her old room with its purple daisy wallpaper. And I slept in Kyle's room with its torn Lone Ranger wallpaper. I didn't sleep too much, just stared at the wallpaper. Sometimes, I pulled out my bag of marijuana and smoked a joint to give myself a tiny thrill at the thought of smoking an illegal drug in Kyle's room. I also liked to imagine Henry in a 1950's Montgomery Wards or Sears buying cute, thematic wallpaper for his children. The dope helped me imagine.

When the last old horse died, I dragged its body behind my pickup to a gravesite, and the bald-headed man bulldozing the road to the creek scooped out a grave, pushed the horse's body into the hole, then covered it up. The horse's death gave Kyle another idea. He put ads in the *Austin American* and *The San Antonio Express* offering the stables and horse care to the city people rich enough to afford a horse. Victoria and I, of course, would be his horse attendants. I could see that, with Kyle now directing our finances, we would make money.

Henry consented to everything. He went in and out of Brackenridge hospital but spent most of his dying time in his room. I don't know what Henry did or thought, trapped in his room, but after a few tokes, I'd imagine him looking out his window at the bald man tearing a road to the creek and at the horse's burial. He must have listened to the scraping sound of Victoria pulling his furniture around his house, and the choking and sputtering of her tinkering with the old Comet. At night, if he was awake from his pain and not delirious, he might have heard me pull up in my pickup, coming back from drinking beer in front of the Alemeda Saddle shop or from my meetings Dianne Natividad. He said nothing more than what he needed to, while his cancer and his own thoughts chewed up his guts.

On one of the Saturday evenings when I had decided to stay home, the sun just going down, I walked past Henry's door, and he yelled in a gargling fashion for me to come in. I walked in and smelled the sickness. Victoria didn't have the time or the chemicals to clean like a hospital did. "Would you mind, sitting down?" he asked. I sat in the chair Victoria had positioned at the foot of his bed, so he could lift his head up or stick a pillow under it and see whom he was talking to.

"What's on your mind, Henry?" I asked.

"I'd like a beer," he said.

"Doc Hillier says a beer would just make you sick."

"I didn't say 'Get me one.' I just said I'd *like* to have one."

"Something else I could get you?"

Henry looked out his window and squinted at the dusk. I looked out the window after him and saw the lightning bugs flashing in the haze of a cooling summer day. Henry looked around at me then shifted his eyes toward his old hat hanging on his foot-end bedpost. I looked at his hat too. "Try it on," he said.

I stood, picked the hat off the bedpost, twirled it around in my hands, and put it on my head. It slipped a little too far down on my head and smelled of sweat, which now smelled healthy. Henry giggled, then coughed, then giggled again. "It looks silly on a hippie boy like you."

"Yeah," I said, took the hat off, sat down, and lay the hat in my lap, crown down. I looked down into the hat and could see a tiny tatter at the point of the crown. "I never liked hats," I said.

Henry reached for the small, dangling chain of a night lamp, pulled it, and I could see his yellow face. "Why don't you keep that one?" I picked up the hat in my right hand put it on my head again. "A hat store will give you some foam to stuff under the sweat band to make it fit better. Consider it the thing I will you." I took the hat off and put it in my lap.

"Henry, I better get going. I want to get into town." Henry paid no attention to me but stared up at the ceiling. "My mother was a Christian woman, but I never trusted a word of it cause it turned my mother Jesus crazy."

I leaned back in my chair. "I know, Henry. You've

told me."

"Yeah," Henry said, squinted at me, then looked back up at the ceiling. "Well, I want to tell it again."

"Okay, Henry."

"You know who was responsible for me buying this place?"

"Who?" I asked.

"You ever heard me mention Shorty Martins?"

"No," I said.

"He was a drunken, worthless cowboy. Was uglier than a shaved ass dog and not but about five feet tall. Had to get a special made boys' saddle to fit his ass on a horse. But, on a horse, he was a pretty man. He could put the reins in his mouth and fire a pistol from each hand, the way the old Texas Rangers chased Mexicans." Henry stopped his speech and looked at me to see what kind of audience he had. I twirled his hat, crown down, around on my lap. "Cause of him, I just thought horses were the prettiest things to have. So I started a horse farm."

"Do Victoria and Kyle know about Shorty Martins?" I asked.

"No," Henry said. "Never told them. So now I'm telling you."

"Why you telling me?"

Henry squinted through the sickness, through the faded, cloudy, cataract looking film that covered his eyes. "When I was seventeen, and not yet out of school, I tried to stick this finger . . ." Henry held up his trigger finger, laughed, then coughed. "I tried to stick what there then was of this finger down the front of Melinda Sue Wengler's panties. The woman whose panties I did get into was a Mexican." He squinted at me. I stopped twirling his hat in my lap and scooted to edge of my chair. "Mexicans are really okay, but they're fun to cuss. She was a whore too. Ran with her to Arizona."

Henry smiled again, coughed. "The darker the meat

the better it is. Ain't that right?" I squirmed in my chair and wanted to cuss him for teasing me about Dianne Natividad, but Henry went on. "You can't really love 'em. But they are good ol' pieces of ass." He smiled and squinted. "Sometimes a man just can't resist 'em, especially given the right situation." I dropped my eyes to stare into his hat. I couldn't look at him because he had just forgiven me for cheating on his daughter.

"The next woman I had was sweet Rebecca, your wife's mother. And it was real love with Rebecca," he said. He waited for me to reply, maybe to ask him to go on. He looked at me and smiled. "You care at all about this?"

"Go on, Henry," I answered and looked down into his hat.

Henry dropped his chin to his chest, then pulled it back up. "Go to the closet," he told me. "I got a lot to tell."

I stood up, put his hat on the chair, and opened his closet door. A mixed smell of mildew, old age, and sickness rolled out from Henry's clothes, and I took a step back. "What do you want, Henry?"

"Look up above you, up on the shelf."

"Yeah?"

"Kinda push your hand through the old rags and papers up there and feel around for a shoe box."

I stuck my hand into Henry's rags and felt for the shoe box. I expected a mouse trap to snap shut across my fingers as sort of a last joke on me, but I felt the cardboard edge of a shoe box and pulled it out. As I carried the shoe box across the floor to Henry's bed, the door to his room slowly opened, and Victoria stuck her head into the room. She looked at Henry, then at me. I shrugged my shoulders. "Everything all right?"

"Yeah," Henry said.

"Sure, Daddy?"

"Yes, goddamn it," Henry said.

Victoria looked at me, "Roger?"

"I guess so," I said.

Victoria looked back at Henry, then again at me. She had gotten used to my Saturday nights out. She had gotten used to waiting. She had gotten used to a quick chat with the old man before she went to sleep. She had gotten used to waking suddenly, late at night, when Henry screamed from pain or memory. She stepped out of the doorway and slowly closed the door, leaving the room in the faint light of Henry's overhead reading lamp.

"Give me the box," Henry said. I handed him the Thom McAnn shoe box. He opened it. It was full of yellowed envelopes. He sorted through the envelopes, pulled out crumbling stationery or legal paper from one then another of the envelopes, shook his head, and stuffed the letters back into the envelopes, and put the letters back before he looked for others. He culled out one letter, then another, then a third. He squinted to see through the film over his eyes and arranged the letters into a sequence. He jerked his arm stiff and poked the letters at me. I got up to take them. "Read them in the order you got them," he said to me.

The first had a return address, 223 Maestas, Taos, New Mexico. The rest didn't. I pulled the first letter out of the envelope, felt the flimsy paper, saw the faded black ink, and squinted to see the time-dimmed writing. I looked at the end of the two-page letter for a signature. Written in a large, cute scrawl, the kind young girls use, the high school cheerleader type of cursive with open circles or little hearts to dot the *i*'s, was the signature, *Rebecca*. "Jesus, Henry, is this a love letter?"

"Read it."

"Why?"

"Read it."

Dear Henry:
I am writing now to tell you where I am. What money

I had got me from Big Spring to Santa Fe, from there I hitch-hiked to Taos, New Mexico. I am not sure why I came here except that I thought I would like it. I have met a very good man here named Clayton Tanner who has taken care of me. I asked him for directions at the bus stop, and he gave me a complete tour of the area. I was trying for Los Angeles, movies you know, but the money wouldn't stretch. I have not yet found enough guts to write my father. Please tell him that I am okay, and explain, and make your own understanding with him as I will try to make mine with you. Please.

I looked up at Henry, who had his eyes closed. "What date is this?"

Henry opened his eyes, "I'm not sure. Dates kind of run together. 1954, no 1955."

"You don't remember the year she left?"

"The exact year ain't important." He looked at me then added, "1955." I continued to read.

I will honor my agreement as to what we spoke of in my phone call. I fully expected that I gave up my children to you when I left. They are yours to raise. I will not interfere with them or you. I will be gone from now on. I will not write to them. But Henry can I write to you? No, I will write to you. And please find enough forgiveness for me to tell my children about me, about what I am doing. Please Henry, tell Kyle and dear little Victoria about me.

Love, even though I am not living with you,
Rebecca

I folded the letter and stuffed it into the envelope. "Henry, has Victoria seen this?"

"Neither one of my children has seen it."

"How could you hide these from them? She says

right here . . ."

He raised up on an elbow. He locked his head into a position so that his stare was on an even level with mine. "You read it. You know what she did."

"The woman deserves better."

Henry coughed, gargled something in his throat, then lay his head down on his pillow and looked up at the ceiling. His words floated out of his mouth and up toward the ceiling, and I could barely hear them. "You hide one letter cause you are mad. And you hide the rest for several years. Then when you say enough is enough, it is too late, and your kids will be upset at you and their mother."

"You fucked up, Henry."

"Read the next letter." It was typed. The faded purple postmark was 1971.

Dearest Henry:

Once again, please tell the kids of me, better yet show them this letter. Their mom has just received a Ph.D. in cinema studies. Henry, you no doubt are disgusted because I have been going to school all this time to study movies. I remember still that you didn't especially like movies. I have seen hundreds since I left you. My dissertation is on a grand man of the movies whom you'd probably like if you were to meet him. He sends his regards because I did meet him! He is Samuel Fuller. You have probably seen some of his westerns or war movies on T.V.

I've told my mother and father about my degree, and from somewhere, my mother got enough money together to fly her and my sister out for my graduation. My father said that it is a waste of time. Henry, I am surprised that you don't keep up with him.

This has been a very long ten years, and as you guess, I have changed. You will be disgusted to know that I have no job to show for the years. Indeed, I did not even look for a job. Right now, I'm not concerned. Before you scold me, though, remember your own long years of work and search that came to nothing and your own relatively late settling down on your beautiful property. It is too bad that you couldn't, nor could I, see what a terrible choice I was. I've learned a lot about irony, Henry.

My most immediate plans are to return to Clayton Tanner. I promised to try his life and place again. He is a kind man, peaceful and content, and happy where he is. My God, Henry, he sounds like you. Are you still peaceful and content?

I also want to go back to Taos. You would love his place. Did you ever see Taos? Maybe if you had, you would have your property there instead of in Texas. It is almost as good as California. In his back yard, he has pinon and juniper trees. From his bedroom window, you can see a great green and blue mountain; from his front window, you can for miles to the Rio Grande Gorge. The mountains are full of streams. If you ever want to come out, with the kids, just write.

Give my love to the children. Kyle must be about finished with high school now. And I can imagine how pretty Victoria is getting. Do you have any photos?

Love,
Becky.

I didn't stop to talk to Henry after this one but opened the next.

Dear Henry:
I am leaving Clayton and his beautiful Taos. He won't or can't leave. I can be happy in other places, and want to see other places, but he is happy only

in Taos. I pity poor Tanner. You, I know, think that I should stay; maybe you are snickering because you think that I am being served justice. But I have to leave to find out what I can do. To me the most terrible feeling now seems to be constantly wondering "what if."

I am tired of baking bread, of waiting tables, of being someone's girlfriend, or whatever it is they refer to me as here in Taos. I want to use what I have learned. I want to use my degree. You can understand this can't you Henry? If anyone, you have used your talents. Haven't you Henry? At any rate, I can't stay here, and Tanner can't go with me to my two year teaching appointment.

Oh, Henry, how I wish I could talk to you. How I wish I could talk to Kyle and Vickie. Is she Vickie yet, or still Victoria? She will probably want to be called Vickie.

I know things will get better for me, though now I am pretty black. I again wish you well and love.

Becky

I carefully folded this letter and put it back into the envelope.

"You gonna let me read any others?"

"No." Henry had his arms wrapped around the shoe box and squshed it against his chest. I got up, walked around to the side of the bed, and lay the letters on top of Henry's folded arms. The letters sat for a while on top of Henry's crossed wrists while he stared through his dim eyes at some thought or memory. Then he remembered me and smiled. He touched the letters with the tips of his fingers, as though he were trying to pluck a spider web intact from between two tree limbs. He put the letters back in the crumpled box, and sealed the box like the time capsule it was. He covered the box with its lid that said Thom McAnn, then wrapped the ancient rubber band around the box.

"Why me? Why did you show me and not Victoria or Kyle?"

Henry shook his head. "Kyle hates her too much. It's broke between him and her. As for Victoria, a man can't tell his daughter about what he'd done before he married her mother."

"You should tell them."

"But I'm telling you," he said and looked hard at me. "Dying is easier than living. When you have only one thing for sure to do, there is no way to screw up. You can't fuck up dying. It's life you fuck up. I don't got time straight, but I got these memories straight, and I got these letters." He hugged his shoe box. "I showed you because I want you to find Rebecca."

"My God, Henry. Phone her."

"I got no phone number."

"Every city has directory assistance."

"I don't even know what city she is in."

I leaned forward in my chair. "What?"

Henry curled himself forward. "All her letters come through Taos or Oklahoma City, but neither place has a telephone number for her." He curled more toward me and poked an ancient, yellow envelope at me. "Find her," he said. I took the envelope, and he lay back down, grunting as he slowly uncurled his back into a prone position. The envelope had only a Taos P.O. box for a return address. "How could I even start?"

"Find Clayton Tanner."

"How?"

"He's got no phone. I tried to call him myself." Henry pushed himself up a little to look at me hard. "Then I got even sicker. Now I want you to go to Taos and look for him and see if he can help you find Rebecca."

"How do you even know he's still there? What if he is and won't talk? What if he tells me, and Rebecca won't see me?"

Before I could go on, Henry interrupted me: "I'm dying."

He rose up on his weak elbow to stare through the cloudy film in his eyes and judge me as a hard-hearted bastard. "You've always been honest with me, Roger. Who else could do this?"

"Okay, Henry. I'll go if Victoria can manage without me."

Henry looked at me again and smiled; then his smile fell into a frown; and he said with no meanness, "The sad truth, Roger, the truth you got to realize, is she could always manage without you."

* * *

I stayed in Henry's room for as long as he could stay awake, and he told me about Shorty Martins and told me again about Melinda Sue Wengler and his Mamma and Daddy. He told me about Kyle and Victoria when they were young. And late in the night as Henry started falling to sleep, I got up to leave, but he shouted from behind me. "You gonna take the hat?"

With his letter in one hand, I picked the old man's hat up off the chair with the other and left him to his sporadic, tortured snoring. I walked through the dark house and to my own room with the Lone Ranger wallpaper. I stripped to my shorts and lay in my bed and stared at the dim outlines of the Lone Ranger and Tonto and thought about Rebecca. Rebecca led me to think of Victoria. I got out of bed and walked down the dark hall towards my wife's bedroom. Just in my shorts, I felt a slight chill even in the hot Texas night. When I got to Victoria's door, I started to knock, but felt insulted knocking on my own wife's door.

She slept with her head turned to one side, her hair pushed away from her face and behind her head. A faint light coming through the window caught her cheekbones and made them silver. I tip-toed to the side of her bed, thought about shaking her to wake her, but instead kissed her silver cheek. I crawled into bed with her and kissed her on her forehead and again on her cheek to wake her up. She woke startled, gasped just a bit, then relaxed when she recognized me. I rubbed her at her forearm without really touching it, just feeling the fine, short hair on her arm. And after I kissed her long and hard on the mouth and pushed my arm under her then around her shoulders, she asked about what Henry had talked about for so long. I boiled it down.

"Do you think you could find her?" Victoria asked.

"I could try."

"Where would you start?"

"Taos. Henry wants me to go to Taos, try to find Clayton Tanner."

"Would he still be there?"

I turned to look at her. She stared up toward the ceiling, squinting as though seeing something. "Let's go. You and me. Let's go to Taos," I said.

For moment she thought about the idea, and I believe she almost gave herself over to a hellacious, wild fling at dreams and romance, but she came back to sorrow. "You know I can't leave now."

I rolled toward her, stroked her cheek with my finger, and felt the same downy hair that was on her arm. She scooted away from me then rolled to her side to face away from me. "Go, see if you can find her," I heard her say. She rolled around to face me. "Take the truck. I've got the Comet running now."

I kissed her again on the lips, then on the forehead. She gave me a polite kiss but didn't roll away from me. I took a chance and kissed her again. She kissed back and pulled my face down the side of hers, down her neck, and into her shoulder. I lay against her shoulder, and she placed her hand on my face. I resisted sleep to smell her, to feel her at every point where my body touched hers, to try to see her. And after long minutes, we clumsily, like when college kids trying to discover each other, made love. Then, with my arm under her neck, her head resting in the soft part of my shoulder, we stared at the ceiling. For that moment, we were content because we saw a solution. That night, I was kept awake by the excitement that possibility and hope give you.

When Victoria fell asleep, I got up from her bed and walked back to my bedroom, sat on my bed, and smoked a joint. I saw Henry's hat and tried it on. I packed it, some of my clothes, and Henry's ancient letter for the trip to Taos.

Chapter 10:
Taos

On the trip to Taos, my truck choked and spit out black smoke and had trouble ever reaching 55 miles an hour, so I stayed in the right lane and watched diesels and the long, wide cars that West Texans like to drive–Cadillacs, Oldsmobiles, Lincolns, Buicks–whiz by me. Around Seminole, with an air-conditioner that finally gave out, I noticed what else Texas is mostly about: heat and space. I tied a wet handkerchief around my head and squashed Henry's hat over it and choked on the dust that swirled in between the two open windows of my pick up until I got to higher, cooler Roswell, New Mexico. I stayed for the night on a KOA camp bench and wondered if Clayton Tanner might be a ghost or a lie.

I drove the lonely stretch of prairie between Roswell and Santa Fe, then took the high road from Santa Fe to Taos, my truck barely making it up the steeper climbs. I took the wet handkerchief out of Henry's hat and rolled down the windows of the truck to let in the mountain air. I passed villages that looked more like they should be in the Pyrenees than in the Sangre de Cristos. And when I passed the trailer parks and plyboard buildings of Talpa and Ranchos de Taos and into the adobe architecture of Taos, I knew I was no longer in Texas.

I found the cheapest motel that I could, The Sun God Inn, and checked in. I asked a gas station attendant about Tanner's address, 223 Maestas. And he gave me directions to the street.

Maestas was a gravel road that curled around the

base of a mountain, which looked to be the city limits of Taos. Tanner's old house, 223, was a fifties style, split level adobe house that must have at once been a comfortable place to live. Now, the adobe was chipped from not being stuccoed enough. There were spaces between the mud or mortar that held the adobe bricks together; the top level seemed to lean toward the front of the house. As I stepped out of my truck, I felt a chill.

I pulled Henry's hat lower on to my head and pushed back my shoulders and walked through some mud toward the house. A border collie ran from around the back of the house and barked. He stopped in front of me and bared his teeth.

A shirtless, tall, slender man with a shaved head and a gold earring slumped in the door frame. He cocked his head and looked at me a few moments before he said, "Hi."

"Hi," I said and stood looking at the growling border collie.

"Bo, down," he said, then smiled, as if he could talk to animals. The dog slowly backed away then ran behind the house. I took off Henry's hat and walked toward the man. He stepped out from the doorway into the morning chill without his shirt, barefooted, wearing some black nylon pants, and gave an amused stare at my sweatshirt and windbreaker. "Yeah?" he said.

I stuck out my hand as normal people from a civilized state do, and he looked down at it before shaking it. "My name is Roger Jackson, and I'm here looking for a man named Clayton Tanner. He was or is a psychologist, and . . ."

The man smiled, grunted, and said "Huh." He shook my hand again. "He's not here." Then he jerked his head toward his house. I stepped closer toward the doorway. "Go ahead, go in," he said. I stepped through the door, and he followed me in. I wondered if he was an ax murderer or a lunatic or if all people in Taos communicated only in half intelligible syllables. "Kinda cool isn't it," he said and looked at me.

I smiled, "I just got in from Texas."

"Hey, no problem, man."

As I stepped into the living room, I could see across it to the dining room, where a small, slightly plump woman with dirty blonde hair was sipping from a cup of coffee. Then I shifted my gaze to a plate glass door, dirty from Bo's paw prints. As I nodded my head at the woman, Bo ran to the plate glass door, barked, jumped straight up, landed on his back legs, then leaned forward–his front paws out in front of him–caught himself on the plate glass door, and pressed his nose. "Bo," the shaved-head man said. Bo dropped. The man motioned to the woman and smiled, "My old lady, Cindy," he said. Cindy looked up at me with an attractive face that looked to have a more normal and articulate ability to communicate behind it.

I tipped my head, then took off Henry's hat to look, I'm sure, like a bumptious Texan. "Cindy," I said, then thought the mountain air had destroyed my ability to make whole sentences.

"Want a cup of coffee?" Cindy said.

"No thanks," I said.

The bald man walked past me toward the chair and set a coffee cup beside Cindy. He sat down beside the coffee cup and curled his lean body over it. "Have a seat," he said.

"Uh," I said, thinking I was becoming one of them.

"Suit yourself, you know. But why don't you sit down?" I stayed standing.

"So did Tanner send you down to talk philosophy or show business, stay the night, get a meal?" Cindy asked.

"No," I said. "I'm looking for him."

"You hear about him?" Cindy asked

"No not really," I said.

"So?" Cindy said.

"I'm looking for him. Could you tell me where I could find him?"

"Why don't you sit down, man," the man said.

"Sit," Cindy said. Despite the intelligence and sweetness in her face, she was the tough one.

The man raised his bald head from his coffee and said, "Maybe it's not our business, you know. Maybe the man doesn't want to tell us. Okay," he said to Cindy.

"No. No. I'm a friend of a former friend. I'm looking for her, and she used to know Mr. Tanner. It's complex."

"Oh wow," the man said, "Not Becky, huh?"

"Sit," Cindy said. I then sat beside the man. Cindy smiled with intelligence and articulateness again flickering in her eyes and wrinkling her smile lines.

"I'm a theatrical manager and director, and Cindy is an actress, but right now we're doing carpentry," the man with the shaved head said and shrugged his shoulders. Cindy raised her eyes.

"Odds are we stay carpenters," Cindy said and sipped some coffee.

"Faith, man," the bald headed man said to her then looked back at me. "Tanner rents us this place when we can pay. He used to live here." The bald headed man looked slyly at me. "With Becky," he said and smiled. Then, as brain cells choked him with a thought, he turned back to his old lady. "And you don't go into art to make money. It's glory, man."

Then Cindy swiveled around in her chair, got up, and went to the kitchen for another cup of coffee. "Do you know Tanner very well?" I asked, and the man turned back toward me, and Bo, smearing mud, scratched at the door.

"Oh, yeah, real well," the man said.

"Too well," Cindy said from the kitchen.

The bald man looked toward the kitchen to non-verbally scold her with Taos osmosis communication, then said to me, "He comes over here, shoots the shit, you know. Brings friends sometimes, sends friends sometimes. You know it's just all real cool."

"He's weird, though. He takes this Taos shit too serious," Cindy said as she came out of the kitchen, again smiling and showing some intelligence but stoop shouldered from aging faster than her man and growing just a bit fed up with Taos ambiance.

"No shit," I couldn't help but say.

"No shit," she said mildly and kept on smiling at me.

"Where's he live now?" I asked.

Cindy shrugged her shoulders as she sat down with her cup of coffee, and she seemed to straightened her back out of its forward curl. "Huh, I don't know," the bald headed man said. "I know where you can find him though."

"Where?"

"Oh, you just go down to the plaza. Go down there and wait."

"How will I know him?"

"You'll know him."

"How?" I was fed up with Martian communication.

"You sure you don't want a cup of coffee? It's chocolate almond mixed with a little espresso," Cindy said. She got up from the table, went into the kitchen, and came back with a full cup of coffee, smiling again as though pleading for a conversation.

"Maybe I'll have a cup." I thought I'd give in. And surprisingly, after awhile, with the strong coffee and the warm sunbeams that shone through the plate glass door, talking with these left-over hippies became pleasant.

"So where you from?" the man finally asked me.

"Texas, the Hill Country, Austin," I said, trying to identify more to these people than just Texas.

"Hey, that was our second choice to moving here," Cindy said to me and smiled; then leaning on her elbows, looking over the top of her coffee cup that she held level to her nose with both hands, she stared for a quick moment at her old man before her smile and her eyes darted back to me. Marital bliss, I thought.

* * *

At sunset, I bought a six pack and walked around the Taos plaza. With the sun setting, with the altitude, with memories of the humid nights and gulf breezes of central Texas, I shivered in the plaza, drank my beer, and looked at the tourists gathered on the balconies of Oglevie's restaurant and the La Fonda hotel. The local teenagers gathered at the plaza. They set down their boom boxes and began dancing in the centuries old plaza.

An Indian with grey streaks in his braids sat on the opposite bench from me. He glanced at me, turned away, then looked again, "Mooch one of your beers?" I gave him one of my beers.

"Chase your beer?"

"No."

"White people never want to drink with me and every goddamn Indian I know does." He took another sip of the whiskey, then put the bottle back in his pocket. "Where you from?"

"Texas."

"Bullshit place. I lived here most all my life, except for when I grew up in Oklahoma. Been coming to this square for years. I'm Billy." We shook hands.

"Roger Jackson," I said.

"You want to sell me your hat?"

I took Henry's hat off my head and turned it around in my hands. "This hat is nearly forty years old."

"Give you five dollars," he said. I looked back down at Henry's hat and suddenly grew jealous of the sweat stains and the tatters on the points of the crown. "No, I'll keep it.

"Listen, I'm looking for this guy."

"I ain't into that myself, but I know this Mexican."

"No, No. I'm looking for a friend of a friend."

"You married?" Billy asked.

"Yes, but do you know a guy who—"

"She a white woman?"

"Yes."

"I had two wives, neither was white. But one stabbed me in the shoulder when I was asleep. She severed some ligament or such shit, and I had to quit the construction business."

"What'd you do?"

"Stopped fucking all the other women. I really loved her." Billy pushed his rolled-up sleeve over his forearm and showed me the inside of his arm. "Look at this shit." A long scar trailed his vein. "Did that myself when the other wife left. Hurts like hell."

"Why?"

"Scar, man. When the scar heals, you're healed." He shrugged. "But that's mostly Indian bullshit. Now, I go to this counselor."

I looked over at him. "What kind of counselor?"

"A little old white guy. Been here for years. Long as me. Had this hot-looking white woman leave him and just kinda gave up on it, if you know what I mean. He talks to me for free 'cause he likes Indians. You stick around, you'll see him walking this black lab he keeps."

"Is his name Clayton Tanner?"

"Yeah, sure, look for a man with a black dog. A little white guy. He used to be bigger." He held his hand just under my height.

"How do I see him?"

"He's mostly around in the mornings. Just wait on the square. He can fix you, man."

Billy pulled his bottle out of his pocket and took a sip, then leaned forward to cough, forcing his braids to dangle over his shoulders, one with a knife wound. He chugged my beer to put out the fire from his whiskey, then pointed his bottle toward me. "Exchange a snort for another beer." He straightened and swooshed his braids back over his shoulders with the backs of his hands.

It was a mistake, but I pulled another can loose from the plastic. He grabbed the can and shoved the bottle up under my nose. There was no label on it. I held up the bottle to look at the liquor and swirled it around. "It's gin," Billy said. I rubbed the lip with the palm of my hand and raised the neck of the bottle to my lips. Something slick was on the lip of the bottle. I threw my head back and let a big gulp of what Billy said was gin burn its way to my belly.

"Thanks," I said. "Doesn't taste like any gin I ever had. Gin always had this carrot juice taste to me."

"That's cause this is good gin," Billy said. "No carrot juice in this shit."

We both hugged ourselves. "Guess you're cold cause you're Texan. Me, I guess I'm cold cause I'm Kiowa, that's a southern tribe. Kiowas are always in the movies attacking something and killing white people."

"When should I show up to find Tanner?"

"Hey, I know what you're after. Nothing but this local trash hangs out at La Fonda or La Kocina, and somebody ends up cutting somebody. You need a classy joint where white tourists go. You feeling lucky?"

"No."

"The Sagebrush Inn, high class, white babes."

* * *

When I got back to my motel, Billy's advice kept ringing in my ears. From the Sun God Motel's neon sign, you could see the Sagebrush Inn. After a shower, I put on two T-shirts and a clean, long-sleeve shirt and pushed Henry's hat down on to my still wet hair.

Hands in my jeans pockets, my shoulders up around my neck, I walked along the dusty gravel sides of the highway into Taos, stepping over trash from the new

Sonic, the beer bottles, and condoms until I got to the Sagebrush Inn.

The Sagebrush was thick adobe and lumber and decorated like an old Western hotel. Inside was the bar Billy told me to go to. It had a long, saloon-style bar. Cow hides, hats, lariats, and chaps were hung up along the walls. It had over stuffed lounge chairs and hard-backed wooden chairs around tables crowded together to give room for a small stage. A trio played on the stage, and some of the customers two-stepped in between the tables and chairs. It wasn't the drunken, Texas two-step that I was use to, but precise and smooth. I sat at the bar, my back resting against it and a glass of beer resting on my knee.

A pretty woman with a girlish grin and a nice figure, with long brown hair that hung just below her shoulders and untrimmed bangs that hung in her face, sat down beside me. As I looked at her, she swiveled in her chair to face the bar, and our eyes met in the mirror at the back of the bar. She pulled her head away to look at the people dancing.

Finally, when she put a cigarette in her mouth and fished around in her purse for a lighter, I picked up one of the Sagebrush's matchbooks, leaned in front of her, and lit a match. She smiled, then put the cigarette in her mouth and sucked in on it.

"Could I buy you a beer?" she asked.

This was a surprise. "Sure," I said, glad because of my finances. We curled back around to the bar and rested our elbows on it. She dangled her cigarette from one hand. The bartender brought my beer, and I thanked her.

"You're a tourist, I bet," she said.

"How can you tell?"

"You just don't look like a local. Maybe it's your hat."

I took off Henry's hat, then put it on her head, leaned away from her, then looked at her. "You're right."

She reached up and took off the hat, holding it in one hand, her cigarette sticking between her fingers. "You ought to get a new one."

"I'm growing to like it."

"I work in a photography store here in the shopping mall. If you have any pictures you want developed, bring them by."

"I don't even own a camera. I like to remember rather than take a photo."

She smiled, looked out at the band, then turned around to look at me, trying, probably, to get a good look at me without my hat. "Would you like to dance?" I asked.

While we danced, she pressed herself close to me and rested her face on the soft spot of my shoulder, and I tried to steer us around tables while keeping step. I thought about Victoria teaching me to dance years ago. I couldn't remember the last time I had danced with her, and here was this poor girl suffering from my lack of practice. "My name is Roger," I whispered.

"My name is Wendy, Roger. Do you have any pot?" she asked.

"All the pot I have is seven hundred miles away."

"I don't smoke too much, though," she added quickly.

"Neither do I," I said.

After our dance, we got our drinks off the bar and found a table in a corner. As the night wore on, as we bought each other more drinks (she liked tequila sunrises), we reached across the table and held hands. "What do you do for a living?" she asked.

I hesitated then said, "I'm an unemployed lawyer."

Her eyes opened widely for a moment, "Are you going to open an office in Taos?"

"No. I'm a visitor."

She dropped her head, and her eyes looked up at me, making her look like a teenager. "It's a nice place huh?"

"Yeah."

"The Sagebrush is a nice place too," she said. I started to recall Dianne Natividad, then I looked back at Wendy to reassure myself where I was and who I was with. Again, she dropped her head, so she had to raise her eyes to see me, looking like a Brigette Bardot imitator. Her look was something she had used to attract high school football players or blue collar workers out for a beer. She was getting too old for her raised-eye look, and for football players. "I stayed here the first night I was in town. They have a hot tub in back."

It would be so much easier if people who didn't love each other but wanted to pretend that they did wouldn't talk so much. "Perhaps, I better go," I said. Wendy again dropped her head, and I looked into her round, innocent eyes. "Tonight, now?"

"I've got a few phone calls to make."

"Maybe, I better be going too," she said, "I've got work tomorrow." I held her hand, and she said, "If you want a cup of coffee, I live right up the road. Take a left at the Ranchos de Taos cut-off. First road to your right, a Mobile home park, lot twenty-three." She got up and slung her jean jacket over her shoulder, and I watched her butt and the way it moved around on the underside of her jeans.

I walked to the bar, pushed up between two guys, and started my debate. Then I felt someone watching me. I turned and saw this Indian with graying hair tied in braids hanging down over his shoulders. He swooshed the braids back over his shoulders with the back of his hands. It was dark, but I could see that his eyes were red.

He tilted his head and said, "I know Tae Kwan Do." He held up his hands and wiggled his fingers. "I could rip your throat out with my fingers, or I could pray to my ancestors to grant you a safe trip back home."

"I'd rather you pray for me," I said. He shook his

head like he was clearing it and leaned his head closer to mine, "You're the guy looking for Tanner. I seen Billy."

The Indian turned back around to face the bar and banged on it with the flat of his palm. When the bartender came, he ordered two bourbons, straight, neat, one for him, one for me. "Look, maybe you can help me out. Do you know where this mobile home park in Rancho de Taos is?"

"Know right where it is," he said, slammed his flat hand on the bar, brushed his braids back over his shoulders, and ordered another bourbon when the bartender sat our two shots in front of us.

"You haven't drunk that one, yet," I said. He downed it and grabbed the next one.

We each sipped our bourbons, and I got fuzzy-headed. What kept working its way through the fuzz was the fact that some good-looking young woman, who dipped her eyes like Brigette Bardot, was waiting for me. "I've got to go," I said.

"Sip your whiskey," the Indian said. "My whole name is Sam Slow, but that's not my real name. When an Indian takes a white name, he names himself after something you whites value," he said and laughed. "So I took mine from a message to a car. Like my old friend, Billy Yield."

"What's your real name?" I asked.

He smiled in a malicious way and said, "You wouldn't understand."

I took a sip and then paid my tab. I would soon be out of cash if I kept spending like this. "So what do you do around here?" I asked Sam, hoping to take his mind off the whiskey he wanted me to buy him.

"I could make a living around here if I'd dress the part for the tourists and talk shit. You know like in the movies. Some old fart around here wears a goddamn loin cloth wrapped up under his ass. What the hell for? I ain't gonna do that. I'm a fucking artist."

"You mean a real artist at fucking or you just mean you're sensitive or something?"

"Shit no, I'm real, come on out to the Pueblo. I got some paintings out there. I'll make you a good deal." He sipped his bourbon but then added, "But don't tell no white people or Indians who look like they are in charge."

I got interested. "You're really an artist? You can make a living at that?"

"Hell, I made $5,000 six years ago." He banged his hand on the bar. "Bought a truck. Wrecked it right after that."

"What you driving now?"

"Got me a motor scooter."

Sure enough, the drunk Indian had a little moped. With me on the back, holding him around his chest, we drove on the very edge of the highway, on the gravel, in amongst the beer bottles, Sonic wrappers, and condoms. My shoulders hunched up around my neck, and my teeth chattered. The moped grunted worse than my truck and shook sideways, but Sam knew right where he was going, and from the right hand edge of the highway, he cut across one lane, the center stripe, and then the other lane to turn left on the Ranchos de Taos Road.

I begged Sam to stop at the gate. He leaned his moped against the gate and reached into his pocket. He brought out two joints. "I ain't no cheap mooch Indian." He handed me two joints. "White chicks get horny when you even show them this shit. Give 'em peyote, they're your slaves. But I ain't got no peyote." Wendy lived in a trailer park full of broken tricycles and rusting beer cans. Sam walked with me toward number twenty-three. I told him to wait away from the front door, but to make sure I got in.

Before I could walk away, he grabbed my arm and jerked me back to him. "I had a wife who liked to stab me."

"Do every one of you guys have a wife who stabs you?"

"When that bitch stabbed me a second time, she punctured my liver and gave me some kind of poisoning. Had to quit my job again."

"What'd you do to her?"

"Hell, I was bleeding. Couldn't do nothing. I loved her, but I had to leave her after that."

I pulled away from him and walked straight to the door. I heard one of those awful theme songs from an old TV show, the kind that stays in your mind after you've heard it

I jumped back when a sliver of light spread the length of the door. I heard Wendy, "Roger?"

I looked back at Sam, who clasped his hands together and raised them over his head like he was a winning prize fighter, then I looked back at Wendy. "This guy dropped me off. I don't do this too often. And all I want, really, is just maybe a cup of coffee and a little talk." I stopped myself, then looked around my shoulder to see Sam walking down the gravel road of the trailer park. He got his feet tangled in some tricycle or other such kid toy. I heard him say, "Fuck," saw him fall down. Before I could see if he got up, Wendy grabbed my hand and pulled me into her trailer.

We staggered into her trailer, kissed in the living room; then she steered me down her dark hall and into the bedroom. Once in her bed, I closed my eyes and thought about sleep, knew I couldn't yet sleep, and rolled toward Wendy and kissed her.

When our clothes were off us and in a wrinkled bundle of laundry beside the bed, she got on top of me, put her hands behind my head, and pulled her chin over my shoulder. I could feel her arms tightly squeezing me. And in the middle of our pretending that we were lovers, she tried to subdue a gasp that nevertheless came quietly from her lips and echoed in my ear. I tried to see her face yet concentrate on the feeling of sex. I wasn't sure if the gasp was sexual or the pain of a night with another man who turned out not to be Mr. Right. After sex, when people normally expected to whisper intimacies to each other in the dark, Wendy lay on her back and stared at the ceiling. And I, glad at least this night for sex, rolled away from her and went to sleep.

Well, what can I say? I was a young man. I still had hormones giving me orders. My wife was indifferent to me. If anyone, I had betrayed Diane Natividad. Yet this should have been more, should have meant something.

* * *

I woke up too early the next morning. I rolled over to look at Wendy in the dawn light. She had smeared purple mascara making tracks down her cheeks from the corners of her eyes. The make-up on some parts of her face seemed to crack; at other places it sparkled in tiny little crystals in the sunlight. Her breasts were touched up with silicon. She was several years younger than I was and fighting those years. She had gray in her hair.

I slipped into my jeans and walked through her narrow hall toward the trailer's kitchen. I stepped on something sharp but kept myself from saying "shit." I looked under my foot and saw a small, plastic toy soldier. I held it up to my face and looked closely at the little man with the fixed bayonet, another ambush. I walked into the kitchen, sensing where the refrigerator was. "Hi," someone said.

A curly headed boy, about eleven or twelve years old sat at the table drinking from a large glass of milk. "Hi." I said.

"I'm Kevin. Wendy's kid," he said.

I extended my hand across the table and said, "I'm Roger." He shook my hand then took another drink of milk.

"We got some Capt. Crunch if you like that," he said.

"No. No. I don't believe so," I said.

"How about some coffee?" said a voice from the hall door. Wendy was standing against the hall door, smiling now, no longer like the wide-eyed teenager, but like a veteran of these affairs.

"Hi Mom," Kevin said.

"I'd like some coffee," I said.

"Instant is all I have."

"Fine," I said.

Wendy dug into a drawer under her stove and came out with a black pan. She filled it with water and put it on the stove. As she stretched up on her toes to reach into a cabinet for the jar of coffee, the short robe rose up over her full butt, and showed her panties. She quickly tugged at the hem of the robe and dropped to the soles of her feet. I walked up to her, looked into the cabinet for her, and got the jar of coffee.

"Bye, Mom," Kevin said, grabbed some books from off the drainboard, and walked to the door.

"You're too big for a kiss?" Wendy asked, and Kevin walked to her and kissed her on the cheek. In another year or so, he'd be a teenager and would be too big for a goodbye kiss. He would start to bitch about his dumb mother and worry her silly.

"Bye, Roger," he said as he went out the trailer door.

The water started to boil, and I went back to her bedroom to finish dressing. I retrieved Henry's hat from a corner and walked back through the hall and into the kitchen, where Wendy had two cups of instant coffee sitting on the table. "Do you need a spoon, milk, sugar?"

"No," I said. Trying to avoid conversation that might be clumsy, I took a quick sip of coffee and burned my lip and tongue. "Ahh," I said.

"Be careful. It's hot," Wendy said. She sat beside me, no longer ducking her head, no longer forcing her eyes up into the top of their sockets, no longer imitating Brigette Bardot, no longer a fake nineteen as she was the night before in the Sagebrush bar but a hardened thirty-five-year-old (or older). Now that she was in her trailer, she realized I was just another pick up. Maybe she thought I was just another mistake, another loser. I probably was. She looked at me straight in the eye but was polite. "I'm thinking about moving to Seattle," Wendy said. "I hear the schools are a whole lot better than here." She halfway smiled.

When we finished silently drinking our coffee, because I thought it proper, I leaned across the table to kiss her. Not expecting a kiss, she raised her coffee cup to her lips. I stopped, poised above her. She giggled, lowered the coffee cup, and kissed me. Her breath was sour, just as I was sure mine was. She put both hands behind my neck and hugged me.

"Could you stay another day?"

"I'm looking for this man. It's really important that I find him." I dropped my eyes. "And I need a ride."

"Give me time to make myself presentable to the public." I watched her from behind as she walked down her narrow hall. Her butt was indeed big, her legs had some veins lining them, the back of her neck had gotten way too much sun.

After Wendy showered and dressed, we walked to her Chevy, which was parked beside the trailer. I looked toward the entrance and saw a moped leaning against a barbed wire fence post that made one end of the gate. "Shit," I said and started running for the moped. Before I got to it, I saw Sam curled up in the homemade drainage ditch that ran alongside the drive. I bent over him and heard him snoring. I reached and felt his right rib cage. There was this lump on it, not a muscle but some twisted, damaged flesh.

Wendy was beside me and looking down at him too. "Who is that? Should we call the police?"

"No . . ." I said. "No, honey," I added. I looked up at her and smiled. And she closed her eyes while she kissed me on the forehead.

"You know him? Is he a friend?"

"He was my ride last night."

"You want to wake him up?"

"No. I don't want to listen to him."

Still shivering, I reached into my shirt pocket and felt the two crushed joints. I put them in Sam's shirt pocket, then pulled the braids out of his face. "Shit," I said to myself, opened my wallet, pulled out five dollars, and stuck the bill in Sam's pocket. "You're giving your money to that bum?" Wendy asked.

"I guess so," I said.

* * *

That next morning, after a McDonald's breakfast, shivering even more from the morning chill, I waited across from the plaza under the over-hanging balcony of a mall. The plaza was filling with tourists and locals. A poster made by the Queen Bee Print Shop advertised Brother Dave and his spiritual transformation meeting.

Soon, a man in his mid-sixties came down Kit Carson Street walking a big black Lab. The small man had thick white hair combed straight back off his forehead, making curls over his ears, and a pot belly made by age rather than beer. He wore Bermuda shorts and a stained white T shirt with small holes in the arm pits. His nose and cheeks were pink and had tiny traces of veins. He didn't have the squint that Henry and other West Texans developed from the sun. His legs had blue and pink veins like his face. He walked from heel to toe, briskly, with a certain sideways motion, keeping up with the dog. The black lab knew the pace.

He crossed Kit Carson and walked to the square, circled it twice, and I stepped out from under the overhanging balcony to watch him. People waved as he passed them: Indians, Mexicans, businessmen, even some tourists.

As he walked in front of me, I crossed the street and headed toward him as he neared the corner of the plaza. "Mr. Tanner," I said. He turned to look at me, and the lab whined, pointed her nose down, and wagged her tail. She sniffed at my knees, and I patted her head. She looked up, and I cradled her chin in my palm. Clayton Tanner held the leash taut.

"Tanner," he said. "Most people call me just *Tanner*."

"I'm looking for Rebecca . . . Rebecca . . ." I stuttered as I wondered what she might have used as her last name. "Rebecca Bolen," I said.

"Did she send you?"

"I'm her son-in-law, Roger Jackson." Tanner held out his hand for me to shake. I dropped the dog's chin and grabbed Tanner's hand. "I'd like to find her to ask her to come to my home and see her daughter and ex-husband."

"Henry Bolen," Tanner said. "Henry Bolen is the man's name. And Vickie is the daughter's name." He looked at me and smiled.

"You're right," I said, waited as he smiled, kept on pumping my hand, then looked at me for an answer. "Henry wants to see her."

Tanner let go of my hand, backed up a few steps, then sat on the curb of the plaza. His dog ran to him and licked him on the face. He pushed her aside and said, "It is finally time." I thought, for a moment, that he would cry. He looked back up at me and said, "You're not a trickster are you?" Like the other inhabitants, he talked in riddles and ellipses.

"This isn't a trick," I said.

He jumped up and shifted his weight from one foot to the other, sort of a dance or a hop. Then he stopped moving and stuck a finger in the air. "I knew you would come. I saw in my dreams that you would come."

"That's good," was all I could think to say; then he invited me to dinner at his house. I figured that everybody in Taos had smoked, snorted, injected, or swallowed too much.

* * *

Taos wrapped itself around the base of several mountains to its east and looked out over a plain that stretched into mesas and mountain ranges to the west. Tanner's red adobe house, not far from the house he shared with Becky, was high up on the base of the eastern mountains, so from his backyard he could look across the plain. He had a back porch and some grass, but mostly sage brush and a few small piñon surrounded his house.

The expensive, genuine adobe had no second story like his first. It was a house with hardly any walls, full of space. The kitchen, dining room, and living room were all one large room with tile floors, throw rugs, and ceiling beams. He had a study, a large bathroom with a sunken tub, and two vast bedrooms.

We sat outside on his porch and drank beer while he barbecued chicken breasts, and Abbey, the black lab, ran through the sagebrush. I sat in an old iron lawn chair and felt the sweat on my can of Coors while Tanner pointed out the landmarks: Tres Piedras peaks, The Rio Grande Gorge, Mule Ears Peaks. He told me that the Sangre de Cristos were the last peaks of the Rocky Mountains. The peaks to the west and south were not geologically related to the Rockies. When I asked him about calling me a trickster, he told me, without a smile, that most Indians believe that coyotes or foxes are mischievous creatures who can trick the gods. Then he told me that Pueblo was just a label "whites" put on the local Indians, that they were separate and ancient communities and not one tribe.

From his backyard, he could see the rain and the

lightning out across the plain. "Look, look," he said to me and pointed to the rain. I slipped my windbreaker on and watched the rain and the sky with Tanner. Colored by the sunset, the sky shone bright red and orange through the rain and the clouds, and lightning moved across the plain. And I thought Henry would like the idea of watching, every night, the colors in the sky from his own backyard. I tried to imagine his tired old horses into young stallions running through Tanner's sagebrush.

Before the sun went down, we ate outside. We sat at Tanner's iron table with our chicken breasts and rice in front of us. Tanner looked up at the sky, closed his eyes, spread his arms out, and mumbled some prayer to God or Buddha, not minding or noticing I didn't pray with him. He lowered his head when he was through, smiled at me, and ate.

While I shivered in the dusk, we chatted in lantern light about Rebecca. When he talked about her, Tanner looked directly at me, motioned with his hands, repeated himself. When he spoke of himself with her, his eyes dropped, and then he looked up, to digress about the Indians or Taos. "Like the Hindus, some of the Indians believe in reincarnation, and when we come back, we again mate with our old lovers but in a different form," he told me.

I hugged myself and shivered in the dark. He looked at me and said, "Cold?"

"I'm from South Texas," I said. "I'm not used to this weather."

"You can get used to anything," he said, smiled, then walked to the back door. He held it open for me, and I went into the living room. Tanner stepped in and shut the door behind him. Abbey ran up to the closed door, pawed at it once, and whined. We both looked at her sad face. "I'm trying to get her to sleep outside," he said but opened the door to let her in.

Tanner started a fire in his fireplace even though I told him I was warm enough without it. After he got the fire started, he sat down on his sofa and motioned me to the chair next to the fireplace. Abbey curled up between us on a smelly blanket that was obviously hers. Tanner started talking. He floated from association to memory, to preaching, to advice, to therapy, to something like prayer. But he settled on the exact details of the day Becky Bolen left him.

* * *

To Tanner, telling the story was a liturgy he intoned to transcend to his weird gods. Once with his gods, he took no note of the world around him. He and Becky and some pan-like Indian creature ran naked in mountain meadows. If I could put myself in such a world and twist it to suit me, as Tanner did, and replace Becky with her daughter, maybe I'd stare blank-eyed at my guest and babble about my memories and fantasies. I feared that Clayton Tanner had lost his sanity, or at least normalcy.

I pushed Abbey's head out of my lap and got up. Tanner didn't notice me but let his head fall against the back of his sofa and stared at his ceiling (probably through it and into the night sky). I walked into his kitchen and helped myself to another beer from his refrigerator. As I pulled the beer loose from its plastic binding and then closed the door of the refrigerator, I stood in his kitchen without walls and looked across it to the living room, and the fireplace, and Tanner leaning back into his sofa, and the play of shadow and light from the fire, the single lamp, and the moonlight shining in.

I walked back to my chair and sat down. The beer I had drunk was growing stale in my stomach, but I took another sip anyway. Tanner brought his head down from gazing at his ceiling or at God to look at me.

"Do you want to stay?"

"What do you mean?"

"Do you want to stay in Taos? Some people want to stay in Taos. You can tell about people. There are those who want to stay and those who don't. Do you want to stay?"

"I've got a wife and no money," I said.

"I'm now in real estate. I own property and houses all around here. I'll help you out."

I wasn't sure if the offer was genuine or whether Tanner was looking for a convert. Then I worried that he might indeed have seen in me someone ready for retirement and conversion in Taos. And worse, given the night and the firelight and the appealing loneliness of his house, I wasn't sure but that I was fitted for Taos, that Tanner and the left-over hippies and the Indians were on to something.

"No. No. Thank you. I've got to find Becky."

Tanner crossed his arms and went to the refrigerator for another beer. "Would you like another?"

"Sure, one more."

"I don't usually drink as much as this. But at times it feels good to forget you have limits and experience the thing you are doing. Drinking beer is like that."

"I like the way it tastes," I said.

When he came back to the living room with the two beers, I took mine then told him why I had come, "Henry's dying. He wants to see Becky before he dies."

Tanner pulled the tab on his beer and turned his head away from the spew of foamy beer. "Poor man," he said. He looked at me, took a sip, then said, "He wrote me, you know."

"He mentioned you."

"He wrote to everyone for several years; I think."

"Why the hell didn't you tell him where she was?"

"The first time he wrote, I didn't know. Then I knew, and she didn't want me to tell him."

"Why would she do that to him?"

"You'd have to ask her. I don't know. She has her reasons, I am sure."

"Well, what about you? She left you too," I said.

"She had to leave."

"God damn come on," I said, and he looked at me as if to scold me for cussing. "Did you find somebody else?"

"No."

"Were there any women after Becky?"

He smiled then said, "No."

"None?" I asked to get his meaning straight.

"None."

"Didn't you want any? Weren't you lonely? God, weren't you horny?"

"You can get over all of that."

"But who wants to?"

He laughed at me. "Once you do, once all the scar tissue hardens, you're free of it. Then you know peace."

"And you have peace?"

I popped the tab of my beer, and Tanner said, "Yes" without blinking or smirking. And I almost wanted to believe him.

"So where's Becky?" I asked.

"She now teaches in the English Department at Oklahoma State University in Stillwater, Oklahoma."

"What's the drive through Oklahoma look like?" I asked.

"No color, burned out. It's all in black and white, but Stillwater starts to get pretty."

"You've seen her then?"

"No."

I stood and took a drink of beer. "The rest of this one will be for the road."

"You can stay the night here. I have an extra bed."

"I also have a paid-for motel bed." I started to go but then stopped and looked around his place. "You don't have a phone."

"I have one in my office."

"But what if you needed help?"

He shrugged his shoulders then said, "Wait." He jumped up and ran to a drawer. He opened it and pulled out a large, thick, black book. "If you could return this either to me here or my office on Ledoux." He handed me the book, and I flipped the cover open to look at the title page. It was Becky's dissertation. He handed me a card. On it was the address and phone number of The Upper Rio Grande Holistic Guidance Center.

* * *

I drove to the Sun God Motel over the dark dirt road I came on and looked at the stars over the plains and the sun beginning to make faint light between the mountains behind me. Though his life was set by the time the sixties arrived, Tanner was a sixties man. With his restless searching, Henry was a sixties man. Becky belonged to the sixties. Maybe we all have a sixties in us, and what we do with that urge determines the rest of our lives. And maybe, if we try to hold on to that urge after it sours, we lose our hold on sanity or normalcy. I hoped that Becky was closer to normalcy and sanity.

So, in my motel room, I pulled another beer out of the styrofoam ice chest at my bed and read parts of Becky's dissertation. In the preface, she thanked her mother and father and Clayton and Henry along with her advisors and mentors. She mentioned that she hoped she would never lose the enchantment she felt at the movies as a small girl in San Antonio, Texas. Then I read what she had to say about Samuel Fuller. I had never heard of him before but learned to appreciate his movies—*Run of the Arrow*, *China Gate*, *The Steel Helmet*. I had seen some before. But mostly I wondered about this strange woman who found something admirable in gonad-glorifying old movies.

I slept for five hours before I was awakened shortly before noon by the Iranian maid wanting to clean my room. After sending her back outside, I quickly showered and packed. I drove to town and found Ledoux street to drop off Tanner's copy of Becky's dissertation. Ledoux, one street off the square, was narrow with chipped cobblestones poking through the cracked and worn asphalt. His building was a small rebuilt adobe, and The Upper Rio Grande Holistic Guidance Center was up a narrow staircase with tiny steps. When I got up the stairs, I walked into something a little larger than a closet with a desk pushed into a corner. On either side of the desk were doors, one with a sign for a dentist and the other with Clayton Tanner's sign.

The receptionist, a woman about Tanner's age, with silver and turquoise hanging all over her and with streaks of gray in her hair, filed her nails. I also saw her feet in jogging shoes under the desk. I remembered Tanner's story form the night before, and I knew who the woman was. "I'll bet you're Rita Gomez," I said.

"Yes," she said, smiled and put down her file, thus jangling her jewelry. "Would you like to see Dr. Tanner or Dr. Abrams?"

"I want to drop this off. Tanner let me borrow it." I handed her the dissertation.

She took it, tsked, rolled her eyes, and smiled up at me. "This old thing. Still worried about that crazy woman," she said and shook her head. She was aging though her skin didn't hang in fleshy pockets around her face, but stretched tight across it.

"Tanner told me about you." I started to leave but turned around to Rita, "Are you married now, Rita?"

She smiled like a reformed alcoholic and said definitely, "No."

"Congratulations." I said and left her.

What can I say? People still saw sex as recreational. They also saw it leading to a spouse, comfort, or relaxation. I saw it as a night's work. But I was also tempted to find Wendy and stay another night with her.

But my mission and Victoria pushed me east out of Taos. If we all have some sixties in us, then Taos must encourage that thing. But once out of the mountains, once across the long, steep drop from Las Vegas to Tucumcari, I woke up. Taos seemed unreal. Wendy seemed real, but then she had had reality shoved in her face. Close to the Texas border, I was tempted to turn north or to drive right through Oklahoma and forget about finding Becky. And then I realized that I was trying to help Henry and not really fixing my marriage. I had made a promise—foolish as it was—and kept an eye out for Stillwater, Oklahoma.

Chapter 11:
Rebecca

When I got to Stillwater, I called Victoria collect from a pay phone at a Quick Trip Convenience store. She said Henry had asked about me. I told her to tell Henry that I had found Clayton Tanner and was about to find Rebecca. I would tell all, I said, when I came back. Victoria said she missed me and said good-bye way too soon.

I bought some of Oklahoma's infamous, watery near-beer at the Quick Trip and sat under the awning of the QT to drink a can. After shivering in New Mexico, I felt glad to once again be in heat and humidity. I watched the heat waves roll off the asphalt. Before I finished my beer, the guy behind the counter at the Quick Trip came outside and told me I would have to drink my beer somewhere else. A city ordinance prohibited public consumption of alcohol, even the goddamn near-beer. I snuck into my pickup, holding my beer down low, so no one would see it so I wouldn't do time in an Oklahoma jail. I missed Marie's and the old ice houses of the Hill Country, where you could always sit and drink a beer.

Though I was anxious to see Rebecca, I worried about seeing her. I wanted to think about what I would say, how I would introduce myself, how I would act. I could convince myself to be mad and confront her or to beg her to come back with me to the Texas Hill Country and save my marriage. So, I drove around Stillwater to put off seeing her and to think about seeing her.

Stillwater, Oklahoma, seems to have been sand-blasted by the red Oklahoma dirt. Trash and red dirt piled up against the curbs of the streets and filled in the cracks in the sidewalks. But as I got to the campus, and walked from its outskirts and into its heart, I found some beauty. Oklahoma State was prettier and cleaner than the town. But the building where the English department and Rebecca were housed was old, musty, and cracking. I walked up a long flight of stairs into the building that wasn't fully cooled. The air conditioner was trying—you could hear it rumbling—but the deserted building felt muggy. I looked around for students, hoping to ask directions, but I couldn't find any since it was late-afternoon during summer school. I looked at a directory of professors' offices until I saw *Dr. Becky Bolen.*

I walked down the hall, stepping on the creaking wooden slats of the floor, and into a cramped reception room with several office doors surrounding a secretary's desk. Sue Blair's name plate was on her desk, but she wasn't behind it, so I stepped around her desk, a plank in the floor creaking, and looked at Prof. Bolen's door. I cleared my throat, then knocked. The slats in the floor writhed as the person whom I assumed to be my mother-in-law stepped to the door. The door slowly opened.

Her face was still pretty, but wrinkles in her mouth and eyes followed her smile. She wore little make up. Her now silver hair was cut into a short, boyish style. A cigarette dangled out of her mouth. She stepped back from me, cocked one eye, and said, "Come in." She turned away from me and walked toward her desk. Her mid-thigh length skirt rose over each bulge of her hamstrings. I let my eyes drop and saw her calves bulge too. I quickly looked up. Her shoulders curled slightly forward, but she held her head high and rigid. I heard the whoosh of air as she sat into the cushion on the seat of her chair and watched closely as she flicked the ashes of her cigarette into the ashtray on her desk. The slim blonde of Tanner's story flashed into my mind. Then I remembered the advice old men give to young bachelors: "Always look at their mothers, boy." I had never, until now, seen Victoria's mother.

I took off Henry's hat and stepped into her office, also made the boards squeak as I walked to her desk, and sat down in the chair in front of her desk.

"Can I help you?" Her almost wicked-looking smile made me think she knew me.

"Prof. Bolen?"

"I am."

"I'm your son-in-law." I hesitated. She smiled broadly, then the smile crept into one corner of her mouth to make her look devilish and to give her cheek a slight dimple. She stood up and looked at me, then looked down at Henry's hat. She pulled her cigarette away from her mouth and exhaled.

"Could I see your hat?" she asked. I handed her the old Stetson, stained and smelly with Henry's sweat and mine, and she sat down with it in her hands, and her cushion again wooshed. She turned the hat around in her hands, feeling first the brim then the pinch in the crown. "So you inherit Henry's hat, huh, Roger?"

"You know me?" I asked

"I know Henry is dying."

I thought for a moment that she and Tanner might be connected through some metaphysical umbilical cord and would then commune spiritually. He also could have phoned her. "He's asked about you."

Becky giggled. I heard in the giggle the young Rebecca whom Henry and Tanner had fallen in love with, and I saw Victoria at twenty-two. She giggled again, and a cough, like Sam Penschorn's cough, followed the laugh out of her throat. She raised her fist but could not catch the cough.

"Tanner called me from a pay phone in Taos," she

said. "I get a bit of meanness in me sometimes," she said. " 'No pleasure but meanness,' you know. I'm sorry I let you go on."

I recognized the quote, knew it was from something I had read but wasn't sure what. She stuck her hand over the desk for me to shake. I shook it and sat in the chair in front of her desk, the floor groaning some more. She inhaled deeply on the cigarette with her smile in one corner of her mouth and made herself look like a wise guy from a 30's movie. "I've been waiting for you all day," she said. "I was afraid that you wouldn't find me."

"I guess I should have called."

"So you got to be the messenger of death. And here's the seal, the proof of your identity." She held up the hat and giggled, her smile lines showing themselves. She handed the hat back to me. I took it. "I really do recognize that hat. It's almost forty-years old. By god, when I met him he wore that hat." She stretched out her hand, "May I see it once more?" She held out her hand. I handed her the hat back. She again turned it over in her hands, then handed it back to me. I stuck it on my head, even squashed it down a bit.

Rebecca giggled and patted the desk. She stood. She was still thin except for a slight bulge around her belly; her body made angles. It occurred to me that, though she had gotten out of Texas, she had that dried, sun-baked, West Texas appearance. Her refusal to wear much make-up or to dye her hair was left over from the sixties, or it was a refusal to show any pretense. "I'm giddy. Absolutely giddy." I thought she would dance. "Damn," she said and clapped her hands together, fingers up like a child claps. Then, in an action that looked like a trial lawyer's, she put her hands palm down on her desk and leaned across it toward me. "So how is Vickie?"

"Victoria," I said and felt like I was one of her poor freshman students who was trying to defend his F.

"Oh, that's a silly, pretentious name. How is she?"

"What about Henry? He's dying," I said.

"Oh, yes. So he is," she said. "Poor Henry."

"That's what Clayton Tanner first said."

"You like Henry don't you?"

"He's kind of a jerk, a Neanderthal. But he is dying, and, for some goddamn reason, I'm the only person he thinks he can send on this crazy mission."

"So he likes you," she said.

"I'm not sure," I said and thought for a moment. "Maybe we both love his daughter."

"But you're here," she said and kept her smooth smile on her face. "Excuse me. I'm sorry, but right now, I'm just more excited about hearing about my daughter than about Henry."

"Well then, come back with me and see her."

Becky stood and pulled an enormous purse off the floor. She reached down again and pulled a brief case off the floor with her other hand. She grunted, along with the wooden slats of the floor, and straightened up. "We'll discuss this later. Right now I'm going to take you out to eat."

"Now?"

"Yes. I'm starving. I missed lunch because I was waiting for you." She walked from around the desk and held the briefcase out for me. I took it. "You have the light one," she said.

"Thanks," I said and shifted the briefcase's weight.

"Do you have a place to stay?" she asked as she took a straw hat from the hat rack by her desk and put it on.

"No."

"Good. You can stay with me." She stopped as she came around the corner of her desk, thought a moment, smiled again, and said, "It's nice to have relatives in." The floor creaked as we walked out of her office.

* * *

She took me to the most expensive restaurant in

Stillwater, bought us wine, made me order the prime rib. She ate as though she were famished, and as she talked, she did not feel at all embarrassed to point with her fork, usually with a chunk of steak in its tines.

I tried to ask her if she would go back to Fischer with me, but she wouldn't say. I tried to ask her about Henry, why she left, but she kept asking about me and Victoria. "I'm a lawyer," I said.

"Well, wonderful," she said.

"Does Vickie also work?" She thought very quickly, then added, "Does she also have a degree?"

"She's got a degree," I said.

"In what?"

"History and sociology."

"So what does she do?"

I ducked her gaze. She sipped at some wine, stuck a chunk of prime rib in her mouth, stared at me. "I don't practice. I quit so that Victoria could watch Henry when he got sick. We live on and off his property."

"So then you must be poor?"

"You got it."

"Oh, that damn property," she said.

"Yes," I said, "that damn property."

"Victoria deserves to live somewhere nice. A city."

Yes, by god, damn right yes, I felt like saying but said rather sedately, "I know."

Becky looked down at her plate to hunt for another chunk of prime rib but lifted one eye to look at me. "So you're not happy there?"

"I've been to the big city. Hell, I was born in Houston. I don't like being a farmer."

"What about Vickie?"

I just shrugged, but Becky caught on. "So when Henry dies, there'll be a debate?"

"Yes."

Becky nodded, frowned while she thought, and looked like she knew some secret about my wife and me, but for my own good, was not about to let me know. Then she dropped her fork on the edge of her dish, held up her hands, and flapped them. She looked like a cheerleader. She looked like Wendy trying to imitate nineteen-year-old Brigette Bardot. "Kyle, Kyle, Kyle . . . What about Kyle?

"He's not poor," I said. "In fact, he's getting rich."

"Oh, wonderful," she said.

"He doesn't like you," I said and immediately felt sorry. Meanness, as Becky would say, I guess.

"Oh . . . but . . . but . . ." she flapped her hands again, two bits, four bits, six bits a dollar . . . "Children? Grandchildren? What about babies?"

"Kyle has two."

"And you?"

I stared down at my plate, looked at her, and her smooth, smile drooped. "None."

She kept on pumping me about Victoria and Kyle and me. She hardly asked at all about Henry.

* * *

On her way home, she stopped at a liquor store to buy some more wine, a bottle of scotch, and beer for me. With the air conditioner running, no windows open, and Becky smoking and coughing, her old Volvo soon filled with smoke, and I kept clearing my throat. I had left my truck in her parking spot at school. "Oh, sorry," Becky said at last and put her cigarette out in the ash tray already spitting up cigarette butts. "All this non-smoking crap is gonna kill some of us."

In the brilliant orange Oklahoma sunset, I could see the rolling red, clay hills with spotty cedar and some tall elms. We drove over some creeks, also red from the dirt. And as the sunset turned into dusk, I thought that, in the faded light, the land around Stillwater looked something like the Hill Country. It was gentle and soothing, not so dramatic as Taos. It didn't encourage eccentricities, nature worship, or weird gods because of a hypnotic beauty. It was just pretty, as Henry said of his property. It seemed to make promises. It would cooperate with humans—grow their crops, nourish their desires, support their horse farms. I knew then that Henry wouldn't have made it in Taos. The majesty in New Mexico wouldn't have compromised any at all with Henry. Tanner, who was willing to surrender himself to the place where he lived, couldn't have survived in a half-assed landscape that supported human beings and not gods. I'm not sure that I was fit for either place. Maybe Becky was fit for any place.

She turned off Oklahoma State Highway 177 onto a dirt road and drove her old Volvo over several cattle guards and up a small hill. When we crested the hill, she said, "We're home." A low ranch-style house was in front of us. "Would you mind reaching into the glove compartment and feeling around for the garage opener." I found it for her, pointed it at the garage, watched as the door curled open, and wished I had a garage. We pulled into the two-car garage, and I saw her four wheel drive pickup parked in the other space. "I liked Clayton's and Henry's old trucks," she said, shrugged her shoulders, and though I didn't see her face, I was sure she smiled. We went into her dark house from a side door, and she pulled a cord and several drapes opened up to let the bright glare of the setting sun come into the house. I squinted and immediately felt the heat. The air-conditioning bills must be enormous, I thought. When my eyes adjusted to the light, I saw a very pretty piece of Oklahoma that didn't look like the moon. "I had this house designed for this view," Becky said. "I borrowed against my retirement for it."

We were in the dining room. I followed her as she walked by the kitchen and into the living room where she pulled open some more drapes to show more of the view. Her house was mostly furnished with space. She had little furniture, and what she did have was old. The upholstery was worn and faded. The corners of her rooms were filled with stacks of books and magazines that had once interested her but had long since been forgotten. "What would you like to drink?"

"A beer," I said, taking off Henry's hat, and sitting down on her lumpy sofa. I heard the ice clinking against the sides of her glass of scotch and water as she came back into the living room and handed me a beer. She sat down on the floor across from me and next to an ashtray. I scooted toward one end of the couch to give her some room. "Stay," she said and lay across the floor. She rolled on to her back, put the bottom of her glass of scotch to her forehead, and crossed her legs, causing her skirt to rise to the top of her thighs. She pulled off one low-heeled shoe with the toe of the other, then kicked the other shoe off. She had a run near the toe of one foot of her hose. "There should be a pack of cigarettes on the coffee table. How about throwing them to me?" I saw them and flipped them to her. She rolled to her side, sat her drink down, pulled the book of matches from out of the plastic wrap around the pack, and lit up, and immediately coughed. "Why did you come?" she asked.

"To bring you back with me."

"Why?"

"Henry asked me to."

"It's too soon."

"Christ, it's been thirty years. Come back with me and meet your daughter, talk to her, explain to her."

"What about seeing my son?"

"Him too," I said.

"But you said he hates me." Becky stretched. She looked at me, then at Henry's Stetson. "Not yet."

"When?"

"I'll let you know." She pretended she could see into the future.

"What about Henry, then?"

"He lived without me. He can die without me."

"The poor son of a bitch is getting fuzzy-headed. What the hell? Come see him."

Becky curled up from her prone position and scooted her butt across her carpet until she sat with her back against a wall. "Oh, I like you," she said. "I'm glad you married my daughter."

"Is everything funny to you?"

"Everything should be funny."

"Like deserting your children?" It was a mean remark, but with her, this bickering was almost fun.

"You gave up a practice for your wife. What else could you give up?" Becky circled her cigarette in the air and tried to catch its ashes with her ashtray.

"I wouldn't stay away from my children."

"I had a promise to keep."

"Henry showed me your letters."

"All of them?"

"No."

She smiled. "He didn't show you the ones where I pleaded to see the kids. To meet them before they grew up to forget me or hate me." She got up and walked into her bedroom. I thought she might slam the bedroom door and stay locked in the rest of the night, but she came back with two shoe boxes, both lids clamped on with rubber bands. She took the rubber band from around one, and held the open box in front of me. The box was full of letters.

"These are Clayton's," she said. Then she hefted the other box. "These are Henry's."

"He wrote you?"

"All the time. He sent them to Clayton's address—the only one he had. He even wrote Clayton." She bundled the box back up. And I wanted to beg her to let me read her letters and see into her life, Henry's life. "Hell, I called him back. I just never told him where I called from. If I wrote, I sent the letters to Clayton so that they had a Taos postmark." She walked back to the wall, sat with her back against it, her shoe boxes full of letters at her sides, her possum grin on her face. She smashed her cigarette into the ashtray.

I sat back down and squinted at her. "But Henry said you hadn't written in years. He acted as if Clayton might not even exist. He said—"

"Nearly ten years ago, just as you were going to marry or run off with Vickie, his letters stopped. Then last week, Tanner forwarded me another one. Henry had addressed it to me at the old house in Maestas. Tanner's tenants gave it to him. In his letter, Henry said he was dying. He said he asked you to shoot him. I called him. He asked me to come down."

"And you didn't come."

"Of course not."

"Then what the hell am I doing wasting my time here?"

"You're sharp as a tack Roger. He lied to you. He's got you out doing his dirty work. He would never come look for me. Now he's got you doing it." I looked up at her. "He has this amazing ability to get people to help him. They help him and don't even know it. I don't even think he knows it."

I dropped my head and nodded. "But don't you think he really loves you?"

"Sure he does, in a way. But he let my kids grow up without knowing about me. I tried to call them. I tried to write them, but he never would let them read my letters, never would let them talk to me."

"Okay then, damn it. Where's your phone. Right now. Call Victoria."

Becky's smile disappeared and made her face completely smooth. "I promised Henry I wouldn't."

"Jesus Christ. God damn, you're both mean. . . and damn near crazy. So why did you ask me all those questions this afternoon. Why'd you wait until now to tell me."

"Just checking out Henry's story."

I sat down on the sofa, grabbed my beer and heaved the empty can into the dining room.

Becky sat in her corner, didn't smile at me, didn't light up another cigarette. But she pushed herself up, went into the kitchen, and came out with another beer that she handed to me. She sat beside me on the couch and patted my knee. "We do what we do, Roger? I hope you can fix your marriage."

I looked at her. Up close she looked as though she would cry, but neither one of us was yet willing to cry in front of the other. "Have you ever married since?"

"Hell, I never even divorced Henry."

I looked at her and said, "Holy Jesus".

She put her hand around my shoulders. "People have lived with me here. Several graduate students, lovers of different shapes and sizes. One woman." She halted, coughed, deliberately smiled, then winked. And though I didn't know whether the comment was true, said for effect, or for my report to Henry, it loosened me up. "But no one ever stayed very long."

Becky got up, walked back to her cigarette pack, lit up, brought her cigarette and ashtray back to the couch, sat beside me, and told me about her father, old Carl Baumann. Unlike Tanner, she would let me interrupt. She let me offer my view and would consider what I had said. And I felt like curling up under her arm, as if I were one of her lovers or kids.

Late in the night, after piecing together her life and Henry's, both of us drunk, so that I told her about Dianne Natividad and Wendy, she sat next to me. Then she lay down and put her feet in my lap. I said, "So go back with me now and make it all right."

"Roger, don't be silly." She laughed at me.

"God damn. You know you're wrong."

"I'm supposed to be wrong. I'm the villain."

"He's dying, and Victoria will forgive you."

"You've forgotten Kyle, again." She pulled her feet off my lap, sat up, ground her barely smoked cigarette out in the astray on the coffee table, and coughed. "Late at night, these damn things start to bother me. She rubbed her feet. I reached down, pulled them into my lap, and rubbed them.

We had a couple more drinks. She went to sleep on the couch, and I staggered into the guest room to catch some sleep

At breakfast the next morning, while I was buttering toast and sipping coffee and she was grading the papers she had put aside the night before, I asked her if loneliness had been worth it. "Who's lonely?" she asked.

Perhaps I wanted her to confess what a dismal, tragic life hers had been, to admit to some great need that was leaving her hollow, then to follow me home and give her revelation to her daughter and me. "Come back with me," I said once more.

She looked at me as if I were an eager but misguided undergraduate. Her smooth smile appeared. "You play the cards you draw," she said and laughed at her tough guy imitation. "It's been a delight to see you, Roger," she said. "But I know, despite your infidelities, that you want to get back to them. You're a hard day's drive away."

Chapter 12:
Victoria

I drove south from IH 35, out of Oklahoma and into Texas, continuing farther south until I could see the ridges of Balcones Fault start to rise up around Waco. The wind criss-crossed between the two open windows of my cab, and I could feel the humidity in the air. I liked the humid heat I was used to, but something was coming; this wet-rag weather was worse than usual. So I sat in my un-air-conditioned truck and blew little beads of sweat off the tip of my nose and blinked against the salty drip in my eyes. I could feel the grit the sweat left in my pores. I began to remember Austin and Victoria and practicing law. On the way back to a place you are familiar with, you can really get intense in your thinking and remembering.

When I got into view of the Austin skyline, somewhere just south of Georgetown, the traffic on IH 35 started to slow. It was rush hour in Austin and a sauna in my pickup cab. The town had gotten so big, it was such a booming place, that five o clock traffic backed up IH 35 traffic ten miles in either direction.

When I was there, the old hippies who had gotten out of Vietnam migrated to Guadalupe Street and sold brocade pillows to fresh-off-the-farm college students. Nowadays, the hippies have disappeared, perhaps they were in Scholz's beer garden where all radicals, both right and left wing, usually spent their days getting drunk. Maybe they got rich and drove BMWs to overpriced renovated condos just west of The University of Texas campus. Over the years, bums, Iranians mad at the Shah, Iranians mad at the Ayatollah, Haitians, Mexicans, and punk rockers took the hippies' place, each in their own turn. There would always be bizarre but interesting people in Austin, the kind you like to watch but not the kind you would want your kids to know.

Ahead of me a lady in long blue Cadillac, the last of the big ones, inched ahead while her frantic poodle went nuts in her backseat. Some people behind me honked. I heard loud rock music from a car two lanes to the left of me. I looked at him, another poor soul without air conditioning and blowing and wiping at the sweat on his face and arms. For a long time, I thought Austin would be my town.

Since I was in the right lane and stalled in Austin anyway, since Austin was what I thought I wanted, I pulled over, nearly catching the Cadillac in front of me, and drove down Sixth Street until I could find a place to park. Sixth Street was the newest "in" section of Austin. When I first saw Austin, in the late sixties, the "cool" section was up and down Guadalupe Street. Sixth Street had drug dealers and prostitutes. Then sixth street became the gay area. Then it transformed itself again: into an upscale "entertainment" center. Every bar had a theme and a band.

The happy hour crowd was roaming down the sidewalks of Sixth Street grazing on the free hor de vors and watered-down liquor. My T-shirt clung to my sweaty chest; I probably smelled like one of Henry's "hard rode" horses. I walked into a polished brass and wood bar, and reentered a little bit of my old world. A few people wore hats: straws, tennis, or baseball. Henry's sweat-soaked Stetson was out of place. A smiling waitress with the look of a UT student brought me a beer anyway. I tipped her too much and called Victoria. Nobody was home. At home was Henry's death. Here was life.

I carried my foamy draught to a corner of the bar and sat. People started to drift in as the sun lowered, and I looked out the window of the bar. The cops closed the street to vehicles. The sidewalks came to life. Businessmen had loosened ties and sportscoats slung over their arms; some women, also, just off work, fanned themselves. Some wild men, probably college students, slipped out of their shirts and stuffed the tails back into their pants to let the shirts dangle in front or in back of them like loin cloths. One girl took her shirt off too— her breasts bounced as she walked down the crowded sidewalk. People stared for awhile, until the cops cuffed her, wrapped her in her shirt, and took her down to the house. Several punksters were out in their green or blue hair, their wrap around sun glasses, and their safety-pinned noses and ears. But most of the people in the crowd were the new arrivals in Austin, the people with the money. They wore khaki or navy shorts, sandals or running shoes, and loose fitting cotton shirts bought from prestigious stores. I wished for sandals and shorts because my jeans stuck to my legs and climbed up my crotch.

More people came in. The air conditioning was trying, but the people brought the humidity in with them, making the bar just barely cooler than the evening. Jazz started from somewhere farther up into the bar where I couldn't see. It grew louder, and the whole place shook with the music. A waitress balancing a tray above her head stopped by me and asked what I wanted to drink. A bead of sweat rolled down her nose and splattered on her bare chest. Pretending I had money to burn, I ordered a Jack Daniels on the rocks.

I wiped my forehead with the back of my palm and turned around. I bumped noses with a tall black haired woman. "Excuse me," I said.

She eyed me, then said, "No problem."

"Crowded," I shouted above the music.

"This isn't bad," she said. I looked more closely at her and glanced down at her legs. She wore a black lace skirt and a white sleeveless blouse. Her hair was long on one side of her head and short on the other. On her feet, she had black spiked heels. She sipped a piña colada, or grasshopper, or some other repulsive colored frozen drink. She turned away from me to talk to her friend she was talking to before bumping into me.

"One night stands are it, for me," I overheard her say. "No more intimate, emotional, bullshit."

"No shit," the other woman said, leaned forward, and kissed the woman on the mouth. I turned away from them and smiled to myself. There was life in this dripping, hot place. It was like the fertile sludge our ancestor amoeba crawled out of.

But the patrons weren't the sludge of society; they had to have money. The waiters and bartenders were fresh-faced, good-looking UT students (the girls dressed to show off breasts or thighs). And they had no disgust for the people they waited on. They looked enviously at their customers and tried to imitate them, for they knew if they kept their noses clean, didn't party too much and flunk out, majored in the right subjects, a few of them would be the next wave of the young new rich going to the bars on Sixth Street.

The patrons were a consumer cult, but they had a conscience. They could have made bigger bucks in a larger city—Houston, Dallas, New York—any big commercial center. But they gave concessions to dollars, bought their way out, so to speak, to live in Austin or other unique cities—San Diego, Santa Fe, Denver— where life was better. In 1984, they had the best lives available.

My waitress brought my drink; I gave her three dollars and told her to keep the change. I was like the students, though, who ogled these people. In truth, I envied them. But because of what I once was, and maybe because of what I had become, that realization left me repulsed with myself.

Halfway through my drink, a boom sounded so loud it shook the plate glass window of the bar. The people in the crowd turned, knocking each others' drinks over and bumping noses, cheeks, breasts, and chests to look out the window. Then, when the rain poured down, the people in the bar cheered. The first waves of rain hit the street and sidewalk, and steam rose up off the cement and asphalt, and people in the street stared up at the sky to let the rain wash their faces. I gulped down my drink, pushed past the woman in black and white, and went into the rain. I too looked up and let the rain wash the dried sweat and stink off my face. The steam settled and the rain cooled the dusk. I took off my boots and walked through the puddles back to my car. I had lots of company. People all around me sloshed through the rain, kicked at the puddles, and ran their fingers through their wet hair. In Austin that early Friday evening, some undeclared celebration you could see in the people's eyes was going on.

But I was Lazurus come back from the people my in-laws had killed off, and I needed to give my report of the dead. I plugged my forefinger in my ear and dialed with my other forefinger. Again, no one answered. I hoped that my guess was not right. I pulled off my boots and socks, and walked through the rain to Breckenridge Hospital. It was the first time that I had been really cool since Taos.

I stepped into the hospital with my wet clothes dripping on the floor, making a small puddle, and shivered in the cold air-conditioning. I pulled my socks over my wet feet then squeezed my feet into my wet boots. At the reception desk, I asked if Henry Bolen was in. A nurse whispered over her shoulder to another one. They paged a doctor. I told them I was a part of the family, but they made me wait for the doctor. She showed me to a room in I.C.U..

I opened the door to the dark room and saw figures turn to look at me. I recognized Henry though. He was lying in a bed with a nightlight beam shining on his lower chin and chest. Tubes were coming out of his nose and arms. He rolled his head toward me, then rolled it back to look straight up.

I stepped into the room and closed the door behind me. The room was even colder than the hospital. The sweat on my back and chest seemed to turn to tiny icicles. I squinted while my eyes got accustomed to the dark. Suzy sat in a large lounge chair and hugged her shoulders. Kyle and Victoria were standing at the foot of the bed. They were oblivious to the coolness. Henry rolled his head toward me again, and Victoria stepped toward him and whispered to him, "It's Roger, Daddy." Henry slowly turned his head to smile.

"Damn, it's cool in here," I said and felt Kyle's grip on my arm.

I looked at him. He glared at me. I stepped toward Henry and bent toward him, careful not to brush against any of the tubes. He smelled like he was about to explode from all the stink of the chemicals and sickness that had been collecting inside of him for so long. "I found her," I said. Henry stared at me, then his eyes rolled as he looked around the room. "I found out you wrote her by way of Clayton Tanner. I found out she called you. I found out you lied to me . . ."

I felt Kyle's grip on my arm again and heard him mutter, "Goddamn."

"She wouldn't come back with me, Henry," I said. "I tried to get her to come. I tried, Henry." Henry rolled away from me and looked straight up at the ceiling. "She is in Stillwater, Oklahoma. She's a professor there."

I straightened and waited for a reply. Kyle stepped up to me again and whispered. "He doesn't understand. It's like he's not conscious."

I bent over Henry again. His eyes looked vacant and watery. I couldn't tell if he saw me or not or if he did see me and his mind wouldn't or couldn't register me.

I looked up to try to see Victoria, but could see only her form. I straightened, and I heard Victoria mutter in my ear, "Don't make him struggle." I reached out and felt her arm, closed my hand around it, and pulled myself to her. I kissed her on the cheek and tasted the saltiness of tears. "You really did find her?" she asked me.

"Yes," I said. I let my arm slide down Victoria's arm until I came to her hand and grabbed it in both of mine. I raised it to my lips and kissed it.

"Emma," Henry said. We all looked at him.

"What?" I asked, stepped away from Victoria, and bent over Henry. "Yes, Henry?" Kyle shushed me. "No, No, what did he say?" I stepped toward Henry. "Henry, Henry did you say 'Emma'?"

"Every now and then, he just says something," Kyle said. "It's nonsense."

"Emma? Who is Emma?" Victoria asked. She stepped up to her father bent over him, stroked his forehead, ready to hear Henry's last words.

Kyle whispered to me, "Probably one of those young coeds he chased."

Henry looked straight up, but he slowly turned his head toward me and smiled. "Roger," he said. Victoria straightened, raised her hands over her mouth, then pulled herself away from her father. For all that Victoria had done, all the nursing, Henry wanted to see me.

I stepped up to Henry. I felt Victoria's cold palm on my forearm, then felt her whispered breath on my cheek, "He's delirious."

Henry looked at me, smiled at me. He had to be conscious and aware. He had to know that it was me, and he knew that he had told me about Emma. I bent over him, "Henry, Henry, I found her. I found Rebecca. You'd be proud of her."

Henry nodded and grabbed on to my arm, "Emma showed me."

"Yes, Henry, yes." I said as Kyle asked, "Who is Emma?"

"Yes, yes, Henry," I said and became more mixed up than Henry. "And she was right, Henry. She and Shorty were right, and Becky, no, no, Rebecca, she still loves you, despite it all. She'd be here, but. . ." Henry's squeezed my arm. "This is Roger, Henry. This is Roger. I've seen them, talked to them. And you didn't fuck up. You did the best you could. You just didn't know. Wait, I'll get her. I'll get her." Henry nodded.

I pulled away from Henry. "Who is Emma?" Kyle asked. Victoria looked at me in opened-mouth shock. Suzy sat in the lounge chair and cried and hugged herself.

I ran down the hallway of the tenth floor to the elevator and went down to the lobby and a pay phone. I called Becky collect.

Becky accepted my call. "Becky, Becky, he's dying right now."

"Oh, my," I heard her say.

"Get down here."

"I'm sorry, Roger." I heard her say.

"Goddamn it. You can see your kids." I heard her breathing, but she said nothing. "Jesus H. Christ, Becky. What harm can he do you now?"

"Not yet," she said. I hesitated and listened to her breath.

"Goddamn it, Becky, you have a chance to help someone out, to change his whole opinion of his goddamn life, to make his dying a little easier," I said.

I heard Becky's breathing as she paused. "Come on, Roger. Don't be naive. What could I or anybody else do to possibly change anything now? Everybody has to die alone and without anyone's help." I slammed the receiver down.

When I went back to the room and its chill, I saw Kyle and Suzy sitting in two large chairs in front of his bed. Suzy turned her head away, wouldn't look at Henry, and Kyle held her hand. Victoria now sat in a chair next to the bed and watched Henry's face. Henry breathed in long gulps. I didn't see why we had to sit by him and torture ourselves while adding to his indignity. If you really die alone, as Becky said, then Victoria, Kyle, and I ought to leave Henry to himself. I moved to the back of the room in the darker shadows, grew disgusted, and thought I maybe should have shot him to save all of us this misery and embarrassment. The old, hard luck, ignorant cowboy wouldn't want us to watch him.

Henry died that night without us watching. The hospital staff wouldn't let us. We all stayed at Kyle's that night. I was so exhausted that I didn't think that I could hug the edge of Ranch Road 12. I might have driven off devil's backbone.

But that night, on Kyle's fold out sofa, my wife cried into my shoulder and said, "He wanted to talk to you," then fell asleep. With Henry gone, with Becky's message coming like God's out of Oklahoma, I could bring Victoria to Austin with me. And before I went to sleep, I felt sorry for Henry. He had to go through so much shit just to die. And I realized that surely, unless we were very careful and caring, or maybe a little like Becky, most of us would have to go through so much shit just to die.

The next day, between preparations for Henry's funeral, I told Becky's kids as much as I could about Becky and Emma. And when they would listen, I told them about Daryl and Clara Bolen, about Shorty, about Henry's first glance at his property, about Clayton Tanner, but I had to compete with a Lutheran Minister from San Marcos, a funeral home director, calls from friends, and their own grief.

* * *

As we listened to the last prayer being delivered at Fischer cemetery, I thought that, if he had never reached that low point in his life, Henry might have enjoyed his funeral. Victoria squeezed my knee. I turned my head to see her bite her bottom lip. I saw Kyle look at me, then pull his eyes back toward the minister for the Fischer Lutheran Church. Bobby wriggled in his seat next to Kyle, and Christen sat in Suzy's lap. A canopy protected us from the sun, but I still sweated into my freshly cleaned, out-of-date suit. All the seats under the canopy were taken by family; outside the canopy, Sam Penschorn, Pete Proctor, Jack Hillier, and other old German pall bearers bowed their heads and folded their hands; ranchers, real estate developers, rich retirees, even some of the Mexicans came and were praying and sweating into their Sunday best.

Dianne Natividad and Eddie Sanchez held hands and smiled at each other. Discreet Doc Hillier stared at the cattle pasture beyond the cemetery. He had no patience with funerals; he would survive them all: Henry, Pete, Sam. Suzy was the only member of the family to cry. Sam and Pete snorted and rubbed their eyes. Sam coughed and spit into his handkerchief. The young, misplaced minister said "Amen," and I rose with the rest of the family. Doc Hillier was the first of the mourners to shake our hands and pat our backs.

As we drove back to the ranch, some of the members in the procession, in their pickup trucks, crumbling old cars, and shining new ones, followed us on the way back to their homes. They waved as I turned into our gate. I looked at Victoria. She sat silently, staring at our old trailer home. I stopped the truck. She turned her head to look up the low hill at Henry's house. "We moved in with him," she said and got out of the car and walked past the trailer. From a distance, we heard the crunching from the bald man's bulldozer.

Sitting in my truck, with its idle set high so that it wouldn't die on the road, I watched Victoria walk. Her feet slid and curled to the outside edges of her soles as the rocks rolled under her feet. I watched her back, the angular shape of her neck and shoulders, the sideways swing of her arms, the sway of her hips. She was starting to curl forward, like her mother. A slight breeze caught some of her cleaned, now bright blonde hair and blew it toward me. Her white dress made her shimmer and set off her tanned neck and arms. ("I'm not going to buy a brand new black dress just to wear it one time in August heat," she said when Kyle gave her sixty dollars to buy an appropriate mourning dress.)

She stepped on to the veranda, crossed it, opened the screen door, then the front door, and walked into the house, leaving the screen door bouncing against its frame. I saw the future, and I sensed that Becky saw it with me. Victoria would stay. She would tend the cabins or kitchenettes or whatever the hell Kyle would call the family resorts he planned to build beside Fischer creek. She would change the sheets, mop up the spilled beer and baby shit, police the grounds, mow the lawns, and sell cold drinks. Kyle would let her have the house, so she could manage his investments, and he would underpay her. She would air out the house to get rid of Henry's old man smell and eventually refill it with the smell of her own old age. Somehow, in a way I didn't understand that, like Henry, she could be happy here—with or without me, with or without any man. I didn't know why I had chosen her over Austin, why I had even had to choose one or the other, but I drove up to the house and followed her into it. I didn't know why I stayed—except maybe to convince her to let me stay.

* * *

We became orderly and polite to each other. Kyle still

brought his family over for Sunday or Saturday dinners. Without Henry, the dinners were quiet except for Bobby chattering or Christen spitting something. During the week, the bald headed man would come up to the veranda to get a drink from our faucet then go back to his construction. But now, he was joined by the rest of his crew, pouring concrete, hammering, sawing. A Mexican whom I figured to be a "wetback" Kyle had found someplace came to the veranda and, as best as Victoria and I could figure, said he wanted to paint the wooden shack at the entrance to Bolen Resorts properties. We let him, but he knew nothing about painting and left something that looked like hardened pancake syrup all over the shack. That Sunday Kyle had something to cuss about, so dinner wasn't as quiet.

Sam Penschorn and Pete Proctor came by to see if they could do anything for us. I tried to use them as free labor and drove them out to the edge of the property to repair a loose strand of barb wire. But Sam coughed up some of the goo in his lungs, and Pete's hands shook, so I drove them into town to Marie's and bought each of them a beer for helping me. They thanked me and invited me to play dominoes with them. I refused and went back to Henry's property, repaired the fence myself, and mixed more of my sweat with Henry's sweat in the old Stetson.

I no longer visited Dianne Natividad; I just waited for Victoria to bury her father once and for all. But Henry made damn sure we wouldn't forget him quick. As much as we cleaned, left windows open, and ran fans, Henry's old man smell remained. Kyle bought us two air-conditioners and put one in the living room and one in his, now my room. With some air-conditioning and Henry's smell fading, Victoria smiled more, joked some, lost years, I hoped.

Still, we didn't live in all the house. We left the door to Henry's bedroom closed. We referred to it as Henry's room. Christen and Bobby couldn't play in it when they came over, as if we feared that they might somehow be sucked into it and never escape. It became obvious though that we would have to break into it. I was for dynamiting it off the rest of the house. Kyle chided me and begged Victoria to stay out of it and let him and me clear it out. Perhaps he feared some heavy-headed Hollywood ghoul would lunge out at us. I was scared that Henry's ghost might snatch Victoria away. She kept us both out while her practicality and common sense grew strong enough for her to open the door and then to immediately demand that we clean it up. So Kyle, Victoria, and I decided to clean out the room, to parcel out between us what was useable of Henry's, to sell the rest-and to read his letters from Becky.

On a Wednesday morning, Kyle took off work to meet us. He wisely left Suzy and the kids at home. We lined up outside Henry's door. As Kyle opened the door and Victoria stepped in, I patted her shoulder. She dropped her shoulder to let my hand fall off. The smell of Henry was thick. Kyle went immediately to the closet, and I held Victoria around the waist. She moved my hand away and wandered around the room, looking at the walls, the ceiling, the grayed, green carpet, running her fingers along the top of the two night stands, then looking at the streaks she made through the dust. She wasn't aware Kyle or I existed. She was in some trance; time for her was standing still while she tried to commune with her father by drinking in the smell he left in the room.

We cleaned, cleared, and stacked what was left of Henry. But we couldn't find what we most wanted. It would have been like Henry to destroy the Thom McAnn shoe box with the most intimate markers of his life.

Victoria lay on the floor and scooted on her belly up to the bed then reached under. She came out with one sock in her hand. It curled over her finger. "We're not going to find it," she said. "I bet he burned it," I said. Victoria started to laugh. Then I laughed. "What so funny to you two?" Kyle asked.

* * *

I can't remember the exact date, but summer was not yet over—Kyle and Suzy didn't show up for Sunday dinner. I walked in from driving the fence line expecting to smell dinner cooking. I could smell nothing. Victoria sat in a chair beside the kitchen table with her head in her hand.

"Where's Kyle?" I asked.

"They're not coming today," Victoria said.

"So you're not cooking, then?" I asked. Victoria got up and walked away from me. "Well, great then. Let's go out and eat. Hell, let's drive somewhere and eat."

Victoria faced the window over the sink and squinted into the sun shining through the window. She looked down at a pile of dirty dishes, turned on the hot water, and sprayed dish soap on to the dishes. I waited a moment, then came up behind her and wrapped my arms around her waist and pressed my cheek close to hers. "Forget washing those. Let's take a holiday."

"Oh, Roger," Victoria said. The steam from the hot water rose in vapors around our faces. She turned around in my arms to face me and wiped at her eyes with the back of her hand. She left a dab of dish soap suds on her cheek.

"You're crying," I said, shocked because I seldom saw her cry anymore. "Come into the living room."

"Later."

"What the hell is going on?"

She turned inside my arms to face away from me. She breathed deeply then turned off the hot water. "You need to go to Austin and be a lawyer."

"Yes, I would still like to," I said and smiled at the thought.

"I've got to stay here."

"Okay, then, so we stay. I've gotten use to that idea. Not completely. But I'm working on it."

"We just can't make it."

"Sure, we can. Kyle's putting up the money. All we do is watch."

"No, No, No," Victoria said and bounced the bottom of her fist off the drain board. "*We. . . We*, us. We can't make it."

"Turn around here," I said.

"No," she said; then I tugged her, and she circled inside my arms to face me. She was crying. "I've been thinking," she said.

"Goddamn it, didn't my treasure hunt for your mother mean anything?"

"You did that for Henry."

"No goddamn it; I did it for you," I said, and Victoria rubbed at the tears under her eye with the back of her hand.

"I'm sorry. I can live without you."

"Do you want to?"

"Yes," she said without hesitating one goddamn minute. She circled inside my arms again to squint into the noontime sun.

I put my hands on her shoulders. "Can you live without loving somebody?"

"I love people."

"Somebody alive," I said. She sobbed once, gathered strength, and stopped crying.

"Please, Roger," she said firmly, "Let's not get mad or nasty."

"So what the hell am I supposed to do?" I shouted, not so much at her but perhaps to Henry and Becky and Clayton and Wendy from Taos who all seemed to be laughing at me.

"Whatever you want."

"Look, we can be happy. Didn't I tell you about your mother? You want to be like her. We're lucky. I can be happy here now."

I pulled Victoria around, so I could see her. She closed her eyes and spoke. "You see. You see, while you were gone, I thought."

"Goddamn it, no," I screamed. Victoria sniffled to keep from crying. I put my hands on her shoulders, and they rose up and dropped as she sucked in for air.

Victoria put her arms around me. She dropped her voice. "It's best," she said. I pushed away from her, hoping she would hit me, so we could really fight. I paced away from her, turned to look at her, then my anger left as I realized she was leaving me. She put her hands behind her and gained enough composure to say almost matter of factly, "Roger, I'm so sorry, but I want a divorce."

"What about a separation?" I asked.

"It's just not going to work. You know that," Victoria said. She stepped toward me. "The trailer is yours. You can live in it, move it, whatever you want."

"Whatever I want, huh?" I said, leaned against the drain board, and thought suddenly of Becky and what she might say. She would laugh, I knew, in the way she could laugh at her own story.

* * *

I sat on the curb in front of the Alameda saddle shop and waited for Dianne Natividad. Newly broken glass lay on the sidewalk in front of the saddle shop; someone had found another window to break. Just a hint of the coolness that comes from the first big norther was in the night air. The breeze was from the north turning back the damp gulf air and starting thundershowers farther south but leaving Fischer's night dry, cool, and clear. It was a night I decided would be better spent with a woman, any woman.

After Victoria told me what she wanted and exiled me to the trailer, I locked its door after me, turned the air-conditioning all the way up, shut the blinds, listened to the booming clock until I pulled it off the wall and chunked it outside, and drank beer and smoked dope in the dark trailer. So, after several weeks of solitary in the mobile home, I drove into town and sat on the curb of the Alameda saddle shop.

I heard the rattle of Dianne Natividad's old Impala and looked down Wimberly Avenue to see it pulling toward me and putting up a smoke screen of burning oil. She stopped in front of me and smiled. She had an unlit cigarette pasted to her bottom lip. I stood and, without caring or checking who was looking, opened the passenger door and got in.

Dianne Natividad yanked the gear shift lever into drive and pressed the accelerator down hard. We roared out of town on Ranch Road 12, and she pressed harder on the accelerator. As we skidded around curves and risked sending pistons up through the hood, I thought it fitting and romantic to be found dead, smashed up around a tree with Dianne Natividad. The clean wind was pulling Dianne's hair back over the front seat and whipping strands of it in front of her face. "I might start smoking," she said and pointed to the cigarette clinging to her bottom lip.

I propped my upper arm in the open window of the passenger side of the car and said, "Might be something to try."

"You are a smart man, though. I thought you might, you know, tell me about how bad it is for you."

"It can kill you. So can driving."

She laughed, pulled the cigarette off her lip, and threw it out the window. "Want to get some beer?"

"It can kill you too."

She laughed some more and slid around another curve. "I wanted to drive first, man. That cool?"

"Sure."

"I don't see you in awhile. Where you been?"

"Drunk."

"That why you quit?"

"Yeah."

"Sometimes it's good to be drunk."

"Yeah."

"Drinking don't improve your talking, man." She smiled and pushed down on the accelerator.

When we walked into Dianne's apartment, she pulled the cord to the socket with the naked light bulb in it. She smiled at me and plopped on her easy chair. I sat on the sofa and watched the shadows we made in the room. "How's Eddie?"

Dianne grabbed either side of her knit shirt and pulled it over her head. She sat in front of me in her bra, with the rolls of fat already forming in her young belly, and said, "He got into a fight with a bad man in San Antonio." When I first met her, she was nineteen, dark, and attractive. She had walked into Gerald Mendoza's campaign office (I was running his campaign) to see what was going on—because, to a nineteen-year-old stuck in a dead-end town with no real chance of escape, anything new or different might cause some excitement. I gave her some literature and my speech about a solid Hispanic voting block supporting several county officials to work against the old bosses. "Bad shit going down, huh," she had said with her smile and cocky manner. She brought in Eddie Sanchez, and for something to do, a way to be together, or a plan to convince themselves that they were important, they stuffed envelopes and rung the door bells of their neighbors. After I sensed I was losing Victoria, I noticed Dianne Natividad's youth, vibrancy, spirit, and susceptibility to seduction. Then again, maybe the nineteen-year-old stuck in a boring town where sex was practically the only entertainment, seduced me.

"What's going to happen to him?"

"Got to do some time in the county jail." She stood

up and walked toward me, reaching behind her and unfastening her bra. She smiled as she freed her breasts, then giggled as she pushed my face into her chest.

I closed my eyes and tried to imagine Victoria's face above Dianne's breasts. And, after we moved into her bedroom, as I felt the angles of her body, I kept my eyes closed and tried to remember Victoria's face and body during our sex.

As I lay in bed, in those silent moments after love-making with someone I wasn't in love with, hypnotized by shadows, light, and relaxation, I looked away from Dianne and thought, dreamed, or fantasized. Dianne was equally silent. For the first time I could remember, she didn't want to talk afterwards. "Why you with me?" I asked.

"Women gots to have it to." She raised up on one shoulder and drew a circle in my chest with her forefinger.

"You have Eddie?"

"Even in high school I like all men."

"Eddie's a fine young man."

Dianne raised up. "Some crazy, big-ass Vato just jumps him you know. And he don't do nothing. So he hits the *cabrón* back, and two more guys jump in, you know. And poor Eddie got his face all beat to shit."

Still staring away from her, I said, "Did he get to a hospital?"

"Some doctor came into his cell and put some stuff on his face. You know, the police and shit, they just aren't fair."

"Yeah."

"I hear maybe you got some problems."

I rolled toward her, and she rolled toward me, and while we looked at each other, we came close to really caring. "Do you love Eddie?"

She smiled, "Pretty much, I guess. But I love you too, Roger."

I smiled because I admired her simple tact and good

will. "No, you don't love me."

"A little."

"Maybe a little, so I am going to give you a present."

She sat up in bed, making it bounce, smiling like a kid, "What you got, man?"

"You know my trailer?"

"Yeah."

"It's yours and Eddie's. Rent free. Don't let my brother-in-law or anybody else charge you anything or run you out."

"Oh, no, I can't live next to your ol' lady, man."

"She knows about us, and she won't bother you. Ask her for a job. She'll let you and Eddie help her clean and mow and sell Cokes in the summer."

She hung her head as I squinted in the dark to try to see her face. "Where you going?" she said and raised her face that had a few swelling tears in her eyes but that also had a real smile.

"I'm going back to Austin."

Dianne looked intently at me, like she was about to cry. "Take care of your family," she said.

It was the most serious conversation that I ever had with Dianne.

* * *

Since taking "Jackson," off their store front sign, Schmidt and Howard had made enough money to buy the top floor of the house that served as their office. Close enough to campus for providing cheap legal advice to students; newly surrounded by fashionable, remodeled condominiums full of newly transferred northerners worried about city zoning, limitations on development, and divorces; near the legislators' hang-out down the street at Scholz's beer garden; Howard and Schmidt were doing well enough to start families and move to the rural suburbs on the western fringe of Austin. They didn't want another partner to cut into profits, but they let me sleep in an upstairs room and do some clerical work for them and some light-weight legal work: threatening letters, notarizing, small claims court cases.

The window in my upstairs room, faced the thick bough of a old, sprawling Oak. I could look out of it in the mornings that were getting just a bit cooler and drier as fall crept slowly to central Texas, see sparrows and Mexican doves, and listen to their songs and the cicadas buzzing. In the evenings, I could sit on the front porch of the old house and watch the students hustling past me to get to the cheapest happy hours in town and the new-young-rich jogging or bicycling by.

I got drunk a couple of times, smoked dope nightly. But you build up a tolerance, as Clayton Tanner might say, or you get depressed. I also thought it unseemly for a "bright" lawyer looking for a real job to be getting fucked up in a law office, so I gave up dope and cut down on drinking. For consolation, I wrote to Clayton Tanner. He wrote back to say that, to leave love truly behind, you must transcend it. And to transcend it, you must be one with it. I didn't feel like becoming one with anything other than a decent wage. I wrote Becky. She offered a loan. I even telephoned my parents. They also offered a loan. I refused both Becky's and my parent's money.

On a Saturday morning, a month into my exile, I sat on the porch of *Howard & Schmidt's* law office and watched Kyle's big, clumsy Buick Regal drive slowly down my street. I could see Kyle looking through the passenger window at the addresses of the houses. He saw me and struggled to park it on the narrow side street. He got out of the Buick with his hands in his pockets and nodded his head. I waved. He nervously walked up the steps to the porch and sat beside me in a wicker chair. The good late October air was clear and cooling. The mid-town streets were deserted because UT was playing a football game. Kyle had fought the traffic around the stadium to come see me. He sniffed at the air and looked around him. "This area is changing a lot."

"It's still old," I said.

"Lot of restoration and redevelopment. Had I known a few years ago, I'd have moved Suzy and the kids into this area." I smiled and held my tongue.

"You want a cup of coffee or iced tea?" I asked.

"Don't you drink beer anymore?"

"Sure," I said.

After I got him a beer, Kyle leaned his elbows on to his knees, twisted his head away from me, and bounced one foot. He jerked his head toward me, then away, then back to me.

"You want to say something, Kyle?"

"Just dropped by you know. See how you were doing." I nodded my head. "So how you doing?"

"Fine," I said.

"Good," he said.

"Did Victoria ask you to drop by?"

"No, I just thought. . . Yeah, she did ask. And we still go out on Sundays, so I thought I'd let her know tomorrow."

"Tell her that I'm poor, as always, but I have renewed hope."

Kyle nodded and straightened his leg to reach in his pocket. He pulled out a wad a bills. I saw a hundred folded across the top. He held the wad of money cradled in his hands then shoved it toward me. "Here," he said.

I was tempted to grab the money then give a whoop. "Did Victoria ask you to give me money?"

He pushed the money closer toward me. "No. It's my money, my offer."

"Come on Kyle. I don't want Victoria's money."

"It's my money, promise, really. Take it."

"No, Kyle," I said but thought to grab the wad. I touched it when I pushed it back toward him.

Kyle no longer ducked me, but grunted slightly and looked straight at me, like the time he gave me the man-to-man talk about his pregnant sister. "Look, Victoria, Henry, and me, we owe you. I don't want us to have any more debts over our heads. Take it. And anything else you want, you let me know."

I stared down at the money, "Kyle you don't owe me." He fingered the wad and rested it in his palm. He looked at me, trying to give me something.

"What if I tell you I'm feeling sorry for you?" He dangled the money in front of me. "I guess I know what it could be like if my wife suddenly just became uninterested in me."

I patted his shoulder. "No, Kyle. I can't take money from you now." I pulled my hand from his shoulder, then looked at him. "I tell you what, though. I'd like a TV set."

Kyle unfolded his wad, peeled two fifties and handed them to me. He relaxed, leaned back in his wicker chair with his arms stretched over the top of it. "You know, you get on your feet, you ought to go in with me in buying and redoing one of these old houses. Nothing turns a quick buck like good rental property."

"I'll certainly keep it in mind, Kyle," I said, feeling good about letting Kyle help me and, for once, feeling sorry for him.

Chapter 13:
Bolen Resorts

Betty, Buck Cronin's secretary, sits behind her typewriter, stares through her half-framed glasses at the document she is supposedly proofreading, lightly rocks in her squeaking swivel chair, and pretends not to be trying to hear what goes on in Buck Cronin's office. I sit across from Betty, smile at her, and listen myself for some distinct meaningful sound, something other than the low grumble of voices coming from behind Buck's closed door. I have no real reason for being here, but just for once, I want to see the result of my *work*.

Buck's door slowly creaks open, and an arm with a lawyer's blue, pin-striped suit sleeve wrapped around it holds the door open for Kay Menger. She comes through the door with her head hung down. She is trying to keep more tears from running down her cheek and staining the collar of her white blouse. Her eyes seem to have sunken farther into her skull, leaving shadows around them. She too wears a suit. Next, Kay's lawyer, Fred C. Flynn, comes through the door. Kay has not chosen well. And I can see from his drooping jowls and shoulders, his fake smile, the way he hesitantly touches the elbow of his client that Fred C. Flynn has just gotten his ass kicked.

Buck Cronin doesn't smile. He has done this enough to know just the right officious look that hides any gloating, smugness, or elation that he might feel. He is as classy an act as he can be, given his job. Mr. Kay Menger does smile, way too broadly, the kind of taunting smile a jock would smile after he has caught the touchdown pass and wants to point the nose of ball at the defender he has just beaten. He too wears a suit.

I grab my hat and stand as Ms. Kay Menger walks in front of me. She stops to look at me. "I'm the guy who took the pictures," I say. "I am sorry." This admission is why I came. It makes all the pieces fit, shows all the hands. Kay Menger will hurt some more, but at least I can give her the whole truth, the way reality lurked around with me in my pickup and then bit her in the ass. Now, at least she need not wonder where she went wrong.

She looks around her. First at her lawyer, Fred C. Flynn, and he can offer no support, no advice, next at her soon-to-be former husband, who only smiles some more, next at Buck, who looks at me like I've lost my mind. Even Betty looks at me.

I twirl the old Stetson in my hands. "How can you ruin people's lives?" Kay Menger asks me. Inside Buck Cronin's private office, Fred C. Flynn talked for her. Outside, with me, where she can be "unofficial," she can put her confusion and anger into words. This too, I give her.

"Someone leaves you, or you leave someone, and your life will be ruined. At least for awhile. With or without someone like me," I tell her, and Buck Cronin rushes past me to Kay and tries to lead her out of his office.

She breathes deeply as though to get out what she has to say in one breath. "But the point is, though, that you were paid to interfere." Her hand started to shake, her lips quivered. "You were paid to hurt me."

"Ms. Menger," I say, and Kay looks at me. "I'm not really sorry for what I did, but I am sorry." Kay turns away from Buck to look at me. "Do you understand at all?"

She stares at me for just a moment. It is a blank stare,

as though Kay's mind cannot work fast enough to deal with me, the lawyers, the photos, and a ruined life. Her eyebrows knit as she tries to speak. She is desperate. She wants to hurt somebody. She looks down at my hat. "That's an ugly hat."

I look down at my hat as Buck leads the whole party to his office door. As they file out, I walk into Buck's peach and cream colored office and sit in one of the three padded chairs in front of his desk.

Buck comes in and says, "Jesus, Roger. You gone soft, crazy, addled?"

Buck takes off his coat and throws it on the conference table across from his desk. He hooks his index finger over the knot of his tie and pulls at his shirt collar. He sits down as I explain, "Seems I finally did the least I could do."

Buck reaches into his front drawer and pulls out a pack of cigarettes and fumbles with it as he pulls out a cigarette and puts it between his lips. "Now she'll probably tell her neighbors, and you won't be able to drive any place in town without people pulling their kids inside and closing their blinds."

Next Buck reaches into a deeper, longer drawer and pulls out a bottle of scotch and two glasses. He pours both of us a drink, scoots a filled glass close to me, sips his scotch, then lights his cigarette. "What the hell, huh? She gets to keep the kids but loses the house, and nobody goes before a judge."

"Happy ever after," I say.

"Doesn't get any easier," Buck says as a curve of smoke wraps around his head. A vein in his neck seems to push against his buttoned up shirt. Another vein stands out in his forehead as though big spurts of blood gush through it. He's probably due for his first heart attack.

I sip my scotch and get ready to bullshit with Buck in order to help him celebrate and calm down. Buck and I are in the truth business. We ferret it out and then hold it up in front of the faces of the innocent, and if they refuse to recognize the truth, Buck pushes their noses into it. Then, when we can, we leave our jobs and console ourselves with our own fantasies.

I console myself with the thought that Becky will soon be back, and I wonder how to entertain her.

* * *

After two northers passed through and started what there is of a Central Texas winter, I began driving to Fischer on Saturday afternoons. I'd get a beer at Marie's and, usually, drive out Ranch Road 12 to look at Henry's property, but I could never force myself to stop to see Victoria. I knew better than to see her after I worked all week on forgetting about her. On a cold, clear Saturday morning, right before Christmas, right after cold, wet weather hit on a Friday night, I pulled off Ranch Road 12 to look up at the house.

Kyle had put a wooden sign up over the entrance: *Bolen Resorts.* Someone was painting the letters blue and the sign red but had yet to finish the whole sign or all of *Resort.* Dianne Natividad's '72 Chevy Impala was parked in front of the trailer next to Eddie Sanchez's Dodge convertible. The cloth top was torn to strips that hung into the interior of the car. Their clothes were hung on a sagging wire clothesline that they had stretched from the trailer to an iron pole several feet away. Henry's road twisting off Ranch Road 12 had pea gravel spread evenly over it, and more brush and cedar had been cleared from it. The bulldozer was parked on the side of the new road, and next to it was a freshly painted, pre-fab, wooden shack with an open front. Kyle must have pictured Victoria in it, hawking Cokes to the swimmers. Victoria's Comet wasn't parked in front of Henry's house as it usually was.

When I drove back to town, I saw Victoria's Comet

parked in front of the C & J Grocery. I slowed down to see if I could see her, then looked away to the other side of the truck as she walked out of the grocery with her arms loaded with two bags. I couldn't see if she noticed me; she certainly couldn't have waved. But I looked in the rear view mirror as I drove by her and saw her standing by the Comet staring after me. I squinted and slowed to a crawl to try to see her face, her body, to see if she had changed with me gone, but I could see only that she had let her blonde hair grow longer and that her body was as lithe and as thin and as hard as ever.

I pulled in Marie's to give her the chance to see my truck and come to see me if she wanted to; then I debated about stopping at all and slipped the truck in reverse. But I muttered a good goddamn to myself, turned off the motor, and went into Marie's.

It was too cold for the Mexicans to be outside, and no one but Pete, Sam, and ol' Doc Jack Hillier were inside. The large windows that didn't fit squarely into their frames let drafts from outside into the bar. To compensate, Marie had turned on her pot-bellied stove, which used to burn wood but now consumed too much gas, to full strength. As I walked across the floor, I felt the layers of heat and draft. Pete and Sam were at their usual table, and ol' Doc Hillier had joined them for dominoes. Pete shuffled the dominoes with his stiff, horny fingers, and Doc Hillier pulled a cigarette out of Sam's Pall Mall pack and handed it to him. Sam took the cigarette, eased it toward his mouth with his shaking hands, and rested it on his lip. He reached for his lighter, held it in both hands up toward his mouth, and tried to coordinate his quivering lip with his shaking hands. Doc Hillier finally grabbed Sam's hands and held them still long enough for Sam to light the cigarette. "Sam's hands are beginning to quiver like a field lark's ass," I heard Pete say to Jack.

"Looky here," Pete said as he shuffled dominoes. "Ol'

Roger's back in town again." Sam waved a shaky hand, and Doc nodded his head.

"You can come on take fourth, so we can play partners," Sam said. I grabbed a wooden folding chair and unfolded it between Sam and Jack, so I could see out the front windows toward the street.

"How you doing?" Jack asked me.

"Fair," I said.

"That divorce stuff is kind of like getting eat by a wolf and shit off a cliff," Pete said. I was glad to have my divorce out in front of them.

Evelyn came to me from around the bar and sat a Coors Lite in front of me, the brand I usually drank in Marie's, and patted me on the back then hugged me. I squeezed her arm as I looked up at her then reached into my pocket. "First one this morning is on the house," she said and went back behind the bar.

"Forty-two," Pete said, "you be my partner," and we reached into the bone pile for our dominoes. I stood my dominoes up with the backs facing the others and the dots facing me, then looked up and out Marie's front window to see Victoria in her Comet, grocery shopping done, pass by. She must have seen my truck, couldn't have missed it, surely, but she didn't even stop in to say hello.

After the first two games, which Pete and I split with Jack and Sam, I asked the men if they had ever heard Henry mention Shorty Martins. Jack wrinkled his brows, but Pete immediately said, "Oh hell, yeah. He's the cowboy Henry talked about."

"Yeah, yeah," Sam said and pounded the table as he remembered.

"He tell you about the night ol' Shorty convinced him to join the army?" Pete said and raised an elbow.

I lied and said, "no," to let Pete and Sam tell the story and to let Jack Hillier listen.

We played on, then stopped to talk some more, and

Doc Hillier mentioned Emma Shuler. The three beers I had drunk while talking about Shorty and playing dominoes gave me a slightly buzzing head, but not enough from keeping me from recognizing the name that Henry mentioned as he died. "She was a cedar chopper," Doc Hillier said.

The first three beers seduced me into thinking I could have more without thinking of Victoria. But I was wrong, so I drank more and more, and instead of concentrating on the game of forty-two, I could see only her face in my mind and think about the first years I knew her. And as much as I could convince myself, even drunk, that it would be a terrible mistake to drive out to Henry's property, all I wanted to do was see her. Sam got mad at me for losing. "Goddamn watch the spots, Roger."

I began to ask questions: "Who was she seeing?"

"Nobody," Pete said.

"When did she come into town? How was she looking? Was she healthy?"

"Young men got their minds all crowded up with sex. Can't play no dominoes cause of sex on their minds," Pete said and slapped Sam on the back. "You are young your ol' prick gets so hard a cat couldn't scratch it."

"Hell to be old," Sam said. "Don't get no more hard -on's. Just get a thick-on now and then."

"Damned, if I don't know it," Pete said. "Old man told me the other day, making love at his age is like putting an oyster in a parking meter."

"I know an old whore done so many old men, she can play pool with a rope," Sam said to match Pete.

Jack looked at the two of them, then said, "Ya'll two shut up for awhile."

I got up and said, "I'm going to go see her." But ol' Doc Hillier grabbed my arm and tugged with a lot of strength. He hadn't said much during the entire game, "I'm no psychologist. But you shouldn't go see her yet."

Evelyn walked over and said, "Anything wrong?"

"I have to see my wife," I said.

"No you don't," Jack said. "She ain't your wife no more."

"How the hell you know," I said and jerked my arm away from him.

"Come sit down play some more dominoes," Sam said.

"Let him go home," Evelyn said. I looked at her trying to figure out if "home" meant Henry's or Austin.

"Go back to Austin," Jack said. "It'd be best for you."

Sam looked up at me. His eyes were sunken deep into his skull and surrounded by wrinkled, hanging skin; eyes that looked like Henry's when Henry was dying. He looked like sadness and loneliness and too many years of living with both. He grabbed the table to steady his hands and said to me, "You just got to get used to it Roger, boy. Ain't nothing else that you can do." Sam, I could see, would be the next to die.

I had thought, less than a year before, that I had grown tired of the same old stories and jokes from Sam, Pete, and Henry. But I missed Henry's stories. I would even have liked to have looked at his trigger finger. And, in less than a year, these old men no longer seemed mean, just old and tired and trying as desperately as Henry to hold on to some dignity and their past. I had thought that I was separate from these old men, different from them. I had thought that I would rid the world of them. Turns out, I was just like them. So I went home to Austin.

* * *

The soles of my New Balance slap the gravel, and the shock goes into my ankle, up to my knee, settles in my hip. Just moments, running was no effort. I was both my running and beyond it. I was the movement itself. Runner's high. My feet were me, but their movement was no effort. I passed the oriental coed, other joggers.

But the feeling left, or I lost it. My feet plop, strain to maintain my pace.

Why do I jog? Jogging gives you endurance. Endurance leads to strength. To do my job, I need endurance. To keep my job, to live with it, I need strength. Buck Cronin has strength and endurance. Kyle is strong, but his strength comes from his misguided notions, not endurance. Victoria's endurance has made her strong but changed her. Becky had strength first, then endurance. Henry endured only. He never got that strong. Finally, he was weak. Kaye Menger, from what I know, is weak. Clayton Tanner is weak.

For all my jogging and its endurance, I remain weak. Thank God.

* * *

I started jogging when I joined Buck Cronin. With Buck, I honed my craft for finding people and realized our need for endurance. After I joined Buck, my truck started choking when I stopped it on busy streets; then it finally died. For a few days, I jogged to work and borrowed a "junker" from a friend of Buck's to make my rounds. Then I called my parents, and after small talk about health and rain, I told them about my truck and asked for a loan for a down payment. "Why just a loan?" my father asked. "What kind of car do you want? Let me buy it for you."

"Dad, please," I said, "just a loan. A loan is hard enough. Don't buy me anything."

I could hear the rhythm of his voice pick up, the joy in it, "I'll send you a credit card."

"I have a credit card. I just need a loan," I said firmly. "I'll let you know how much."

"Don't worry about money," my father said.

I heard excited breaths from my mother who was listening on the extension line. "Oh, Roger, thank you," she breathed in to regain some graciousness. "I'm so glad you came to your senses about our money."

"It's just a loan," I said.

"Interest free," my father said.

I felt that I was weak. I couldn't maintain my principles about taking money from people. Now, I feel good about letting my parents help me.

I put two thousand down on a brand new blue Toyota truck with a white stripe across its side, a stereo radio and tape player, radial tires, and a working air conditioner. I moved out of the upstairs of Howard & Schmidt's office and into Buck's reasonably cheap townhouse (he gave me a special deal) in exclusive West Austin, where people can pretend that they live in the country. The view from my bedroom window looks over several rooftops to a large, wooded, undeveloped hill. And indeed, I sometimes think that I am living on Hill Country property.

I wrote to Becky about my new job. Rather than write, she called me and congratulated me for over an hour. Then I started to jog. Within a month, I was jogging three miles a day.

With a new truck, a flat belly, and a good job, I thought I was well enough to see Victoria. It was spring, and a hot sun sizzled the dampness left from an all night shower and sent steam rising on the Hill Country limestone. The pastures were full of bluebonnets, Indian Pinks, and sunflowers. Ranch Road 12 was clogged with Austinites or San Antonians out looking at, and occasionally picking, the bluebonnets, a Hill Country tradition. I turned the air on in my new Toyota pickup, breathed in the pungent smell of the new vinyl and cloth, and looked at the pink, blue, yellow, and green coloring on the sides of the hills. I even stopped alongside the road, like some of the old grandmas and little kids, and illegally picked some bluebonnets. I stuck some behind my visor and put some others in the hat band of Henry's Stetson.

The "Bolen's Resort" sign in bright red and blue hung across Henry's cattle guard. Beyond it, farther up the main road, on the new road to the creek, the concession stand with a large lettered *Coke* and *Sno Cones* printed across its sides was bright white in the sun. I turned into Henry's newly bulldozed road under the sign and drove past my old trailer home. Dianne Natividad's '72 Impala, leaning toward a flat tire, seemed to be slowly dying in front of the trailer home. Beer cans, a milk carton, and a rusting barbecue pit were in the front yard. Dianne Natividad was hanging clothes onto the sagging wire lines strung between the trailer and the steel post. I slowed my pickup down to see her. She saw me, smiled broadly, dropped a wet shirt into her laundry basket, and ran toward me.

She rested her elbows against the frame of my open window. "Goddamn, Roger. *Que Pasa?* Like what you been doing?"

"Working for a living."

Dianne stepped back and looked at the truck. "Pretty sharp wheels, man."

"Big times and fast bucks," I said.

"Guess what, man," she said.

"What?"

"I got pregnant, Roger." She stood straight up and patted her belly that was beginning to bulge a little more than normal.

"Eddie's?" I asked.

She slapped at me, "Oh, come on, man, sure." She leaned back into my window. "I'm going to be a good mamma. I guess I'm not going to spend no more nights with you."

"That's grand."

"The funny words, still. I'm going to miss you." I kissed her on the forehead again, then slipped the truck into first to get up the hill.

As I drove away from Dianne and up toward Henry's

house, I looked out of the window to see Eddie Sanchez coming out of the trailer house. He was pulling an undershirt over his head.

I saw Victoria peek out of a window as I pulled up in front of the house. I got out of my truck and looked back down at Eddie's and Dianne's trailer. As I walked up the steps toward the veranda, Victoria opened the door for me and waited by it. She was gaining some of her old weight back. Her cheeks were not as gaunt; the sides of her thighs were pushing against the inside legs of her jeans; she had lost the sun-baked tan she had when I moved out. Her hair was curled. She wore sandals, and her toenails were red. I scraped some of the mud off my running shoes on the top step of the veranda.

"Where's your boots?" Victoria asked and smiled.

"I jog now. Have three pairs of these."

"No boots?"

"Just my old pair."

I took a step toward her, and she backed up. "Is there a purpose or is this just a visit?"

"A social call to my ex-wife."

"Good. That's fine. I'm glad to see you. Come in," she said and turned into the doorway. I followed her in and shut the door behind me.

The living room had been repainted and some ferns in pots were placed in several corners. The old couch was re-upholstered. "Kyle insisted," Victoria said when she saw me looking. I smiled because I had guessed Kyle was responsible. "I have fresh lemonade and beer," she said.

I sat in the newly re-upholstered couch and rubbed the rough texture of the cloth and smelled its newness. I looked at the ceiling and the walls and could see none of the cracks in the paint and plaster nor could I smell any of the old man odor of Henry. Victoria came back out of the kitchen with two lemonades, handed me one, and sat on the other end of the couch. "Does the rest of the house look like this?" I asked.

"Henry's bedroom is the same, but Kyle pulled down all of our old kiddie wallpaper."

"No more Lone Ranger?"

"I miss it."

Victoria cocked her head to one side and stared at me. "The hat still looks good on you," she said. I chuckled, took Henry's hat off and twirled it in my hands, then leaned it so she could see the bluebonnets. The point at the pinch in the crown had torn more and formed a bigger hole. "The bluebonnets add some dash. . . I was glad you got it."

"So how's life?" I asked

She shrugged her shoulders, then said, "Kyle tells me you're doing well."

"Okay."

"Is it good enough for you?"

"Is this still good enough for you?"

Her smiled disappeared. "I want to be friendly to you."

"Just a question."

Her smile came back, and I tried to look pleasant too and regretted coming. "I thought I wouldn't be nervous around you." Victoria stopped talking and smiling and looked away from me. "I guess I'm not ready to see you."

"Nonsense," she said but didn't look at me. "There's no reason to get hung up on all of this. We know each other. We've got to be friends."

"Maybe it's this house."

She turned to look and me, took my hand, and said, "Well then, why don't we get in your new truck, and I'll show you the changes."

* * *

I was glad to get out of the house, to look at the place, to have something trivial to talk about. And my new Toyota took the bumps in Henry's back road real well. I turned off the air and rolled down the windows. The sun shone through the windshield and side windows in beams full of motes while dust blew up behind the truck. Victoria's pinkening cheeks caught the sunlight and turned red, her blonde hair, recently curled, lit up her face and made her eyes even bluer.

As we came back by the house, Victoria told me that Kyle had given up on the stables; no one in San Antonio or Austin wanted to be so far away from his horses. So the stables were crumbling, but Kyle planned to bulldoze them and build a lighted tennis court. I drove down the road from Henry's house and turned down Kyle's new road. The bald-headed fat man had bulldozed it smooth and scattered pea gravel over it, so you didn't need a truck to get to Bolen Resorts.

Kyle had cleared out the brush and left only the tall cottonwoods and cypress. He planted carpet grass, ferns, and hedges. He even built a native stone sidewalk to his Resort. Kyle had built four small duplexes with back porches facing Fischer creek. He had a pier with a diving board hanging over the deep pool. He had a swing set, and several ropes strung up in the limbs of the tall trees, so kids could play Tarzan and swing out over the river and splash into the water. We got out of the truck and stepped into the grass. Victoria reached down to take off her sandals and walked barefooted in the carpet grass. "It's cool," she said.

I sat down it the grass and pulled off my tennis shoes and socks and walked barefooted with her around the cabins. I stopped walking. "I feel better now."

"See. Good. No reason we can't be friends." The word *friends* hurt like a stab wound from the inside out.

I swallowed hard and followed her to the pier. We walked out to its edge over the deep green pool where we had skinny dipped. She stared into the water, and I sat down, then lay down on my back to listen to the cicadas and the rapids from farther up the creek. The sun felt good on my face, so I took my shirt off and wadded it up for a pillow. Victoria sat down on the diving board. "Jesus, this is nice," I said. "It's been nearly a year since I've been in Hill Country water."

"Go for it," Victoria said.

I stood unbuckled my jeans, slid out of the legs, and pulled off my underwear. Victoria silently looked at me, gasped, and quickly scooted to one side as I stepped past her and on to the diving board. She laughed as I tested the spring of the board. "You're crazy," she said, and I dove off.

The seventy-degree water sent a chill down my neck, through my back, and into by butt and legs. But as I took a couple of strokes under the water, I got used to the chill and felt cooled. I broke to the top of the water, shook my head, and began to swim. The feel of spring-fed, limestone-purified, cold but revitalizing Hill Country water came back to me. It is a pleasure that makes you concentrate just on it, nothing else, no problems. I tread water. Then I saw Victoria standing naked on the edge of the diving board.

I looked through the drops of water that clung to my eyelashes and clouded my vision to see her take a test spring on the board. She was not growing younger as I had thought. Her breasts and hips were starting to sag. Her thighs were starting to round out, like she had padding under her skin. She had a curling puffiness just under the belt line. With the water out of my eyes, I saw the sun highlight the wrinkles forming around her chin and above her upper lip. She was, in fact, losing youth and starting to mature. She looked a little more like her mother. And I was suddenly sad that I was not seeing her age nor aging with her.

She dove into the water in front of me and came up beside me laughing. I dunked her and started to swim for the shallow water. She swam after me. "Roger, this is crazy," she yelled after me.

I got to waist-deep water, stood, turned toward her to see her swim up to me. She stood beside me, smiling at me. Then her smile disappeared, and she said, "Roger?" She folded her hands over her breasts, suddenly blushed, and stared down at the water.

I stepped toward her as fast as I could in the water, sent a wake behind me, wrapped my arms around her, and kissed her. Her arms trapped in front of her chest, she tried to push me away, wriggled, and turned her head away from me. We made swirls and splashes of water as I tried to twist her back around toward me to kiss her. I kissed her neck, but she jerked her head around and gave me a bump on my lip. I let go of her and slowly eased away from her. She hit me in the shoulder with the heel of her hand, pushed me; then we both stopped to stare at each other; she again folded her hands over her breasts, and I turned and sloshed through the water to the bank.

I stepped into the grass, walked to the pier and lay belly down on the pier. She walked to the bank and sat on it with her arms still folded over her breasts. "Damn, I guess I'm sorry," I said after awhile. Victoria looked up a me but said nothing.

"I'm sorry, Roger."

"Jesus fucking Christ," I said. "What's wrong with us?" An answer, a discussion would have helped, but she withdrew into one hazy silence. "What just happened? What did I do? Do you have another man?" She said nothing. So I put on my clothes and walked across the carpet grass toward my truck without looking back at Victoria.

* * *

That night in Buck Cronin's townhouse in West Austin, I stared at the ceiling of my dark bedroom until late in the night, caught in something that was not sleep but was not consciousness either. In the dark and in that peculiar state where you can sense things but do nothing about the sensations, I thought I felt or heard somebody in the room. I knew better than to open my eyes, for I knew if did, my mind would conjure up Victoria and make her stand in front of me, or worse, lie down beside me. When the lights came on, I damn near shit green twinkies.

Rather than Victoria, Eddie Sanchez was standing in front of my bed. His long, ragged hair was a tangled mess on top of his head. A mustache, which was just long hairs, curled over his top lip and into his mouth. The sleeves of his shirt were unbuttoned and twisted on his arms. One side of his front shirt tail hung out. The redness in his eyes, his crooked stare gave away his drunkenness. He held a knife in his hand.

"Hello, Eddie," I said.

"Fuck you, man," he said.

"What's the knife for?"

"It's how I got in here, *pendejo*."

"You ought to put it up."

"I maybe out to put it up your ass."

I rose up in bed and tried to think of what to do. "Put it up. No reason to do anything."

"All that political shit you talk is a bunch of shit. What good's it do you now?" He stepped toward me. "What you think of me now, huh? You think I'm some no-good Mexican?"

"I think you're drunk."

He chuckled, shrugged his shoulder. He stepped back, leaned against the wall, then slid his back down it until he was sitting on the floor, his knees up under his chin. He folded the knife up and stuck it into his pocket. "I can be bad, you know. But I'm too drunk to be bad now."

"I know," I said, folded the sheet and bedspread off of me, and sat up in bed.

"So now we all know about me. What about you,

man? Huh? Huh, man?" he asked.

I leaned against the back board of my bed and crossed my legs in front of me. "I'm just trying to get by, Eddie. Just like you."

"Bull shit. You white patty, son of a bitch. You talk shit about *La Raza* and fairness and shit and you fuck my old lady."

I saw what the problem was. "Is that what you're here about?"

"No shit. You pretty smart."

"Eddie, it was nothing between us."

"She told me," he said and hung his head. "She told me she was really nothing to you. How can she be shit to a big time white guy with a new truck. You don't want some poor Mexican girl."

I was growing tired of his self pity. I had enough of my own. "Stop your crying Eddie. You're not cut out for it."

He chuckled a bit. "You think you know so much, huh," he said and pointed at me. "You give me a place to live. You give me a job. It's nigger work, not like what you do, but it's a job. Why?"

"Because I like you. Eddie, I—"

He interrupted me, "You always talk bullshit. I should never taken your trailer, man. Should have told Dianne never take shit from *gringos* who talk shit. Better to steal from shit talking *gringos*."

"It's a gift, goddamn it. I wouldn't have done it, if . . ."

"More bullshit. It was a gift for Dianne. It was to piss off your ol' lady. It was a Hail Mary. But it wasn't no gift for me."

"Get out of here, Eddie," I said.

Eddie stood up. "Still talking shit," he said. "You know what I was going to do? Huh? I was going to steal your new truck and haul my ass to Houston. But I thought maybe I wanted to see you."

"What about Dianne?"

"Fuck her," Eddie said. "You so smart, you tell me if I should stay with Dianne. She don't fuck just you, you know."

"Eddie, I know a woman who could tell you about the high price you have to pay for running out on a family."

"You talking shit again. You ran out on your old lady."

"I was kicked out."

Eddie looked at me, cocked his head. "Got to be a reason you got kicked out."

I shrugged my shoulder, "Unlucky, I guess."

"More bullshit."

I looked away from Eddie, no longer concerned with him, and at my dark ceiling. I looked back at him to see that he was looking away from me, no longer really concerned with me but talking to himself. "So how you feel now? You just seen your old lady, and now you sleeping by yourself. How you feel?"

"I feel like shit, Eddie, " I said.

"What if you could go back?'

I thought for a moment and saw the impossibility of ever going back. "I'd kick you out of the trailer, whip your ass, whatever it would take."

Eddie laughed. "So why did you keep fucking Dianne?"

"Cause I talk shit, Eddie. And Dianne liked it."

Eddie chuckled, pulled his knife out of his pocket, and leaned into my footboard. He threw the folded up knife on the foot of my bed. "I guess maybe I talk some shit, too."

He turned and opened the door. "I'll open the front door for you," I said.

"No. I got in. I get myself out," he said, flipped off the light, and walked into my dark house. I sat on the side of the bed, then got up, felt along the wall, went into the dark hall, down the stairs, and looked out the front window of my townhouse at Eddie backing out of my driveway in Dianne's '72 Chevy Impala.

* * *

By June, I was up to five miles. I learned to like the humidity that beaded my body with sweat, making me aware of my body and my fatigue. And I followed the other joggers to Baron Springs, paid my buck fifty, and swam a few laps in the cool water. After swimming, I could lie in the carpet grass around Barton Springs, listen to the cicadas in the trees, close my eyes, and let the sun dry me.

I called my parents once a week. Each ran to a telephone (they had three in the house), so they could talk to me at the same time. Sometimes they talked to each other over the extensions. And I promised, before summer was out, I would spend a few days at home. I even looked forward to being back in River Oaks, sitting outside in the old gazebo and looking up at their prancing squirrels. I stopped going for weekend drives to Fischer.

I wrote Clayton Tanner and told him how crazy I got. I got a return letter saying that all Taos was praying to an assortment of gods for me. I wrote to Becky but got no answer. Then, in mid August, a year after Henry died, Becky Bolen called me. It was time now, she said, for her to see her kids. She wanted me to make arrangements and "escort" her to the southside of San Antonio and to Henry's property, which had now become Bolen's Resort.

Chapter 14:
Highland Park

Yesterday, I spotted her among the other passengers unloading from the Oklahoma City flight. She wore a wide-brimmed straw hat with a chin strap. She carried her purse and a hat box. She held the hat box out to me. Inside was a genuine Monte Cristo straw hat. It was a gift from Becky. She had sent Clayton Tanner to a hat shop in Santa Fe and had him order the finely-woven, soft straw hat. It was the most expensive piece of clothing that I owned. Henry's hat hung from a peg on my wall.

"Try it on," she said. It felt good the moment I put it on my head. Becky smiled in that shit-eating way of hers, wrinkles spread from the corners of her eyes, and I couldn't help but wrap my arms around her. She had gained weight.

When I stepped back from her, I saw that her stomach had rounded more and her hips had spread out more. She saw me looking. "Put on some weight," she said.

"You look fine," I said.

"You know why though?"

"Why?"

"I quit smoking," she said proudly.

I stood back and looked at her. "That's right. I didn't even notice. No smoke. Nothing in your mouth."

"No cough." She stuck out one hip, making her body a series of angles. "I threw them," she says. "I went into my backyard and just threw them. My last pack. Haven't touched them since."

"You'll feel better?"

"Hell, life is too short. Damn disgusting habit. And after this trip, I start on a diet. First cigarettes go, now fat."

We went to the baggage claim area, I reached for her suitcase, and she pulled it away from me. "I've been carrying my own luggage for a long time, now." She lugged it all the way to my new Toyota truck. Once we got to it, I grabbed the suitcase and slung it over the side and into the back. Her suitcase was incredibly heavy.

For dinner, I treated her to Mexican food. She ate the large plate with a flauta on the side. She damn near finished everything and said, "I'm a pig, but you just can't get good Mexican food in Oklahoma. I miss it."

This morning, even though I have my air-conditioner on high, she rolls down the window of my Toyota truck and lets the air whip her short hair around. We are on an investigation as well as a holiday. It is not yet noon, and we have taken the small, winding roads off to the West of I-35 from Austin to San Marcos. I ask if she would like to go by Fischer, but she wants to save that trip. We take the backroads along I-35 from San Antonio to San Antonio. We both get a sense that soon, there would be no backroads.

She rolls up her window. Her short hair is in a mess around head and across her forehead. She smiles and reminds me of those dogs that like to stick their noses out through a crack in the window. She enjoys everything in the present. Now we were on her way to look at Carl Baumann's home and maybe, if Becky had the directions straight, the Baumann's family plot in St. John's Lutheran Church's cemetery.

I liked San Antonio. It is so different but so close to the Hill Country. The old Germans like Carl Baumann came in to the city from off their farms and took some control away from the Anglos who had taken control from the

Mexicans. They turned it from a frontier settlement into a cosmopolitan and mercantile city. Then the Mexicans came back. In the seventies, after the Mexicans discovered the clout of their money and political power and voted the old *patrons* out of office, after liquor by the drink passed and thirsty conventioneers and even more tourists invaded the city, the Mexicans cashed in on the Hispanic heritage in the city and got even more power. So it was a city constantly changing what it was and what it thought it was, yet always basing the changes on some constants.

We made it through the spaghetti-like maze of San Antonio freeways and downtown streets, but finally got to the southeast side of town where old ice houses, the predecessors of Seven Eleven and all the other convenience stores, still dot some of the corners. They are a part of the city's heritage. In an old city that had to cope with heat and humidity long before air conditioning, ice houses were cool places to sit in the summertime and have a beer or a soda. They all have picnic tables under scraggly trees. And if you parked your car in front of them, someone would still run to your window or shout at you from inside for your order. The southside squats below the escarpment, which stops just north of downtown. The southside used to be farmable land, and then, for a while, it developed some prestigious areas, back when Becky was a girl. Now the new residents move farther and farther north, outside of the city's limits, for a better view from higher land, for more malls, mega-screen movie theaters, chain restaurants, and new middle-class housing. Anyone could move to the northside with enough money; the Westside was the "Mexican" side of town, the east was the Black area, the Southeast side around Highland Park had Mexicans, blacks , and left-over dying off, old Germans, Czechs, and Poles. This area of town is a lazy, slow, no man's land.

I drive into Highland Park subdivision and Becky bounces in her seat. Like those dogs, she presses her nose against my window to drink in what she sees. The city has long since gobbled up any distinct housing districts on the southside of town. Neighborhoods were destroyed as cities and freeways grew. But on either corner of Pine and Highland Avenue are two tall palms whose trunks are scarred from cars plowing into them and stained black from exhaust fumes. Next to the trees are two tall concrete pillars. Now marked with graffiti sprayed and chipped into the stone, the pillars at one time declared the boundaries of then prestigious Highland Park.

I pass McKinley, Schleigh, and finally get to Hicks and turn down the block. "There, there," Becky shouts, turns to look at me. "Shotzie wrecked her bicycle there, and I had let her peddle me back. I was on the handlebars. Scared to death." The houses are mostly squat bungalows with steep roofs, but some have flat Spanish tile roofs. They are stuccoed or lined with native brick–large, flat, mortared limestone rocks. Left over from an age when architects weren't afraid to be gaudy, they have arches, towers, terraces, sculptures, columns, and artificial brick wishing wells. All have porches and large trees, the only escape from heat in the days before air conditioning. From what I see of the residents, they are mostly the newly prospered Mexicans from the Westside who got enough money together to buy a new house uptown from a ghetto. Skilled workers, they did their own electrical work or carpentry, added their own touches like statues of Madonnas and saints in the front yards. And living next to them, in an uneasy alliance, were the old people who had moved in when the area was still fashionable and who had not yet died or moved off. These older residents were the ones who, like Henry's neighbors and old Carl Baumann, liked to cuss Mexicans.

"There it is. There it is." Becky turns to looks at me, claps her hands in front of her, almost like a little girl, and swivels around like that old dog to look at her childhood house. It is a native brick house with a porch that stretches across its length and a black iron railing around the porch. A more-or-less sculpted pine tree spreads a few limbs over the top of the porch, and a large pecan tree shades the front yard, making a few bare spots in the lawn where the sun can't reach the grass. In other places, the lawn is thick Bermuda and carpet grass and carefully cut back from the sidewalk that leads to the porch. The house next door has kids' toys, a car battery, and a bare lawn with threads of carpet grass overgrowing the sidewalk. These people couldn't afford me or Buck Cronin. They see a priest, bear through, beat up somebody.

"Let's go in," Becky says.

"Someone lives there."

"We'll knock first," Becky says and is out the door before I can open mine. She skips across the front lawn and peers into a window. I step up to the house and ring the doorbell. A Mexican man, a little younger than me, answers the door. His thick black hair, immaculately cut, matches his black horned-rim glasses. He wears a finely cut beige suit, light blue shirt, and bright blue-dotted, red tie. Becky is behind me, peering over my shoulder. The man opens the door smiling and pushes open the screen door. "We're sorry to bother you," I say.

"Can I help you?" he says politely.

"I'd just like to talk to you, if I could. Maybe look at your house."

"We've just gotten back from, mass," the man says, sounding as though I was committing a sacrilege for trying to hustle him on a holy day.

"Oh, hell," Becky says and jumps around from behind me. She puts her hand out to the man, beams at him. "I grew up here. I want to see it again." He pushes the screen door farther open, and I look at the glossy shine on his cordovan shoes. "I'm Roger Jackson," I say.

"Johnny Ruiz," he says and sticks his hand out of the screen door. His smile drops.

"And I'm Becky Bolen."

Johnny Ruiz smiles, "Becky, Becky something. I talked to you once when we closed the deal." Becky nods. "You had just put your father in a nursing home."

"Yes, yes," she says.

Johnny Ruiz holds the door open, and I step to one side to let Becky rush in ahead of me. The house has the old-style ten foot high ceilings. The living room has a lush shag carpet in a color that matches Johnny Ruiz's suit. His walls are a freshly painted bright white. One has a picture of Christ, another of the Virgin Mary. The furniture is polished Early American with a bright mahogany tint. In the dining room, a china cabinet displays the china, probably given as a wedding gift, and a dining room table has a lace table cloth draped over it and a chandelier hanging over it. The sofa is plush satin with large throw pillows. A large TV commands all the seats in the house to point toward it. "This is wonderful," Becky says. "My parents never had it so nice."

Johnny smiles, puffs up. "The house didn't look like this when I bought it. Paint, furniture, carpet is all ours. But next month, we get a new carpet. Shag is out of fashion."

"What did the house look like?" Becky asks. Johnny lets his smile drop. "No, really. What kind of shape was it in." He hesitates.

"Go on," I say.

"It stunk more than looked," Johnny said. "Your father didn't put out the trash. Just let it pile up. The paint and sheet rock had cracked. The walls were stained. It was for the best that you moved your father into a place that could take care of him."

"Did you ever meet him?" I ask.

"I saw him," Johnny says. "He looked . . . kind of crazy."

"He's dead now," Becky says. "For some time."

"I figured as much."

Two girls come in from the dining room. Both wear ruffled white dresses and matching red shoes and ribbons. A dark, attractive woman walks up behind them and puts her hands against their backs. Johnny turns to see them, "Mr. Jackson, Mrs. Bolen, this is my wife, Alice, and my daughters, Carmen and Ashley. We've just gotten back from church." I nod my head. He says to his wife, "Her father used to live here." He looks at his wife, and she pulls the little girls into the kitchen.

"Please," he says and motions us into the dining room. "Perhaps, later, you might look around; now though, would you like some coffee and brunch?" He smiles, "Maybe a beer?" Just as he finishes speaking, Alice carries in a silver tray with a three cups of coffee, and Ashley and Carmen carry in two white bakery sacks. Alice holds the tray in front of me.

"We don't want to interrupt, anything," I say.

"Please," Alice says. As I take my cup, the two girls tear open the sacks. "Carmen, Ashley, not so anxious," Alice says to the two girls. "Offer some to our guests first."

Ashley comes to me and holds an open bag in front of me. "On the tray," Alice says. "Put the *pan dulce* on the tray." Becky lets her head roll back and laughs. Johnny and Carmen laugh.

Ashley looks at all of us. "You said," Ashley says.

"It's okay," Becky says. "This is just fine." She reaches into the bag and pulls out one of the Mexican pastries. I look in the bag at the pastel colored *pan dulce*. I pulled out a flat crisp *buñelo*. Alice hands me a cloth napkin.

"Sit, sit," Johnny says, and Becky quickly squirms into a chair. I follow. Then the Ruiz girls sit around us.

Johnny says, "We always eat something sweet after

mass." He laughs. I bite into the pastry and sip my coffee, and Alice opens the front blind to let sunlight spill into the front room. Ashley and Carmen each grab into the bag and stick pastry into their mouths. "Help yourself," Johnny says.

"Really, we feel terrible about barging in on you people," I say. Alice sits down. Becky devours the pasty, grabs for more, practically slurps the coffee. As she chews, she smiles and looks around the dinner room.

"No problem," Johnny said as he reached for some pastry.

After we finish, Alice and the girls pile the napkins and silverware into the tray and take it into the kitchen. Ashley immediately runs back and sits in her father's lap. I see Alice peek in at us and Johnny shoo her back into the kitchen with his glance. He looks at Becky. "So few people appreciate families anymore. Where they came from."

"There wasn't much to appreciate in mine," Becky says. Johnny's smile drops. I can see that Becky wants to smoke.

"So how long have you lived here then?" I ask.

"Nearly twelve years," he says.

I nod my head.

"So why here?" Becky asks and leans across the table on her elbows.

Johnny smiles at her. "I'm a Westsider, man," he says proudly with a mock accent like Eddie Sanchez's. "You know what that means?"

"I'm not sure."

"It means I'm a Mexican. My father could barely speak English when I was born, and now I'm a C.P.A."

"Really," I say.

"Yeah," he says, "I could have bought a house on the Northside, lived with Anglos. But the price here was a lot better. It's less crowded here. No traffic jams. Some say the schools aren't as good, but . . ." He shrugs his shoulders. "I send my girls to private Catholic school. And the people here aren't so rich. This is still a neighborhood."

Eventually, Johnny shows us around the house: the den, the dining room, his bedroom, the kitchen. I stay in the kitchen to look at the yellow tile that coated the drainboard and the large ventilation hood over the stove. A square spot in the wall has been touched up and repainted but was still noticeable. Johnny points to it. Becky answers for him, "An old water cooler was in here." I try to see this Becky, instead of the young Becky whom I can't conjure up, telling old Carl Bauman and Doris that she wants a divorce from Henry Bolen. I try to see Schatzi in her wet hair, getting up to walk away to her privacy and suicide. But I can't really see them because Johnny Ruiz has worked so hard at transforming the house into a part of his modest dreams.

"It was rusted right into the wood and didn't work anymore," Johnny says. "I put in central heat." The back door in the kitchen leads to the back porch, which is bright with yellow and white wicker lawn furniture. The back yard is bright with flowers and plants. Becky runs into the back yard, smells the flowers, looks at the pecan tree. She walks up to it, rubs it at the height where she must have felt it as a six-year-old. Johnny invites me to stay until two o'clock when his relatives will come by. The men and women sit in the backyard, and drink beer, and the kids take turns swinging a stick at a *piñata* or playing softball in the street, and at six, everyone eats tamales or hamburgers or barbeque.

I say we have to get back. And I look at Becky as she searches in vain for the fake cement wishing well and a brick goldfish pond. They have either crumbled or Johnny has torn them down.

* * *

The St. John's cemetery is on the eastside, the

blacks' part of town. The cemetery is overgrown with weeds. Some tombstones have the obscene graffiti of wild, angry black boys. Some are cracked and tumbled over. A large statue of an angel is missing its head and the tip of a wing. I drive around for a while then park my car when Becky says, "Stop." I grab my new straw hat from the seat of the truck.

Becky smiles at me in my new hat. "It looks good on you." She positions her wide-brimmed straw hat on her head, then pulls the clasp up the strings underneath it. "Henry's hat looks pretty disgusting, Roger." We get out and walk among the crumbling graves of forgotten old Germans, sweat staining our clothes. Becky stops next to a curb with not a tombstone but a raised marble slab with "Baumann" written across it.

Becky smiles and jerks her head toward the tombstones. A bubble of sweat flies off of her nose. Carl is buried next to Doris. Across from them is Carl's mother and father, Otto and Hertha. And next to them, is Schatzi. A tombstone of the same height and marble stands next to Shatzi. "*Becky* Bolen" is written across it. It has a birth date and an open-ended date. Next to Becky's tombstone is a blank tombstone. "They're cheaper, the more you buy at one time," Becky says, chuckles, and squats.

"Who's the blank one for?" I ask.

"It ends with that grave. I don't know who would want it, though." She pushes herself up by placing her hands on her knee and groaning as she raises herself. She looks at me. "So I don't know who it's for."

"Kyle? Victoria?"

"They'll probably want to be buried next to their father."

I look at her, do not drop my look. "Probably."

"So do you want it?"

"What?"

"You're kind of like me. Stuck, so far. I pretty well

266

know where I will be planted, where I am planted. You probably don't. But I've got an extra seat—if you want it."

"I'll let you know," I say. I take my new straw hat out and tip it, as though to pour out the sweat. Then we turn to walk back to my truck.

We see an old black gardener hoeing at some weeds. Even on Sunday, probably because he has nothing else, nowhere to go, he is working in *his* cemetery. But surely, the underpaid, retired workingman, knows he's too old to ever defeat the weeds, dried grass, dying flowers, and crumbling tombstones in St. John's. And through the crooked rows of tombstones, mausoleums, and family plots, two black boys, barely in their teens, drink Big Red soda waters and shout to each other about who was the baddest player on the San Antonio Spurs basketball team. One carries a basketball under his arm. The other carries one of those Easter baskets you buy for kids at the dime stores and super markets, the kind with dark green, stringy plastic grass; purple, pull-apart, plastic Easter eggs with candy inside; and those hollow, chocolate Easter bunnies. From her face, I know that Becky wonders along with me where he got an Easter basket in late summer.

For all they know, they are in a park. Maybe they are right. A park makes a hell of a lot more sense than family plots. Like raising horses or hoeing a crumbling all-white cemetery in an all-black section of town just because it is something to do, a family plot is silly. Maybe Becky took me to San Antonio to see the futility of pissing out your territory then saying "mine." The scent of your piss would always soak into the land, and the land would always out live you. A plot, whether a house in Highland Park or property in the Hill Country, is just like a plot in a crumbling, forgotten cemetery. I understand the humor and the meaning behind the view from Becky's toilet seat.

The old gardener gets up and yells at the boys to get out of the cemetery, "Don't you boys know you is in a graveyard." I look at Becky beside me. I think of Johnny Ruiz. And I think of the Baumann house that became the Ruiz house.

Dividing cemeteries into plots and families or making land or houses into property might be silly, but people who are weaker than Becky, who get hung up in Taos or the Hill Country, who stay in love, need the plots and property. The Johnny Ruiz family, I'd guess, make their plots and property important, something nobody in ol' Carl's family could do, something Henry almost did. But then again, Johnny Ruiz might be struck by divorce, depression, or death before today is through, and he might move out of his Highland Park house.

Suddenly, I see Becky. She crosses her arms, across her chest, drips sweat from her face, smiles at me with that shit-eating grin, and makes me wonder if I need a plot.

Chapter 15:
Henry

I lie back in a reclining lawn chair and rest my can of beer on my stomach. I feel the wetness of the bottle on my T shirt. Becky sits across from me in the regular lawn chair and sips her glass of wine. She insisted on the bottle of wine. She now insists that I become a bit more civilized and learn to drink wine.

"I just started drinking beer, again. I quit for a while," I say.

"Why in the world did you ever stop?" she asks, shifts around in my lawn chair, and frowns. We have just gotten back from Deep Eddy pool, so Becky is in her drying swim suit. Her suit, which she must have bought when she was still smoking, clings to her and folds over at her waist and butt.

"I read that drinking doesn't help with depression," I answer.

"Nonsense. You either drank too much or too little. You need to forget about her." Becky lifts her nose slightly in the air in a condescending manner and lifts one leg. A few wrinkles surround her knee, but her skin still tightly wraps her still shapely legs.

"Easy for you to say."

She smiles as though I were still an undergraduate, then says, "Yeah, it is easy for me to say. I'm sorry."

Becky squirms in her chair.

A few lightening bugs float around us, but no mosquitoes are out. It is a nice night. But I risk the pleasantness by asking a serious question. "So what are your plans?"

"Guess, I'll just play it by ear," Becky says and looks straight at me. "I want to try Kyle first. I have a few tricks up my sleeve to get him . Then I'll try Victoria."

"And why didn't you try to help Henry?" I ask.

Becky chuckles, "In the last letter, Henry said that he thought you turned out to be all right but that he didn't think that you cared for him very much. I see he was wrong about you."

Becky hesitates and stares at me as though she has found me out. "At the time, I didn't," I say. "But now I kind of miss him."

"After he's dead," I say.

Becky smiles, leans back into the chair. "So what's the difference between me and you?" Becky asks. "We both let him die."

I raise myself up. "That's not right. That's not the way it was."

Becky sips her wine; then that devious smile stretches one corner of her mouth.

"I'm not as stupid as I seem around you," I say and smile back at her.

Becky drains her glass, stands, the chair sighing, and says, "I'm tired. I think I'll call it a night."

"I think I'll stay out a while longer. I have trouble with sleep."

Becky steps toward me and the back door, but before she goes in, she grabs my hand and squeezes it. "I'm sorry," she says. I look up at her and see Victoria; I straighten and stretch toward her. My kiss hits her cheek instead of her forehead, where I was aiming. She closes her eyes, and I stay stretched, taut, and slightly nervous. Her lips come very near mine. I feel her breath, but I cannot quite tell if her lips are gently, discreetly kissing my own. She slowly pulls back, quivers a little, and I relax in my chair. Some better judgment or some residual old-style Christianity keeps us from flinging off our clothes, running into my bedroom, and pretending that we could be lovers. "I wish you were older, Roger," Becky says.

I squeeze her hand and say, "I wish you were younger." She laughs and goes inside. The old saying bumps into the back of my forehead, "Look at their mammas, boys." I just had, and I saw the best of both Victoria and Becky. We are both old enough, and we have both seen enough to know that our friendship has certain limits. To go beyond those limits would be risky for both of us. It was hard enough just to meet her. Still, we were close because we were peripheral to Henry's family. And then the voices of Jack Hillier, Sam Penschorn, and Pete Proctor told me, "Don't even go there."

* * *

For a week, we play in Austin. I take Becky to work with me, introduce her to Buck Cronin. She rents a car and spends several days shopping, swimming, and driving around the area. And I called Kyle then Vickie to arrange meetings. Kyle's was first.

Becky and I walk into the Jim's, refreshed by our swim in Barton Creek, our hair still wet. "Jim's" is a chain of coffeehouses. They helped force the closing of Austin's old Nighthawk Restaurant, the one where politicians and professors would meet to negotiate and work out deals. The old Nighthawk would have been more appropriate for this negotiation.

While Becky rubbernecks, looking and guessing about her son, I see Kyle sitting in a booth with his back to us. I take Becky's arm and guide her toward Kyle. Becky halts as we near him and grabs my arm. She whispers to me, "This is a good idea, right?"

"To tell you the truth, I'm not really sure. No telling what Kyle'll do."

"Well, Jesus. You think I can handle him."

"You're his mother."

Becky pulls on my arm and says, "Let's go."

Kyle turns around to look at us when we get to his table. He wears a short sleeve shirt and a loosened tie. His sportcoat is slung over the back of the booth . He quickly looks down at his glass of water, then up at me. "Kyle," I say, "This is your mother." I gesture toward Becky. Kyle stands up. Becky slides into the booth, opposite from Kyle. I sit beside her, and Kyle sits down across from us. I want to rearrange the seating because I feel trapped between them, but I take off my new straw hat, my gift from Becky, and lay it, crown down, on the table.

Kyle stares down at his plate and lifts a glass of water to his lips. He takes another sip of his water, then turns to look away from us. "Please Kyle," Becky says. Kyle turns to face her but says nothing. "Thank you, Kyle" Becky stutters, "I'm proud of you. Henry was proud of you. Roger's told me all you've done. It's marvelous." Kyle still says nothing but only takes a drink of water. "Come on now, Kyle," Becky says. "I know you cannot think of me as your mother. But show me and Roger some courtesy." I am afraid Kyle will hit me because he can't punch a woman. Instead, he turns to Becky and frowns. She smiles.

"I haven't done much compared to becoming a college professor," Kyle growls then freezes Becky's glance with his stare.

"Come on, Kyle," I say. "Lighten up."

"You aren't in this family anymore."

Becky taps her knuckles on the table. "Roger spent more time with you than I did," she says, and I want to kiss her. Kyle turns away from both of us, then looks quickly at me, as though to apologize for his remark. And he may have apologized , but he wouldn't in front of his mother.

"Please, Kyle," Becky says. "I've paid for my desertion.

I really have."

"You could have come back."

"How?"

"You shouldn't have left."

"I had to."

"How in the hell did you *have* to?" Kyle says to her.

Becky takes a deep breath. "I couldn't live with Henry anymore. I tried to stay . . ."

Kyle interrupts her, and says, "Bullshit," then looks like an embarrassed five-year-old caught cussing in front of his mother. Kyle lifts his head and looks directly at Becky, "I cussed you most my life. I'm not about to stop now."

"How about some forgiveness, man," I say, then bite off my words to resist pleading with Kyle.

Kyle looks at me. "This isn't your concern," he says and points across the table at me.

"Kyle," I say, "take your finger out of my face." He glares at me; then he curls his finger into his fist; he puts his palm down on the table, and I feel sorry for being mean to him and adding to the unpleasantness. "Thank you," was all I could think to say. He starts to slide his hand toward his lap, and Becky gently puts her hand on top of his. He jerks his hand out from under hers.

"Why do you want to stir shit up?" he says to Becky with a suppressed yell. Several waitresses and customers, though, turn to look at us. Kyle lowers his voice. "Everything here, everything about me and Victoria is just fine without you. Go back to Oklahoma or wherever it was you came from."

"Okay then, Kyle," Becky says. "I see how it's to be." She reaches into her purse and begins to pull out bank notes and legal papers. "In another ten years, I'm going to retire. When I do, I'm going to get a quite sizable retirement fund. I plan to walk into a bank and deposit it all. I also have some substantial savings and investments." She starts to throw the bank notes and deeds in front of Kyle.

A waitress walks up and says, "Are you ready to order?"

"Go away," I say, then add, "please." She looks at me for a moment with an open mouth, then goes away.

"It all goes to your kids, when I die, Kyle," Becky says. Kyle reaches for the notes and holds them in his hands. "Roger and I are going to rewrite my will tonight." If there was one way to get to Kyle, this was it. This was Kyle's method.

"No, don't. I don't want it," Kyle says.

"Please, Kyle, consider," I say.

Becky bows her head then continues, "Until, I do die, I'm going to start two separate trust funds. One for each kid. At eighteen or in case of an emergency, they get it." She pats the notes. "For this, I want to see my grand kids and meet your wife."

Kyle looks at me. "No, goddamn it, you can't do this. I won't let you. You can't buy me," Kyle says. Poor Kyle, I fear, had already sold himself.

"Kyle, this is absurd," I say.

"I'm not trying to buy you; I'm just trying," Becky sighs.

"No," Kyle says. "I will take care of my family. I don't want you around them. They're mine. Stay away," Kyle hesitates; even he must see the absurdity of what he had said. "No money. No visits."

Becky hangs her head, and Kyle won't look at her. He stands, grabs his sportcoat, and walks toward the door. I get up and run after him. Just as he walks outside, I catch his arm. "Come back inside, Kyle."

"No," he says, jerks his hand out of my grip, and turns away from me.

I put my hand on his shoulder and say to his back. "This isn't just about money," I say.

He hangs his head and mumbles, "I know that. If it

was just about money, I'd let her do it."

I let go of his arm, and he walks away from me, his head hanging and bobbing, his sportcoat slung over his shoulder. He looks almost like Henry on his last ride.

He trots the last few steps to his car and turns to look at me. He is already sweating. He turns away from me, opens the door of his Buick Regal, wads his sportcoat into a ball, and throws it into the car. He climbs in and drives away. As he pulls out of the driveway of the Jim's Restaurant, Becky steps beside me. She holds my hat.

"I guess I lost him," she says.

"I'm sorry."

She feebly shrugs her shoulders, and I sling my arm around them. "It wasn't your fault," I say.

"Huh," she says. "The hell it wasn't. Sometimes the payments just don't stop."

"He's pig-headed," I say.

Becky smiles, "I did try, though, didn't I?" Her smile drops, and she looks at me for an honest answer.

"You done good," I say. I don't lie, and I wish that my forgiveness of them both, for sins real or imagined, could have mattered to either of them. She hands me my hat.

*　*　*

Becky sits on the passenger side of my pickup with her hands folded in her lap and smiles calmly. For her meeting with her daughter, Becky wears a yellow, sleeveless sun dress. Her wide-brimmed straw hat with the chin straps sets in between us. My hat lies, crown down, next to it. She is composed, cool, chatty. I sweat even with the air conditioning on. My hands are so greasy with sweat that I can barely keep them on the steering wheel. My back is stuck to the back of the seat. "I could take a bus," Becky says.

When I called Victoria and asked if I could bring her mother and Victoria agreed, my stomach twisted itself into this knot. Passing through San Marcos, I relaxed just a bit, put in a tape, and tried to mouth the words of the song Willie Nelson sang. Becky lightly hummed along with Willie: "One night of love don't make up for six nights alone."

As we pass Fischer, Becky looks at Marie's guarding Wimberly Ave, the Fischer cut off from Ranch Road 12, smiles, and points. "Marie's," she says. I glance over and see a crowd of cars around it, cars I don't recognize. Even a BMW is parked at Marie's.

"I've never seen it that crowded."

"Oh God, it hasn't even changed. It hasn't changed." Becky says and taps on the window.

"Nothing ever changes in Fischer," I say, but I am not looking hard enough.

We pass the over-grown, brush filled Lutheran Cemetery where Henry is buried. I pull off to the side of the road, then pull a U to go back to the cemetery. "Where are we going?" Becky says.

"I thought you might want to see Henry's grave. I know you like cemeteries." Becky smiles at me.

As we pull in, Becky squints, "I remember this place."

We drive over the rutted gravel road that winds around several scrub oaks to Henry's plot. We get out of the cab at the same time and walk toward the grave. I take off my new straw hat and, with my hand, wipe my sweat off my face and from the inside of the hat. Becky looks at me and says, "It's hot today." Kyle bought Henry the plot and a flat, shiny marble tombstone. There is room for Kyle, Suzy, and Victoria in the family plot. I am the obvious omission. Kyle must have known Victoria and I would split, or he never really considered me a part of his family when he bought the plot, or he just didn't want me hanging around him for eternity.

I smile at Becky, and she walks up to the marker and looks down at it and the artificial flowers placed in a vase beside it. "I always thought he'd have himself buried on his land," she says.

"He never said. Victoria kind of wanted to bury him by the horse stables," I say, and Becky laughs. "Kyle wouldn't let her, though. He said a grave would scare tourists."

"And on the other hand, it might have become a curio, added authenticity. Anyway, Henry's probably happy here. He lived most of his life for the Hill Country. He's in it now." She giggles, "Hell, he's a part of it. He's happy." She stoops down on one knee and pulls the artificial flowers off the grave. As she tries to stand, her knees creak loud enough for me to hear them. I step up to her, take her elbow, and help her up. "Bursitis," she says, bends over, and rubs her knee.

"A friend of Henry's always says it's hell to get old," I say.

She smiles and says, "I don't plan to get old yet—despite what Sam Penschorn says." She slings the flowers in her hand out beside the grave and says, "Henry shouldn't have artificial flowers."

"Kyle got them. They're perpetual," I say.

"Why should the dead have to worry about perpetuity?" she asks. I shrug my shoulders; we chuckle and go back to the pick up.

* * *

We pull off the road and into a line of cars turning into Bolen Resorts. Becky puts her hand over her eyes and stares ahead. Another car pulls behind us. Mostly, the cars are filled with teenagers and inner tubes. Bolen Resorts caught on. I have not been back since this spring. I made a vow. But I read about Bolen Resorts in the business section of *The Austin American*. The article praised Kyle's ingenuity. When we get to the entrance, Dianne Natividad, her belly bulging, steps up to my window. I roll the window down. "Three dollars per car load," she says, then recognizes me.

"Roger!"

"Hi, Dianne," I say. Becky hands me three dollars from her side of the truck.

"I've got it," I say and dig in my pocket.

"Oh, shit no," Dianne says, then covers her mouth with her hand. "I got to stop cussing on the job. You get in free," she says.

"When's the baby coming?"

Dianne pats her belly with her fist, which is stuffed with bills. "October."

"Wonderful," I say. She laughs at me and a car honks. I wave to her and drive up the hill. Becky turns around to look at Dianne, and in the rear view mirror, I see her watch me drive up the hill. The car behind me honks at her, and she turns around and shoots the finger at the surprised teenagers. Becky turns to look at me with one eye cocked. "An old friend," I say.

"I can see that."

As the cars enter Bolen Resorts, their back tires kick up the dust on Henry's road and drip oil, thus staining Henry's gravel and making the place smell like a gas station. Some hot shits squeal their tires to make more dust and create the smell of burning rubber. The road to Bolen Resorts turns off Henry's gravel road and on to Kyle's newly bulldozed road, where Eddie Sanchez, choking on the dust, leans on the counter of the Coke shack. I wave to him as I continue up the road toward the house, and he lazily waves to me, then smiles and shrugs his shoulders. After we clear the Coke stand, Becky points out her window. "The stables are gone," she says.

In their place are several tents from overnight campers. "Jesus, Christ, Kyle," I mutter to myself. "This is fucking Yellowstone Park."

Becky crosses her arms and looks up the road toward the house. "The house. The house is the same."

I look up the road at the house. Victoria's orange

Comet is parked in front. "It's the same," I say. "Victoria got that car started herself." We both smile.

I stop in front of the veranda and grab the steering wheel with both hands while Becky grabs her hat, gets out, and walks toward the house. As she walks in front of the pickup, she looks back in at me. She walks to my open window and looks in, the wide brim of the hat making a shadow across her eyes, making her look sinister.. "I could do this alone," she says. I shake my head, and she steps aside as I open my door. I grab my new hat, push it down on my head, and stop outside of my truck. Becky follows me up the steps and across the veranda to the front door.

As always, the front door is open to let the early morning breeze blow through the screen door and into the living room and kitchen. I knock on the screen door; it rattles in its frame. Victoria answers the door. She wears the white dress she had worn at Henry's funeral, jogging shoes, and a straw cowboy hat. I stand back to look at her. Her costume at first looks incongruous, weird. But then, as she smiles, and I look at her hair and full, pink face, I see that her clothes add to her charm. I look down at her jogging shoes, "I started jogging, too, about a mile down Ranch Road 12 and back. Besides, the shoes just feel good."

I step back, and she steps out and lets the screen door slam shut behind her. She grabs my hand with both of hers, and raises them just under her chin; then she kisses me on the cheek. "That's a *friendly* kiss for my *ex*-husband. Nothing more, Roger." I hate her patronizing me. Worse, I hate the polite tone she uses. And I hate the kiss.

Victoria looks up at me, "I like the hat."

I pull off the hat her mother gave me, "Henry's just gave out."

"Did you see what Kyle's done?"

"He's making money," I say as I clutch her hand. She

feels the squeeze and loosens her grip. I drop her hand and put my hat back on my head.

"Last night, a couple of college kids unrolled their sleeping bags right here on the porch. They were gonna drink some wine then 'crash' here. I came out about ten and chased them off." She tries to go on, but she looks over my shoulder to see Becky standing in back of me.

I hesitate for a moment as Victoria turns to me. I want some time alone with her. But I turn to look at Becky, who is biting her bottom lip. Becky lifts her head up then lowers it slowly, as if doing a complete vertical pan of Victoria. Then her jaws relax, she raises her hands, and puts them together like she is praying. "Victoria," I say, "this is your mother." The two women face each other. Victoria sticks out her hands and Becky takes them. I step to one side.

"Vickie," Becky says.

"I'm so glad to meet you," Victoria says.

Becky smiles, slips her arm around Victoria's waist, and both women turn to look at the line of cars turning into Bolen Resorts. "I'd like to see a little of the place," Becky says.

Goddamn, I say to myself, just like that and they are friends, like Becky never left.

"I can drive you," Victoria says.

Becky looks at her daughter, forgetting I am around, and says, "I'd kind of like to walk."

Becky walks down the steps of the veranda, and Victoria follows.

"We could walk down to the creek," Victoria says. "or the pool, but it will be full of tourists."

Becky turns to look at her and says, "Let's avoid the crowd. How about the upper pasture?" Victoria smiles, drops her head slightly back, and laughs, shaking her blonde hair on the tops of her shoulders. I stare at her, snap a photo in my mind of her smile, what I haven't seen in so long.

They turn up the road and walk up around the house. I go to the corner of the veranda. Victoria wraps her hand around her mother's arm, just above the elbow, and they continue up the hill.

I jump over the railing of the veranda to watch them, feeling excommunicated. The two women's feet slide and curl out on the rolling rocks. Becky is steady and strong. I can almost see through her yellow dress, and I can see her shapely, sweaty legs stick to the hem of her dress and the beads of sweat on her back. Then I watch the angular shape of Victoria's neck, the sideways swing of her free arm, the sway of her expanding hips.

The morning breeze catches some of Victoria's clean, bright blonde hair from under her straw hat and blows it toward me. Her white dress becomes translucent in the sunlight, makes her shimmer. She is her mother's daughter. Who knows, perhaps Victoria will be buried in St. John's Cemetery beside her mother.

I know as I watch them that I am no longer needed. My friendship with Becky has its limits. Victoria has just met her mother, and for the moment, their relation knows no bounds.

I realize too that the two women can exclude us from their lives. They don't need Henry, poor ol' Clayton Tanner, square-headed ol' Carl Baumann, Kyle, or me. We could never really harm them. They are better equipped for surviving and suffering. But the sight of them walking up the hill, arm in arm, is like a vision, something like the sights that Tanner must have had when he communed with his weird gods or something like the hopeless wishes or memories that rolled around in Henry's head as he died. Neither Henry nor Tanner will see this, though they would have wanted to. I watch for them, for all of us. I click another photo in my mind.

I walk to my truck to drive back to Austin. I will call later. Victoria will get her mother back to my house or to the airport when she is ready to go. Irony sucks.

* * *

I stop at Marie's on the way back to see what the crowd is about. When I walk in, Evelyn comes up to me, grabs my arm, and kisses me. "Nice to see one of the old gang," she says. "Tell Kyle, he sure is making us some money with that Bolen Resorts idea." She steps back and spreads out her arms. She has on a T-shirt with "Where the hell is Fischer?" written across her chest. She jerks her thumb toward the bar. Marie has a line of T-shirts on hangers behind the bar. "Bolen Resorts," "Nowhere but Fischer," and "Marie's Tavern" the red, green, yellow, and purple shirts say. Some have glitter pasted to them. Evelyn pats my back and walks to a table of kids sipping beer. I look through the screen of Marie's and see groups of college kids gathered at the picnic tables where the Mexicans used to sit. I look at the faces inside the crowded bar and finally spot Pete Proctor and ol' Doc Hillier sitting by themselves in a corner.

When I walk up, Pete says, "I be goddamned." I sit down beside them. "I'm damn glad to see a regular come in," Pete says. "Nothing comes in here but these goddamn, stiff-dick teenagers with fake I.D.s. They even took over the Mexicans' place out back. The ol' Mexican boys don't even come here no more."

"Kyle was right," Doc Hillier says. "Things change."

"To hell with Kyle," Pete says. "He'd a never done this while his daddy was alive." Doc Hillier sips his beer.

I raise my hand and shout for a beer. Evelyn appears with a Coors Light, and I hand her a dollar. She smiles, "Price has gone up," she says.

"You are goddamned to hell right," Pete says. "Gettin' so a poor man can't drink here no more."

"A dollar and a quarter," Evelyn says. I give her another dollar and tell her to keep the change.

"Show–off big spender," Pete says.

I sit down beside them and sip my cool beer. It tastes good for a change. "Where's Sam?" I ask.

"Poor old bastard is at home coughing up his lungs," Pete says. "I told him those goddamned cigarettes would kill him." Pete is worried about Sam and has obviously been cussing everything. "Time is a son of a bitch," he says.

"If you're looking back at it, it's not so bad, but if you wasted it, or you're stuck in it, then it's a son of a bitch," imperturbable Doc Hillier says, looks at me, and smiles. Doc Hillier will never die.

"Yeah," I say and think of how well Victoria and Becky deal with time.

"I think Hillier talks shit," Pete says.

I drink my beer and order a second. Doc Hillier and I drink silently, and Pete cusses. I would have liked to have stayed, gotten pleasantly instead of depressed drunk, and pushed Pete into telling a few stories. But Pete is not in the mood, and I want to get back to Austin. So after my third beer, I wish Sam well, wave to Evelyn, and tell Jack and Pete goodbye.

As I step out of Marie's, I look down Ranch Road 12 toward Henry's property. I think about Henry in his grave. And he makes me worry about me.

As I drive to Austin, I'm pretty sure that I have this story about my in-laws, about West Texas and the Hill Country, about people I never really knew right. That's what I do, take photos of people I don't know cheating on each other and put together stories for lawyers. I think I'm pretty good at those stories, so why wouldn't I be good at this story that is also about me?

Something in us gives us the urge to acquire our own property—whether that property is in the Hill Country, Taos, or River Oaks. It must be the same urge that makes us want to find a lover, commune with some god (probably of our own devising), write a novel, compose a symphony, suck up life in our own liberating fashion.

And when we fail at acquiring our property, as we most often do, something else in us makes us reactionary, defensive, falsely and hypocritically religious, stingy with our hearts and our possessions. Maybe, like Sam and Pete and Henry, if we tell the same stories often enough, we can soften the failure. Becky knew this. And she knew that you must not resent that something in you for going sour.

I am pushing forty and have no property—or have lost it. But if I ever do, I hope that, like Becky, I can give it all up if I need to. Henry never let anything go. So he had to go through a lot of shit to die.

So Becky was wrong about Henry. Henry is not happy in his plot of Hill Country. He is thrashing around inside his coffin. I saw him lose faith in his land, and when the land was no longer enough, I saw him yearn for some final vision to give him clarity. But I got Henry's vision: the two women, his daughter and wife, walking up his gravel road. He had willed that vision—that task—to me. He also willed me his hat. I put my new hat on my head and pull the brim down to shield my eyes from the sun's glare through my windshield, and I am finally completely glad that I did not shoot Henry Bolen so that I could be around to help him die. Now I have to drive into my own future and find my own Hill Country Property and struggle to keep it or give it up—to be Becky, or Henry, or Victoria.

Photo: Baswell Ben Griggs

Jim Sanderson has published three collections of short stories: *Semi-Private Rooms* (Pig Iron Press, 1994); *Faded Love* (Ink Brush Press, 2010), and *Trashy Behavior* (Lamar University Press, 2013). He has published six novels: *El Camino del Rio* (University of New Mexico Press, 1998), *Safe Delivery* (University of New Mexico Press, 2000); *La Mordida* (University of New Mexico Press, 2002); *Nevin's History: A Novel of Texas* (Texas Tech University Press, 2004); *Dolph's Team* (Ink Brush Press, 2011); *Nothing to Lose* (TCU Press, 2014). And he has published an essay collection: *A West Texas Soapbox* (1998).

He is presently serving as the chair of the English and Modern Language Department for Lamar University.

See website: http://sites.google.com/site/jim2sanderson/home